THE LATIN SUB,
Impure Thoughts
and
One Man's Definition
Of Mortal Sin

THE LATIN SUB,
Impure Thoughts
and
One Man's Definition
Of Mortal Sin

A Collection of Short Stories by

STEVEN McBREARTY

Adelaide Books
New York/ Lisbon

2017

The Latin Sub, Impure Thoughts, and One Man's Definition
of Mortal Sin
A Collection of Short Stories
By Steven McBrearty

Copyright © 2017 By Steven McBrearty

Published by Adelaide Books, New York / Lisbon
An imprint of the Istina Group DBA
adelaidebooks.org

Editor-in-Chief
Stevan V. Nikolic

For any information, please address Adelaide Books
at info@adelaidebooks.org

ISBN13: 978-0-9995164-4-7
ISBN10: 0-9995164-4-2

Printed in the United States of America

Contents

PUBLISHING CREDITS

These stories have originally appeared in the following magazines and publications:

The Latin Sub - *Adelaide Literary Journal*, Sept. 2017

The Sacker – *Short Story Writer's Showcase*, 1999; also selected for reading in a Texas University Scholastic League reading contest.

Kingston, the Lizard, the Man – *Stories that Lift*, 1999; voice recorded on the web pages of the magazine

Skipper and Ken Visit Barbie's Pad – *Austin Chronicle;* honorable mention in Austin Chronicle short story contest, 1999)

Jane Fountain – *Coq and Bull*, June 2009; honorable mention in the magazine's literary contest

The Plumber – *Belle Reve literary journal*, July 2014

To Paris at 2:00 A.M. – *Every Day Fiction*, September 2017

Christmas Eve – *34th Parallel magazine*, March 2016

Exploding Astrodome Scoreboard – *Belle Reve literary journal*, April 2013

Roadside Restroom – *Straylight Literary Journal*, April 2011; Honorable mention in Glimmer Train Family Matters competition, spring 2009.

Pray Hard, Kick Ass Hard – *The Paragon Review*, May 2016

The Short Horn # 3 - *Flatman Crooked journal*, May 2008

East of Paris, West of Berlin – published in *Potpourri magazine*, June 2001; listed as best of Potpourri collection.

Vietnam Vets - *34th Parallel magazine*, April 2013.

Other stories have been published in the *Mississippi Review*, *Disappearing City Review* (Christmas Day on a City Bus was featured prose, April 2009), Slugfest ltd., and others.

The Latin Sub

There was a sub that day in freshman Latin class at St. Aloysius High in suburban San Antonio, Texas, so all hell had broken loose. Spitballs were flying, there were arm wrestling matches on desks, a trash can basketball game had broken out in a corner. Desks were rearranged for impromptu conference groups.

The sub was a painfully-thin, prematurely-balding man who lost control of the class immediately. His protruding Adam's Apple bobbed up and down spasmodically. The underarms of his starched white discount store dress shirt were soaked in perspiration, his shiny black polyester slacks were hiked up high over white sports socks and brown tasseled loafers. His name was Mr. Waldo, the name itself the inspiration for put-downs and derision. I felt sorry for Mr. Waldo. I pitied him. I identified with him. He was somebody who was never going to command respect or command an audience. He had a wife and young child, he had told us, and I felt sorry for them, too. You could only hope they would be blinded to what a dufus their husband and father was.

I sat rigidly at my desk, letting my thoughts wander. It was all I could do. It was like a Zen exercise, walling myself off from the chaos surrounding me. I didn't like chaos. I didn't want disorder. Maybe there was something wrong with the adolescent me, but I didn't want to spend the day feeling as though I had accomplished nothing. Time was limited, after all. Life was short. Besides, disorder provided ample opportunities for my classmates to zero in on criticism of my personality, my character, my fragile ego, my looks. Classmates swarmed around me as in the climactic scene from Little Big Men, but I remained stationed at my desk, pretending to be absorbed in the fascinating world of Latin parts of speech.

St. Al's was an all-boy's Catholic high school located in Castle Hills, a ritzy new suburb outside the "Loop" in far north San Antonio, a zip code laden heavily with doctors and lawyers and split-level ranch styles with three- and four-car garages, small houses themselves. (My dad being an accountant, we lived seven or eight miles away in a less glamorous subdivision, with only one level and a two-car garage, driving in each morning through a hectic freeway rush hour). The school was a brand spanking new facility, designed in a clean-line, cheerful 1960s contemporary style, a sort of space program/Southern California motif, with a glassed-in entrance and dark reflective windows all around like some cool character wearing sunglasses. A slender, representational, unmanned cross adorned the entranceway, high up. Two-story ceilings on the inner corridor and a glass wall around the library provided an airy, hi-tech feel, almost as if the library were a command center for NASA, with students and librarians striding around inside like programmers and scientists working to keep the mission on course. Classroom walls were painted vibrant, life-affirming colors. The desks were tablet arms, with space beneath for storage. The school was staffed by Christian Brothers—they're the ones who make the wine—with lay teachers filling in the gaps. There was a companion girl's school, St. Agatha's Academy, but it was separated by a half-mile of uphill no-man's land, wooded hills and jutting rocks and cactus. At the end of the school day, students from St. Al's trekked through this thicket to visit St. Agatha's girls on the other side. It was like a journey to Valhalla. Unfortunately, I had been unable to go there recently, due to football practice.

Mr. Waldo stood facing the white writing board, conjugating Latin verbs in a low monotone and with a printed scrawl. His head was cocked a little to one side, as if admiring his handiwork, the phenomenon of Latin grammar. One large spitball, then another, hit the board beside him. Then a volley of spitballs came, with one striking him on the back of the head. He whirled, marker in hand, face contorted in surprise and fury.

"Who threw that?" Mr. Waldo demanded. He stood there, pinching the marker hard between two fingers of his right hand.

"Fire!" somebody yelled. A paper fire had erupted in a trash bucket in the back corner of the room.

"For heaven's sake," Mr. Waldo said, his head shake a sad, sarcastic commentary on our pampered pedigree. "What kind of families do you kids have?"

"Get some water!" somebody said.

"Use your shoe!" somebody said.

"Use your Latin book!" a third person said.

"Fire!" somebody shouted. The entire class took up the chant, like a football cheer. "Fire! Fire! Fire!"

It was at this precise moment that the school principal, Brother Ramsey, entered the classroom—or, rather, materialized in the back doorway of the classroom, like Banquo's ghost. Brother Ramsey was a simian-like man, a man we compared to Neanderthal Man, with a prognathous jaw and long, dangling arms and an intimidating, perpetual five o'clock shadow. He was feared by all, students and faculty alike, for his pugnacious style, his combative approach to every interaction. He entered unobtrusively, unannounced, standing silent in the doorway. He stood unnoticed for a long while, the madness inside continuing. Smoke from the now-extinguished trash can fire (somebody had actually used his shoe) drifted around the room, pushed by currents from ceiling-mounted air conditioner vents. Mr. Waldo tried shouting to restore order. Order was not restored. But as eyes turned and word about Brother Ramsey got around, the classroom turned eerily, unnaturally quiet. It was like the silencing of a crowd at a play when the opening curtain rises. Somebody coughed. Somebody sneezed. Students scurried back to their desks or stood frozen in place, like figures in wax. Brother Ramsey stood with a commanding posture, grinning diabolically. There was going to be mayhem. There was going to be bloodshed.

"So, it seems that the children play while the elves are away," Brother Ramsey said, in his precise, guttural monotone. Never had that little nursery rhyme seemed so ominous.

Then he moved in, preternaturally quick, picking up one of my classmates by the shoulders and depositing him in an empty desk. He grabbed another classmate by the ear, dragging him to a desk. Everyone who wasn't in a desk went there immediately, as in a deadly serious game of musical chairs. Brother Ramsey's eyes roamed the room, searching for miscreants. His eyes were like destruction rays focusing on victims. For the remainder of the class period, he sat scrunched-up in a too-small classroom chair, like an elephant in a bubble bath, long arms dangling. Mr. Waldo's Latin conjugations were received now by a chorus of eager, responsive students, waving their hands energetically for attention. There was never such an alert, attentive Latin class in the history of humankind. As the buzzer ending the class period sounded, everyone filed out in a somber, submissive tone, as in a religious ritual. You could almost smell incense in the air.

Fortunately for us, Brother Ramsey was an anomaly at our school, a throwback to a dying era of hard-ass, Baltimore catechism, sin-and-confess Catholicism. We were changing along with the times, with Vatican II, with the counter-culture movement, with new technologies and TV and transportation advances. We were about as peace and love now as the hippies, as communal as an Israeli kibbutz. Imbued with the enlightened tenor of the times, most of the teaching brothers were sensitive, forward-thinking, progressive-minded men, earnest in their desire to impart a sense of genuine Christian love to their young charges.

Brother Xavier was the freshman religion teacher at the school. I've never forgotten his first class that September, my very first day as a high school student. Brother Xavier was a handsome, broad-shouldered man, probably in his mid-30s, with tight golden curls on his head and bulging biceps, an athlete in his own schoolboy days, he had suggested modestly, as a point of orientation. He wore his plain brown cassock casually, jauntily, even roguishly if that were possible, his knees pushing through as if to establish that he could have been a first-rate lady's man if he hadn't dedicated his life to serving God.

As we settled into our desks that first day, Brother Xavier played a popular folk rock song on a portable turntable stationed on his teacher's desk: "A World of Our Own," by The Seekers. The refrain reads as follows:

We'll build a world of our own that no one else can share
All our sorrows we'll leave far behind us there
And I know you will find there'll be peace of mind
When we live in a world of our own

After the song had played several times, Brother Xavier camped down on his desk, right leg swinging. Throwing the room open for discussion, he requested opinions on the song's message, did we think this was the ideal, what we should all strive for? Romantics all, everybody emphatically said yes, we wanted to find somebody to love and to be with that person exclusively—in effect, to build a world of our own. Brother Xavier's leg stopped swinging. He placed his hands beside him on the desk top. No, he said, God doesn't want us to wall ourselves off from the world. He wants us to strive to make the world a better place for others, not just seek selfish pleasure for ourselves. It was a punch to the jaw, a profound, sobering revelation that I took to heart.

This day—the day of the Latin sub—one of the students asked Brother Xavier for a definition of mortal sin. A mortal sin was one that condemned the perpetuator to an eternity in hell if not repented (properly) and forgiven. Mortal sins ran the gamut from murder and grand theft to impure thoughts, with impure thoughts seeming to loom large in the sin hierarchy. (That's what the nuns taught us, anyway.) Considering adolescent boys were assailed constantly by impure thoughts, we lived in constant fear of going to hell. Brother Xavier fingered the oversized black rosary sashed around his waist like a belt. He seemed to consider his words carefully before responding.

"Mortal sin?" he said. "I wouldn't worry so much about impure thoughts and sexual desires. I'll tell you what's a mortal sin. I was riding the street car down Canal Street in New Orleans one afternoon. The street car stopped by a group of black kids playing penny-pitch in the gutter. Some old white guy leaned out the window and spit, and said, *'Niggers!'* That's a mortal sin."

I understood. I felt liberated. I felt alive in a different way, an upbeat, optimistic, newly-cognizant way. Destroying somebody, destroying somebody's spirit was a mortal sin, not some random, fleeting, natural brain wave of desire. I left class walking on air. I wasn't going to hell, after all.

Buoyed by my free pass, my new lease on life, I decided

decided to make the trek up the hill to St. Agatha's when the school day ended. Normally, I was unable to because of football practice, but with a flare-up of an asthmatic condition (and a small bit of play acting), I had a doctor's excuse to skip that day. My mother couldn't pick me up until 4:30, so I had some free time on my hands. I had told her I would be studying. The thought of heading up the hill to St. Agatha's filled me suddenly with optimism and hope. The path to St. Agatha's represented hope itself, the rank, ribald possibility of love and acceptance—and maybe more. I hadn't been up there since the first days of school back in early September. And after Brother Xavier's religion class, I felt that I was doing the Lord's work; I was doing this to save my soul.

As I crossed over railroad tracks before entering the woods I stood briefly watching the football team toiling away on the practice fields in the distance below. I could hear the coaches shouting, the piercing bleat of their whistles, the grunts of the players and the thud of their pads as they hit each other or the blocking sleds. I could see the players flop onto the ground and roll around while the coaches preened over them in their tight white shorts and cleated shoes. Watching them from this vantage point football seemed meaningless. I had joined the team because I enjoyed playing sports, but also because I thought it would make me a heroic figure, a popular big man on campus. But I discovered quickly that there were others who were stronger and faster than me, who cared more than me, who seemed to relish the hustle and the horseplay of the locker room. I hated the locker room hijinks. I disbelieved the claims of character-building, that treating players like a piece of wet dog crap somehow created strong-willed, upstanding individuals. I thought it created a distrust for all authority, a breeding ground for rebellion.

I surfaced fifteen minutes later onto the St. Agatha's campus, high atop a plateau overlooking a broad swath of northside San Antonio. You could see cars moving along Loop 410—from this vantage point they appeared to plug along at a slow and stately speed—and the newly-constructed spate of office buildings lining the roadway.

The school itself was a throwback to an earlier Catholic school style, with a statue of St. Agatha, Martyr, on a pedestal out front and florid paintings of our Holy Father and Jesus and the Apostles on the inside halls. It was a different world here, a feminine world animated by nuns and permeated by the delightful (if unsettling) sights and sounds of adolescent females. (The unsettling part was the reason why our two schools were segregated by sex.) The girls wore plaid uniform skirts and starched white blouses, unintentionally sexy. After school, those blouses became untucked, hanging loose. The top buttons were unfastened. The nuns here were a different breed from the ones who taught me in high school, looser, a bit more hip. Their habits were less confining, almost like regular clothes. Their wimple was really just a scarf, revealing wisps of hair, humanizing them. Even the calves of their legs showed, and their shoes were ordinary tennis shoes, not orthodontic-looking clodhoppers. They stood sleeves rolled up, hands on hips, feet spread, surveying their charges in a relaxed and self-assured manner. They had a sense of humor. They had a sense of irony. Some nuns seemed to have developed a kind of level-headed woman-to-woman relationship with their students, a bluff and bantering back-and-forth with an implied understanding of hormones and adolescent mood swings. And though they were protective of their girls, they accepted us St. Al's guys gate-crashing here as a natural, normal course of events. If they learned your name, they called you "Mister Kevin" or "Mister Steve" or whatever, in a tone that made you feel honored somehow, valued. There was even one young, pretty-ish nun, Sister Rita, for whom I harbored a romantic fantasy, that she would throw off her habit and renounce her vows and run away with me. She would have to drive, of course.

"Nice day," I told Sister Rita, observationally. Very adult-like, very mature.

"Nice day," Sister Rita responded. Smart, snappy conversation!

St. Agatha's was hopping that day, swarming with St. Al's students, angled afternoon sunshine interspersed with the long, soft shadows of autumn. It was a fall festival atmosphere, almost, a zone of laughter and merriment and bonhomie. The girls in their white blouses, St. Al's guys in our own uniforms of white pullover shirts and black slacks. This was where I belonged, I thought. This was how I could please God, save my soul. To hell with football practice. I quit the football team in my mind, right then and there.

After finishing my chat with Sister Rita—I thought there were subtle signs of a future rendezvous there—I took off in pursuit of love, joy, hedonistic pleasures. Or a smile, at least, from a pretty girl. I wandered into a crowd of guys teasing some girls. They laughed in tittered and response to schoolboy jibes, but they were holding their own, firing back jokes and risqué banter. I tried to think of something smart and clever to say, some way to pitch in, but my brain had gone into shutdown mode. I couldn't think of a single thing. I moved onto another group, standing on the fringe, hoping that a different vibe would give me some kind of entre there. It didn't happen. I felt shut out.

Several failed forays later, I was beginning to feel like an imposter there. I blundered from group to group, hoping to make an impact. But it was as if I didn't know the code. I had been away too long. I seemed invisible. I hadn't paid club dues. I hovered on the edge of groups of guys talking and bantering with girls, confident and cocky. I wished I could be confident and cocky. I began to wonder if I was even quite human. People walked by me, oblivious. I said things nobody responded to. Girls avoided eye contact. Even Sister Rita seemed indifferent to my plight, turning her head cruelly when I stopped by for an encouraging remark.

Depressed, defeated, I tried to rationalize my situation as just bad luck. The wrong crowd there today. In a different crowd, I would be a star. But I wasn't sure who I expected the right crowd to be. I turned back to the woods for a long, solitary hike back to the St. Al's parking lot, where my mother would pick me up. There was nobody to say goodbye to. Nobody who cared. My spirits were crushed. I felt like some sad animal, slinking back to its solitary den.

Then I heard my name called: "Kevin. Hey." I turned to see a girl I had met last summer, Denise Biancardi. She was standing apart from the other girls, smiling, fingering her crucifix. Her top button was unbuttoned. Her shirttail was untucked. It was as if the afternoon sun were a spotlight shining on her, illuminating her, making her special. A thrill of expectation shot up my spine.

"Remember me?" she said.

"Denise!" I said. "Hi! What's going on?"

We had met back in mid-summer at a barbecue mixer for incoming St. Al's and St. Agatha students, outside on the infield of the St. Al's baseball field. Wearing aprons over their cassocks, the Christian Brothers barbecued hamburgers while St. Agatha's nuns circulated about in chaperone style. It was a vastly different vibe from my grade school experience, a promise that life going forward could be something more than simply following rules and confession and five Hail Mary's afterwards. Sizzling hamburgers and barbecue smoke afforded a festive air. Her hair was straight and dark brunette, almost black. I remember thinking she was pretty, in a wholesome but savvy and smart-girl kind of way. And there seemed to be a cast of kindness in her dark eyes, some safety there, a guarantee of non-judgment, unlike some of the other girls I had known who seemed to thrive on biting, injurious remarks. We were shy together at first, but warmed up quickly, relating stories about our parents and families and dogs. She told me that her father owned an Italian restaurant on Broadway, one of the main strips into downtown, and that her entire family worked there, five kids and uncles and aunts included. It made me admire her even more, that she was a working girl. I could see that in her— or thought I could, anyway. I told her that my father was an accountant and a cheapskate, so cheap that we had only one telephone, centrally located so that everybody in the house could eavesdrop on you talking. She was the oldest child in the family. I was, too. She liked to play tennis. I did, too! "Let's play sometime," she said. "That sounds like fun!" I said. It sounded like a romantic adventure, just her and me out on a court together. As afternoon morphed into night, the semi-darkness and the surrounding cacophony of voices seemed to create a kind of shroud of intimacy around us. We could do and say things we had never said or done before. Sitting on the grass, half-eaten hamburgers on paper plates beside us, we touched each other off and on, experimentally, on the arm, the shoulder, the face, the foot. It was as if a kind of spell had come over us, a witching hour where anything goes. As darkness descended, we entered a skit contest with the subject matter: "Students Entering High School." Our entry was received with laughter and applause. But in the confusion afterwards, she slipped away and I never got a chance to get her number or tell her goodbye. I hadn't seen her again until just now.

"How are you doing?" she said now.

"OK," I said. "How about you?"

"I'm doing OK," she said. "I haven't seen you up here before."

"I always have football practice," I said. I shrugged. "I'm kind of sick today so I couldn't go."

"I hope not too sick," she said.

"No," I said. "It's just some allergies or something that I always get. Sometimes I get asthma. The doctor said I shouldn't run today."

"Well, glad you're here, then," she said.

"I'm glad I'm here," I said. I stood still, facing her, feet planted. I wasn't going anywhere now. She fingered the crucifix around her neck. We seemed to be treading on new ground here, a paradigm for a different kind of relationship.

"I had fun talking to you at that mixer last summer," she said.

"You did? I had fun, too."

"I thought our skit was pretty good. I thought it was the best one, really."

"I thought so, too!"

We had edged closer to each other, facing each other tentatively, uncertainly. She held her hair behind her head with one hand. I stood staring into her eyes, eyes that seemed to confirm my own feelings, feelings of longing and affection. Desire rose up in me like an unstoppable force. For just this little while, everything seemed right. Neither of us was moving. Neither of us wanted to move. Neither of us seemed uncomfortable. It was a sweet, unexpected feeling, not being uncomfortable with somebody. I was uncomfortable with everybody.

Without really thinking then, I lunged forward, aiming for something I had heretofore only dreamed about—a kiss on the lips with a girl. She came forward to meet me. Our lips puckered and touched. I pulled back, then went in for a more comprehensive follow-up kiss. It put a charge in me. I felt alive in a way I had never known before. We moved back, staring at each other, staring in wonderment and delight. We lingered briefly, wanting more—at least I wanted more—but fearing that a nun would intervene and then we would be put through an interrogation that would no doubt rival those at the height of the Spanish Inquisition.

Then I saw the watch on her arm. I returned to reality.

"What time is it?" I said.

"It's 4:30," she said.

"Oh, crap," I said. "My mom's picking me up back at the St. Al's parking lot. I better go."

"You better go," she said.

I grasped her fingertips briefly before tearing out for the woods. We had made no plans for the future, no proposal for another meeting, nothing. It didn't really matter. I didn't need anything else just then. I was totally happy. My life was pretty much complete. I scrambled through the trees and brush downhill to the St. Al's campus in a state of near-ecstasy. My senses were alive to a new dimension, a new world, a world where I was a respected and respectable human being. Maybe Brother Xavier was only partly right. Maybe a world of one's own was just a starting point, a launching pad for going out into the world. I felt equipped now to save souls.

As I emerged, crossing back over the railroad tracks, I saw our car, our white Pontiac Bonneville station wagon, 400 cubic inches of unbridled 1960s-era horsepower, parked in the side lot by the gym. I saw my mother in the driver's seat, waiting. Her window was rolled down part way. Like everybody back then, she was smoking, exhaling out the open window. She was a typical mother of the times, I suppose, hair cut rather short on the sides and back and permed into an impenetrable hive glued together by industrial strength hair spray. She was over-reactive and over-protective, perpetually worried, a bit of a nut. I considered her as a kind of amateur Erma Bombeck, firing off one-liners on issues of topical importance. I don't think she really had much of a life outside our house. I don't know what kind of a life of the mind she had. It all seemed fine to me. I was too young to question her life-style. I had no idea what adults went through. I guess I thought they had most problems solved.

I slowed down when I was within view, combing my hair, tucking in my shirt, wiping perspiration from my face with a handkerchief from my pocket. Then I saw Mr. Waldo, walking from the school lugging his beat-up old satchel.

"Hey, Mr. Waldo!" I said. He turned, abruptly, almost angrily, it seemed, as if expecting just another rebuff from a blockhead student. He looked weary. He looked beat. He couldn't take dealing any longer with snotty, privileged adolescents any longer.

"Hello, son," he said.

"I learned a lot in your class today," I said.

"That's nice," he said, after pausing for a moment. "That's good to hear." He nodded briefly before trudging along. I watched him get into an old, dented Ford sedan. The door stuck when he opened it. I knew he didn't have much money. I knew his life must be difficult. I thought perhaps I had made him feel good, changed something for the better in his mind.

I entered through the passenger-side door of the car greeting my mother with a nod. She craned her head around to see me. She held her cigarette loosely, precariously, with a long ash, at an angle that threatened to ignite the interior car fabric. Her face had assumed a concerned appearance that raised my hackles against any release of data. It was like she was peering into my soul and finding everything bad and nefarious there.

"*There* you are!" she said. "Where have you been?"

"I just took a short walk," I said. "Coach thought it would be good."

"You're not supposed to be running."

"I wasn't running. It was just a walk."

"You're bleeding," she said.

I glanced down at my arm. Blood was trickling down from a scratch on my wrist where I must have caught it on a thorn or bush. I hadn't noticed in my ecstatic state. I pushed down on it with my fingers.

"I brushed against something," I said.

"You'll need to clean it up."

"I will," I said. "I'll clean it up." I frowned, as if to display concern for my own carelessness and slipshod approach to my health.

"Well, how are you?" she said. "How did it go today."

"Fine," I said. "OK. There was a sub in Latin class."

"How was that?" she said.

I shrugged.

"OK," I said. "I don't like it when there's a sub." She nodded, in a way that seemed design to ferret out additional information. I didn't want to give her any.

"I never did, either," she said. "Is that it?"

"That's about it," I said.

Nodding uncertainly, she started the car and began to back out slowly. With a car that size, and my mother at the controls, the backing out procedure seemed to require immense quantities of time and concentration. I slumped back in the back seat, separating myself from her, scanning the freewayscape as it flew by. My life was good now. I was ready to go out into the world and save souls.

In the Time of the Revolution

My mother I hoped to be able to save in the time of the Revolution. She was a sweet, smart, trusting individual, my mother, forward-thinking in her own way, just now breaking through the turgid bonds of middle-class American existence, beginning to explore new avenues for satisfaction and fulfillment. She had her negatives, among them being married to my father, a stodgy, tightwad CPA for an office supplies firm, but all things considered she would be worth keeping around. Slightly plump, girdled, perpetually on a diet, she wore her hair in a kind of bouffant wave, with bangs, and these oblong rhinestone eyeglasses that would need to be replaced. Still, she was hip in her own way, hip in an astute, sage, sensible, jolly, senior-citizen's way (hell, she was 46), alert to me as a struggling young adult, indulgent to my whims and fancies. Lately she had been dabbling in such mind-opening activities as yoga and book club and community theater. (She played a very jovial Mrs. Gibbs character in "Our Town.")

This particular revolution was occurring in the year 1971, a year marked by Vietnam War protests and the release of the Pentagon Papers and continuing cultural changes. Change had been percolating for a number of years now, even in my hometown San Antonio, deep in the backwater of south central Texas. There were baggies of pot and panes of acid and long hair on men and women shedding bras, and we were going to change the world. A new order was beginning. The old order was falling away. And it all seemed to have happened organically, a huge unstoppable gusher of change fueled by television, new technology, and a perception of life entirely unprecedented in the annals of humankind. I was 19, a tender, callow 19, filled with anxieties and unfulfilled dreams.

My mother seemed to believe that I was some kind of wanton libertine, a blissful, guilt-free product of the free-thinking moral standards of the times. I didn't want to totally dispossess her of this notion.

"I know what you young people are like nowadays," she said, moseying over as I sat eating breakfast one weekday morning.

"What?" I said.

"You know."

"I don't know," I said. "What are you talking about?"

She smiled mysteriously, enigmatically, like a fortune teller conducting a séance. She was wearing her famous Guatemalan peasant's dress, decorated in bright, jagged bands of color. The dress seemed a statement of her moving forward, catching the waves of change coursing through the contemporary, post-Eisenhower world. She moved in a certain way in that dress that she didn't move in any other article of clothing, swishing around with a smart, determined, cheerful demeanor. I doubt there were many actual Guatemalan peasants with my oh-so-American mother's sense of sunny self-sufficiency.

"Do I have to say it?" she said. She swished her dress around like some over-the-hill belly dancer. "I'm not naïve. I read about all this stuff and watch it on TV. Sex. The Sexual Revolution."

My face burned, my hands shook as I lowered the fork from my face. I looked down at my bacon and eggs, pensively. I didn't want to disappoint my own mother. I wanted her to feel good about me, about my relationships and sexual exploits, that I was as popular and dissolute and debauched (in a good old red-blooded American way) as the next guy. I shrugged.

"Well . . ." I said, implying the distinct possibility that all she had suggested was true. My bite of egg tasted like cardboard. My mother placed her hands on my shoulder and kneaded.

"I just want you to be careful," she said. "I don't want you to end up with some kind of horrible disease."

"I'll be careful, Mother," I said. I shrugged again.

If only I had the chance . . . this other revolution, the Sexual Revolution, was a touchy topic for me. The truth being that I was a poser in this realm, a pretender, a dilettante. I, too, had read the stories and watched TV and heard people talking, and my resulting inferiority complex rendered me diminished and depressed.

Mother moved away, swishing her peasant dress. I shoveled down the remainder of my breakfast in a reverie of self-consciousness.

I gathered up my keys and wallet and backpack and hopped into my Ford Mustang—a high school graduation gift—parked on the street. In my down-time from the Revo-lution, I went to school. I was a freshman at San Antonio Community College (SAC), still living at home, a situation that was embarrassing, ego deflating, tragically traumatic. After high school, I was qualified academically to attend a four-year institution—my top choice being the University of Texas at Austin, where Communist infiltrators lurked in building hallways—but as first-born child my parents weren't prepared for me to move out yet—and my father was cheap, classically, majestically cheap. Despite earning a solidly middle-class income, he wouldn't commit to paying for me to go away to college until my junior year. My old corner bedroom, with its writing desk facing a bay window and a black-and-white TV, felt like a white-collar prison now. You could come and go, but you always had to return. Everything good and exciting seemed far, far away.

I drove to class that morning brooding under a toxic cloud of insecurity and apprehension. SAC was located along a broad, bustling thoroughfare just north of down-town San Antonio, a several-block cluster of contemporary, geometrically-shaped buildings, with glass facades three- and four- and five-stories tall, soaring atrium lobbies with wall sculptures visible within. Everything about the campus be-spoke "functional." It was functional and practical and efficient, training center more than college, a place where dreams went dormant, where dreams went to die. Everybody there seemed either in some peculiar situation or oblivious, everybody was ready to get out and off to a "real" college. After classes, I drove downtown where I worked as a clerk for a title company, a position my father had arranged for me. It was all very trite and stale and humdrum, a lame, lackluster experience.

I was conflicted regarding my role in the Revolution. Under the hard-core shell of the revolutionary was a young man who wished to succeed in life in an appallingly traditional way. I wanted a career, to get married, to live in a charming, middle-class neighborhood, raise children, then retire to a hassle-free dotage where I played tennis all day long and drank beer. In a concession to the cause, I pledged to never earn more than $75,000 a year—$475,000 in today's dollars—and to refrain from certain other superfluous ostentations. Uncertain how my fellow revolutionaries would perceive such strategies, I kept them to myself.

One afternoon, I attended a lecture by legendary civil rights attorney William Kunstler, in a downtown San Antonio Mexican restaurant. Kunstler's wild shoulder-length shock of graying hair and brusque New Yorker accent intimidated me. At one point, he suggested that we, the members of the audience, should prepare to take itinerant revolutionaries into our homes, as an in-kind contribution to the cause. I had immediate concerns about this proposed activity, both logistically and philosophically. I feared the process might begin right then and there. I shrunk back in my chair, trying to remain inconspicuous. I guess the sad fact was that I was more Romantic than Revolutionary. Despite all indications to the contrary, I believed that love could conquer all.

I parked my car on a quiet street in a staid old inner-city neighborhood of white clapboard houses with postage-stamp lawns and high front porches supported by classical Greek columns, Doric and Ionic and Corinthian. I walked to class reluctantly, backpack dangling from one hand, barely attached. I looked on it as a neutral object, as a cumbersome appendage, like a piece of luggage at the airport. It was a requirement. It was not a friend. My blue collared pullover shirt seemed somehow simultaneously gaudy and mundane. The hem of my blue jeans dragged on the pavement. My mother's words zinging in my ears, I felt like some prize chump, the least cool person in the history of the world. I felt that I had to explain myself to everyone, put myself into context. I felt like I was a long, long way from ever achieving anything, either personally or professionally.

It was a cheerful, sun-kissed May day, the sky a pure azure blue, soft, wispy clouds tracking across like chariots of ancient gods. It was the kind of day that if you felt good, you felt spectacular, energy spiking through you like a life force, but if you felt bad you felt left out, shunned by everybody's bubble of happiness.

My first class was Economics 101, taught by a handsome baby-faced professor who resembled a junior VP at a branch insurance firm, dark hair slicked back, the slacks of his 3-piece herringbone suit tight and hiked up high around the ankles. The auditorium was an amphitheater, rows of seats in a semi-circle, each pastel-colored chair equipped with a foldable tablet arm. Track lights overhead were controlled by a motor and a dimmer switch. A white matte video screen in front moved up and down on a roller.

The lecture focused on supply and demand, scarcity, opportunity costs, elasticity of supply, among other topics that would go by the boards in the time of the revolution. I zoned out immediately, thoughts meandering around such themes as my (potential) sexual prowess and my entire future existence, both of which appeared bleak at the moment. Everything seemed bleak. The ever-expanding universe was hurtling toward infinite size, some undefined final resolution. My personal universe seemed to be contracting to the size of a proton. We were going different directions.

After class, I dragged myself over to the SUB (Student Union Building) for a cup of strong black coffee. And possibly a shot of heroin, if available.

On the sidewalk outside the SUB a pair of scruffy dudes sat at a folding table with a hanging banner that read, "US OUT NOW," and a pile of pamphlets, poorly-printed. One of the dudes shouted out as I passed by, "Hey man, come find out what's going down."

Trapped, I sidled over to the table where I grabbed a pamphlet and smiled, offering a peace V sign to signify my revolutionary bona fides. One of the dudes smiled conspiratorially, flipping his uncombed earlobe-length hair in a way that couldn't have occurred a decade earlier.

"Be ready for something big going down later," he said.

"I will," I said. Entering the SUB, I stuffed the pamphlet into my backpack.

The SUB was bustling this late-morning hour, a fragrant aroma of fried eggs and bacon and buttered biscuits wafting through like a siren song for starving students.

Silverware clinked, coffee cups clanked, cooks shouted out orders. The hustle-bustle annoyed me somehow, everybody seemed happy, paired-up, chatting, contented members of some established group. I felt like a loner, an interloper, a man without a country or a faith. I picked a plastic tray from a stack and started through the crowded cafeteria line, sliding my tray along the metal rails. Though I had eaten breakfast already, I impulse-purchased a large glazed cinnamon roll along with a coffee, aiming for a sugar rush. It was the closest thing to heroin that I could get.

I paid a girl straddling a stool at a cash register, chewing gum. I joked with her while handing her money and she looked at me quizzically before opening her cash drawer and passing me change. She never stopped chewing. I was a dud again.

I turned from the check-out counter abruptly, bumping trays with a frail, formless young woman in bib overalls and with purple streaks in her chin-length hair. My coffee shook and jiggled on the tray. I reached out with one hand. She frowned reactively. We both apologized, but it was that kind of strained, offended apology that left you feeling angry and annoyed.

Shaken myself, I was carrying my tray to a table when I saw a girl I recognized from my English literature class moving toward me. I shuffle-stepped briefly before girding myself for conversation, what would surely be an awful conversation, a pointless conversation. Another blow to my ego. Another beat down.

I had never spoken to her directly, though in class we had some back-and-forth exchanges over the course materials, sitting at our desks, and I had been impressed with her sensible, sometimes sharp-edged observations about their meanings and their relationships to life. She was an attractive girl, blond and tanned and very suburban-looking, a swimmer or a dancer or a tennis player, I presumed. In fact, I had fantasized about her regularly, meeting with her and kissing her and more. But I wasn't prepared to talk to her right now. I wasn't prepared to talk to anybody.

She walked right up to me, smiling aggressively, a bit too extrovertedly, I thought. I smiled back, grimly. She wore a red nylon backpack strapped to her back, affording her an exceptionally upright, provocative posture. Her bosom—braless, I presumed—pushed out from a white blouse of silky material. The blouse ended just above her belly button. She wore blue jeans—of course—tattered a little, with a hole in one knee. But laundered neatly. Her blown-dry hair was pushed back behind her ears. She didn't look like somebody who openly opposed the Revolution, but maybe she didn't think about it much either. I thought I knew her type—hair, clothes, cars, makeup, long hours of gossip on a Princess telephone at night. Not that any of that bothered me. I could adapt to that style.

"Hi Dave," she said. I was flattered that she remembered my name—inordinately flattered. My face turned red.

"Hi Kate," I said. Kate Hudson was her name, the name of someone who had obviously never suffered a moment of pain or deprivation in her life. I wondered how long it would take her to discover what a dull, inept person I was.

"I haven't seen you in here much."

"I know," I said. I gestured gawkily with my tray. "I don't come in here much. I usually go to the library between classes." As soon as I said that I knew it sounded finicky, pedantic, rather precious. I might as well have said I liked to pick daisies in a field.

"That's good," she said. "Diligent."

"I don't know," I said, waving my tray again. "Maybe just stupid."

She laughed.

"I know you're not stupid," she said.

I laughed, too loudly, too coarsely. Man, I was stupid.

"Are you going to sit down?" she said. "Can I join you?"

"Oh—sure," I said. "Where do you want to go?"

She glanced around. She was probably thinking, "God, do I have to do everything?"

"How about that table back there?" she said. She motioned to a small square table in a corner. I nodded OK. My nod felt forced and stiff.

"Looks good," I said.

I trudged alongside her feeling nervous, sluggish, self-conscious, trying to figure out how long I was going to have to sit there, what I was going to say. I actually just wanted to stew in my own thoughts. I didn't know why exactly, but I was very private regarding my eating habits. I didn't like just anybody to see me eat. It was hard to explain. Eating seemed to expose something in me, something flawed and guilty and weak. It was like a peek into my soul, a soul blotched by deficiencies and rejections and inadequate application of skills. Not only could I not take people into my home, I couldn't even take them to my table. After a desultory walk, we settled into opposite sides of a square, specked-Formica table with wobbly metal legs. I promptly smacked one of the metal legs with one of my own. A crescendo of happy talk from satisfied and satiated fellow students seemed to mock us as we sat.

Our first few lines of conversation were pure boilerplate, derived from our shared classroom experience.

"Dr. Whitbread is a groovy guy."

"Yeah, he's funny, too."

"I liked that time he collapsed on his desk after reading the poem."

"He's really made me appreciate 19th century literature."

"I know. He makes is all seem so relevant to today."

I sighed inwardly. I knew how this would go. It seemed OK now, but soon would degenerate into another in a long line of abject failure with girls. Against the somber backdrop of the Revolution this was meaningless, of course, but unfortunately, sadly, I couldn't seem to keep it from mattering to me. I was going to have to pretend that I knew something, that I was something, that I had achieved something. I tried to put on my best pose. It was one thing to pose for my mother, who wanted to believe the best and thus was easily fooled, something else again to pose with a girl my own age. She would analyze me, see through me, dissect me like a frog on a laboratory table. Then at the end she would crush me with a comment about a boyfriend, of course, no doubt a cool and confident character with a hot car and money and unlimited freedom, and I would be left muttering something small and inconsequential. After-wards, she would never even make eye contact with me again. I would just be somebody on the far side of the class. She would leave class quickly, avoiding me.

But then she leaned forward, resting on her elbows. She smiled. Her eyes seemed to shine, reflecting some new-found form of affection, something alien to me. She seemed unusually close to me, almost in my plate. It was like sitting in the front row of the movie theater, staring up at the screen. Her backpack was on the floor now. Then she did something that I found rather strange—she picked off a piece of my cinnamon roll with her left hand and held it near her mouth.

"You don't mind, do you?" she said.

"Oh—no," I said, shaking my head uncertainly. "Of course not."

She put the piece of cinnamon roll in her mouth and chewed, chewed dramatically, chewed radiantly, chewed with an arching eye movement, chewed like somebody auditioning for a spot in a French comedy of manners. A tour de force of chewing. After she swallowed, she smiled, as if to define just how delighted she was by her achievement.

"Delicious!" she said.

"Fantastic!" I said.

Her pose was lushly sensual, sending shivers down my body. It was almost as if she were puckering her lips for a kiss. The tilt of her body seemed like a solicitation, an invitation to approach. And then she did something even stranger than taking a piece of my cinnamon roll. She began to cry. First I saw tears trickling down from the corners of her eyes, she sighed, her bosom heaved, then she put her head in her hands and sobbed openly. One big blop fell on the table and she wiped it away with her hand. Another blop fell and I wiped it away. I panicked, thinking perhaps I had invaded her space, absconded her responsibility.

"Is everything OK?" I said. What an idiot! Of course everything wasn't OK. But what should I say? I touched her lightly on the elbow. That seemed a safe place. She lifted her head, eyes bleary.

"It's so stupid," she said.

"I'm sure it's not stupid," I said.

I don't know why I'm bothering you," she said. "You just always seemed so smart and nice."

"Thanks—" I said. "I'm not so sure about that."

She wiped another tear from her eye.

"You probably don't want to hear what's going on with me," she said.

"I do," I said. "I do want to hear." She reached out her hand to me.

"It's just so stupid," she said. "It's just that I feel like I'm never going to go anywhere. My whole life is going to be a waste."

"Your life's not going to be a waste."

She sat up then. She composed herself. She wiped her eyes with a napkin from the table. My napkin, actually. She told me her story then, starting slow, then the words spilling out like water from a hidden spring. She seemed to want to tell me, to trust me, to consider me somebody worth telling her story to. The raucous sounds of the SUB seemed to fade away, leaving only Kate and me, alone in the cosmos.

She told me that she felt like she was posing, that she didn't belong, that while other people were cool and confident, she was uncertain and insecure. Her family was barely middle class. Her father was an electrician and they lived in a small house in a sketchy neighborhood with one bathroom and one phone. She had to buy her own car—a clunker. She had to pay for her own clothes. As she talked, I stopped being so nervous around her, so self-conscious. I began to understand that she was vulnerable, and hurting, and uncertain—just like me! She had been posing, too. Something changed, something clicked inside me then. My energy level soared. I felt myself return from the abyss. My life seemed to be starting anew.

"And now," she said, "they say I'll have to pay my way through all four years of college. I'll never get out of here . . .I know, it's so selfish."

"It's not selfish," I said.

I looked longingly at her, sitting across the table from me. This seemed like a breakthrough of some kind, a discovery, an apotheosis. I felt elevated to a new status. I was a legitimate human being. I stood up, leaning over the table. I grabbed her shoulders. I wanted her to know that I was with her. I wanted her to know that I understood.

From that moment on, we were clued in to each other. The rest of our time at the table was all happy talk, plans and preparation and positive vibes.

"You can do it," I said. "You can get a grant, a loan, a part-time job. I've got to do that, too. I'll help you figure it out."

"You will?" she said.

"For sure," I said. "I want to."

"Oh, that's great!" she said. "That's groovy!"

When we walked outside into dazzling late-morning sunshine, the world had changed. This ordinary place, these nondescript classroom buildings, this paved walkway, seemed sacred now, a shrine, a holy place. I was a new man, a new man in a new world. Everything seemed in front of me now, my life filled with possibilities. The future looked positive, upbeat. And yet, for one of the few times in my life, I didn't want to leave the present. I had no additional wants or needs. I bumped gently against Kate as we walked, which was itself a kind of corroboration, an acknowledgement of approval. No matter what happened in the future, I had something. I had something now.

In the distance, far up on the shrub-lined mall, we saw something unfamiliar, out of the ordinary. There was a commotion of some kind, a disturbance, a rolling tide of people moving toward us, gesturing and chanting. It was like a multi-footed, multi-handed creature, some mythological late-20th century beast. Above it seemed to float a kind of apparition, a papier-mâché figure in reality, that upon advancing closer we could see was an effigy of President Richard Nixon, his trademark jowls covered in a clownish five o'clock beard. It was a war protest! It was the Revolution! I guess it was what the guy at the table was hinting at when he said something big would be "going down" later. My pulse quickened as I looked at Kate apprehensively. This was uncharted territory. I had been waiting for the Revolution to come to my campus, but now that it was here, I felt tentative and uncertain. I didn't know what Kate would think. We had never discussed such things. But as the throng approached, she took my hand and nodded.

"Go for it?" she said.

"In there?" I said.

"Yeah!" she said.

"OK!" I said.

We merged in at the edge of the crowd as they shuffled by, and now we found ourselves among them, a part of them, chanting and clapping, marching through the main mall of the campus. It seemed almost like a real campus now. The smell of marijuana smoke drifted through on a lazy spring breeze. Non-participants lined the walkway like parade watchers, some faces curious, some admiring, some set hard in anger and disapproval. They represented the great schism of our times—new paradigm vs. old-style conventional values.

Surging with emotion, we shook our fists and shouted, "U.S. out now!" "Nixon is a dick!" I felt proud and justified, a genuine certified member of the counter-culture. (Even though I still lived at home.) I was making a difference! I was changing the world! Yet glancing over to Kate on my right, I felt a twinge of regret, of disappointment, of lost opportunity. From profile view, she seemed oblivious to me now, caught up in her own emotion. I felt that I had lost her somehow. Our affection had been subsumed in a larger cause. She shouted and clapped, unaware of me.

We reached the edge of campus and crossed over onto city streets, turning north onto San Pedro Avenue, a broad, divided thoroughfare than ran from the far northern suburbs all the way downtown. We spilled over the median onto the northbound lanes, stopping oncoming cars. Traffic bottled up behind us. Horns blared. Drivers shouted. A city bus idled in the far right southbound lane, exhaling diesel fumes, straining to go. We walked among the trapped cars like in a movie about space invaders. It was strange and thrilling and exhilarating, moving through this forbidden land, something far apart from our mundane everyday existence. We continued on for several city blocks, ignoring red lights and Don't Walk signs and drivers waving wildly for us to move out of the way. An Action TV news van trundled along the sidewalk beside us, broadcasting the rebellion. We had broken through the bonds of conventional civilization to a new plane of awareness.

Abruptly, though, everybody stopped, people tumbling one into another. There were shouts and screams up ahead, the type of panicked cries that accompany a disaster.

"Tear gas!" somebody shouted. "They're gassing us!"

"Pigs! The pigs are loose!"

There was confusion and chaos as cops in riot gear lobbed tear gas from canisters into the crowd. Puffs of smoke hung in the air like noxious fog. Cops waded into the crowd, swinging billy clubs.

"He's bleeding!"

"Shit! We've got people down."

Those in the vanguard were tackled and cuffed with hands behind and thrown to the pavement, then dragged off into paddy wagons parked nearby. Kate grabbed my hand and we ran at right angles from San Pedro Avenue as everybody scattered. We pushed hard, stumbling a time or two but pulling ourselves back up, running until we found ourselves alone on an isolated back street, not far from where my car was parked. Our breathing subsided as we slowed to a walk. It seemed a kind of paradise there, a place of peace and harmony and reconciliation. A ceasefire there. We were all by ourselves. Nobody on earth knew where we were. Before the days of cell phones and computers, we were unreachable. The sunlight was of an ethereal quality, like sunlight in a pristine valley in a far-off corner of the world. Birds—our enthusiastic allies—twittered merrily in the trees. The discordant sounds from the peace rally had faded away. We weren't being pursued. We had escaped. We were safe. There would be no anguished, urgent phone calls to parents for bail-outs. We stopped outside a white, two-story clapboard house and sat down on the curb. Our hips were only inches apart.

"Wow," Kate said.

"Wow," I said.

Kate smiled. I smiled. I thrilled as her eyes seemed to disclose some new, more refined brand of affection. The feeling of enchantment we had discovered back in the SUB began to return. I glanced over to her, beside me on the curb. She stretched out her legs. She didn't make any movement to leave. She looked like she wanted to stay with me. I tapped my foot on the pavement, uncertain as to next steps. I tried to think of something to say, something smart and snappy and suave. I couldn't think of anything. I felt embarrassed suddenly, as when Adam and Eve discovered they were naked in the Garden of Eden.

Then Kate did something that was perhaps more surprising even than what she had done before—she leaned over to kiss me on the mouth. My psyche soared as her lips touched mine. The kiss was a foretaste of heaven itself. She threw her arms around me. I was helpless in her arms. I didn't want to move. I wanted to stay right there forever.

When I returned home from working at the title company my mother was cooking something piquant and stew-like for dinner.

"Hungry?" she said, stirring a heavy pot.

"You bet!" I said. I wrapped my arms around her back and we tangoed briefly, like Astaire and Rogers, like Kelley and Hayward. She couldn't know exactly what was going on, but she may have had some inkling. She would be worth keeping in the time of the Revolution.

The Sacker

[Important Note: This sacker's career occurred during the heyday of sacking, before the introduction of plastic bags, along with scanning devices, changed the world.]

As a 17-year-old sacker in the formalized caste system of Handy-Andy Supermarket No. 23, 4225 Fredericksburg Rd., San Antonio, TX., I was low man on a slick and crowded totem pole. Produce managers, cashiers, checkers, merchandise supervisors, shift managers, even stockers (that breed of one-celled paramecium-like matter) felt they were superior, Hamlet to my Polonius, McBeth to my badly-flawed McDuff.

Ironically, the skills required for superior, error-free sacking are rare among the general populace. Sacking requires a sense of proportion, spatial balance, and appreciation of geometric form, as well as an intricate ensemble of fine motor skills. You can't just slouch up there and start sacking, like an off-the-cuff speech. First, one must carefully assess the sacking job—number of items, their temperature, moisture content, mass, and bulk. One must set one's mind to the task, not unlike an actor getting "into character" before a theatrical production. Then, under conditions of immense and unrelenting pressure, one begins. One must begin. The foundation is laid: heavier items on the bottom, lighter items on top. Too many items, the bag tears. Too few items, and precious trees are wasted, along with precious pennies for the store. (Precious pennies being a predominant theme among the grocery hierarchy.) There are other general rules, but "feel" is essential, not unlike (I would presume) that innate knack required by a crack photographer in sizing up a subject, or a left-fielder in gunning down a runner at home plate. I "feel" not just anyone has the temperament, the discipline, or the physical tools required to sack. I don't wish to sound harsh and judgmental, but frankly, sacking is not for everyone.

Saturday morning behind the counter, the usual chaotic maelstrom—somewhere just outside the Seventh Circle of Hell. My immature mind, focused on several Dream Girls noted earlier that morning, was blasted from its reverie like reveille at dawn.

"Hey, Butt Face," said Calvin Meadows, my checker, without turning his head. I was stationed behind the counter, feet spread, shoulders hunched, hands swinging loose in front—poised for action. I rocked to and fro slightly, swiveling, ready to move in any direction. Over the counter, if necessary.

"What?" I responded, but only after a small but significant pause, to signal unmistakably I wasn't on his payroll.

"Get me a roll of quarters, will you?" I remained silent

for a long moment, again. Boy, I was getting awfully skilled at that.

"Okay," I said, finally. I sighed and shook my head before shuffling over to the office, a small, square window with a slot for sliding money in and out. The cashier inside was busy stamping checks with an automatic numbering machine.

"Whaddya need?" he said, without bothering to look up. The cashier was a hot-shot guy with a flattop and big forearms who had been working there about thirty years, though I guess he was only about 20 or so. He seemed destined to be a career grocery store guy.

"Roll of quarters," I said. To the cashier, I always spoke with an extreme economy of words—the fewer the better. If I could get by with a grunt, I'd grunt. I was convinced he understood only a few regular English words, although he had a fabulous storehouse of grocery store jargon. He was the Ben Jonson of the grocery trade. Of course, he was irritated to hear my request. He was always irritated. I could see the perspiration on his furrowed brow. The color of his skin was like some off-brand of boiled pate.

"Whaddya need quarters for?" he asked, as if quarters were some rare and exotic commerce used for a desperate, outlawed medical treatment. His mouth contorted like a fish.

"Meadows wants 'em," I said, implicating Cal with a dark, sinister motive. I said this with a rather naughty interior laugh, understanding the cashier considered Cal the very lowest form of grocery store fauna, except for me, of course. The cashier rolled his eyes sarcastically, his bushy eyebrows flexing outward.

"Doesn't he ever want anything but rolls of quarters?" the cashier said. "God, he's breaking me." Even in my impaired condition, broken down by having to deal with inane associates, I enjoyed his remark, how the cashier took this ordinary business transaction as a kind of personal offense, as if releasing the store's legal tender actually broke him. Finally, terribly aggrieved, he pushed a single roll of pink-wrapped quarters through the slot and returned to stamping the back sides of checks. This was probably the closest thing to poetry to him, stamping checks. I considered offering thanks, but gratitude seemed inappropriate, almost mocking, under the circumstances. I trudged back to the check-out counter and held out my hand, feeling somehow chastened. I was always feeling chastened.

"Open them," Cal said.

"Open them?" I repeated dumbly, staring at the roll in my hand as if it contained a ticking uranium lode. I forgot to mention that my manual dexterity was on a par with your basic trilobites.

"You think I got time?" he said, cackling hideously. God, he was a supercilious bastard. Tall, gangly, with dark peach fuzz clinging vaguely to his pimply cheeks, and a high receding hairline above a long and narrow scalp, though he was a senior citizen of approximately 18. I couldn't think of a single objective reason why he should be such an ego-inflated, overbearing clod. Why didn't he have the inferiority complex, instead of me?

He stood there, obdurately inspecting his precious cash

box while I rapped the roll of coins on the rounded metal rim of the check-out counter, grumbling ferociously just below hearing range. After all, sacking was my thing—I had no training in this particular discipline. Nothing happened. I tried again—nothing. Cal inserted his cash box into the drawer and closed it with a whump. One more try, and now the roll split open, spewing coins like a malfunctioning geyser. The checker held his head at a peculiar cocked angle which signified extreme disdain.

"Oh, God," Cal said, grimacing fiendishly. "What have you done?" Though it was perfectly obvious what I had done. Quarters were everywhere, more quarters than could possibly have been in the roll, rolling, spinning on their edges, gyrating all over the floor like obscene dancers. Hunched over, I scrambled to control them as a line of customers began to form. It seemed that customers were drawn to my counter like mayflies to a high-power spotlight.

Cal said to the next customer: "He's famous for his fine motor skills." He gazed at me with an expression of complete contempt. "Oh, Lordy, you've got those things everywhere."

I began scooping up the coins as best I could, scuttling along the floor like the Hunchback of Notre Dame. Finally, from a kneeling position, I handed the final quarter to Cal, turning it over with a swashbuckling defiance that belied my total discomfort. Then I clapped him on the back in a show of false camaraderie and crawled out from behind the counter, now on all fours.

Just then—as my luck would have it—the store manager stalked by in his usual condition of high alert, scanning the aisles like a motion detector with his sharp, beady, bifocaled eyes.

Mr. P, as we called him (for Petrowicz, or some such moniker nobody could pronounce), talked on the go, arranging a row of canned goods here, stocking paper bags there, straightening somebody's necktie with a quick and fidgety hand. His age was indeterminate—somewhere between thirty-five and fifty-five was the best I could determine. Certainly his sex drive was on a par with that of a lichen. Which was probably a good thing—he was here ten hours or more a day, six days a week, minimum. Career managers were hired for their ability not to have a personal life.

Seeing me, he smacked his forehead with the butt of his hand and shook his head sideways in a pantomime of disbelief and wonder. It was as though he were viewing the scene of a major natural disaster, a fissure in the earth, perhaps.

"God Almighty, Son!" he proclaimed. He spoke in loud proclamations for everybody to hear. He always called me "son." It might be noted also that Mr. P tended to notice only the negative aspects of employee behavior. "Your shirt's not tucked in." "Your tie needs straightening." "Get a haircut." These were his stock and standard remarks as he motored by prior to disappearing through the swinging metal doors into the warehouse area. Obviously, crawling out from behind the check-out counter during a time of heavy customer activity was not specified as proper deportment in the employee handbook, which Mr. P had memorized page and paragraph.

"I—" I began to stammer, groping for an explanation. But like a boxer who had his opponent flailing on the ropes, Mr. P gave me no time to regroup.

"Would you care to explain what you were doing on the floor?"

"Well, I—I" I said. I gestured foolishly with my hands.

"What sort of spectacle were you trying to present?"

"I don't know," I groveled.

"Do you understand that from the moment you step foot on this floor you represent the organization to the public?"

"Yes, sir," I said. "I understand that, sir."

A fortunate thing occurred, then. Mr. P was distracted by a customer, blocking his path with her body and a saccharine smile. The consummate corporate politician, Mr. P always had his hand in a customer's hand, or around a customer's back, staring in with practiced intensity.

This particular customer was one of our store celebrities, both because of her eccentric appearance and because she could spend entire days shopping, sometimes. Reports of her location would be relayed gleefully around the store: "She's entering Cosmetics, now." "She just made the turn into Frozen Goods." "It's looking like Produce will be her next stop." Sometimes she left the store with a loaded cart, sometimes she bought nothing at all. Or one item. Or ten. Rumor had it she was a wealthy widow, so everybody was ordered to be on their best behavior in her presence.

A frail, elderly matron type, she was spectacularly overdressed today in a long, black silk gown, a pearl necklace, and a mink stole, the hem fraying at the bottom. A wave at the bottom of her frosted hair resembled a pipeline for surfers and her lips were as red as Bing cherries. She waved to Mr. P, a stilted, stiff little wave way up by her shoulder, and he waved back. Afterwards, he grimaced, involuntarily.

"Hel-l-o, Mrs. Bednarski!" boomed Mr. P, in the particular type of broadcasting voice he reserved for public consumption. Everybody had to know how masterfully he could handle customers. "How are you today?" But immediately you could see his anxiety level rising as he began to evaluate the time factor involved in conversing with Mrs. Bednarski.

"I'm good, Mr. Petrowicz," Mrs. Bednarski said, enunciating each word laboriously in her thin, dotty, old lady's accent. She accepted Mr. P's hand in hers and massaged it gently between her scaly thumb and index finger, as everybody under the age of senility cringed with nausea. "But I do have one, teeny, tiny, little complaint. Not a complaint, even, really. Just one small recommendation. Something you might consider."

"And what's that, Mrs. Bednarski?" Mr. P said. The anguish in his face was counter-balanced by his effort to please her as he watched the seconds ticking away. Seconds during which he could be prowling the floor, adjusting shelves, kicking butt. The kicking butt factor loomed large in all of his in-store relationships.

"We-l-l," she drawled out the words in a kind of superannuated little girl's voice. "In the produce aisle, the way the lettuce is stacked . . ."

Mr. P wiped his brow ferociously with his free hand as Mrs. Bednarski droned on. Perspiration poured off his face and stained the underarms of his white dress shirt. I took the opportunity to slip away to the far side of the store.

Mr. P didn't forget about me, though—when he finally broke loose, he tracked me down in the Generics aisle, where I pretended to price-check 32-oz. jars of apricot preserves. There, he laid his enormous reptilian hand on my right shoulder, facing me, as though I were about to be knighted.

"McKelvey," he pronounced, solemnly. He still didn't know my name—he was reading off the nameplate on my breast pocket.

"Sir," I said.

"Do something with your life," he said.

"Yes, sir," I agreed. "I will, sir." He pushed my shoulder backwards and forwards, like a lever.

"You seem to have some rather major problems, McKelvey," he said. He read my name on the breastplate again. "Anything at home bothering you? Parents quarreling? Girlfriend troubles?"

"No, sir," I said.

"Sure about that?"

"Yes, sir," I said. He looked me up and down for long seconds, appraising me.

"I'm glad to hear it," he said, squeezing my shoulder until I winced. "Then let's get with it."

"I will, sir," I said. "I'll get with it right away, sir." Nodding ominously, he released my shoulder and turned to walk away. I breathed a sigh of relief. But then he stopped abruptly, pivoting on his heel. He had the most remarkable pivoting action outside of the U.S. Marines.

"You know something, McKelvey?" he said.

"What's that, sir?" I said.

"I had been thinking of promoting you to checker," he said. "But now I'm going to have to reconsider. I'm going to have to watch you for awhile."

"Yes, sir," I said. "I understand, sir."

"I'm glad you do," he said. "Get back to work now."

"I will, sir," I said. "I'll get back to work, sir." Perhaps it was symbolic that when I glanced down I noticed that my left shoelace was untied.

"Tie your shoe, Son," Mr. P said.

"Yes, sir," I said. "I will, sir."

The remainder of that fateful Saturday I sacked with a bruised and sullen pride, my terrible secret intact. Yes, I was the most senior sacker in the history of the store to have never been promoted to checker. I didn't understand why, exactly—I had brains, savvy, style. Upon lengthy rumination, I could come to only one conclusion—I was too smart to be promoted. A major swell of pride rolled through my chest as I made my final decision.

"I'm quitting." I dropped the bombshell without warning.

"What's that?" said Mr. P, suddenly hard of hearing. He leaned over slightly at the neck and shoulders, as if they were connected on a hinge.

"I'm turning in the old grocery sack," I said, melodramatically, actually pretending I had a sack to hand to him. "This is my final day. My final hour, in fact. My final minute."

Anticipating a protest, a valiant but doomed lobbying effort, a last-second, hard-sell blitz, a kind of fraternity rush, I stood defiantly, prepared to resist. But Mr. P merely exten -ded his hand for me to shake, a conciliatory, let-bygones-be -bygones, wrap-it-up hand. He seemed relieved, actually.

"Good luck, Son," he said. "Sorry things didn't work out for you here." I shook weakly, my gaze fixed sheepishly approximately three inches to the left of his nose. I fought the impulse to punch him squarely in that rather fleshy appendage.

"Me, too," I said, deflated. I continued, stupidly. "Maybe I'll see if there's any openings again, sometime."

"Give me a call if you do," Mr. P said, though obviously he didn't mean it, relaxing his grip and moving on quickly to address Calvin Meadows, who had edged up beside him to pose some stupid checker-related question. I was unable to return his obnoxiously eager stare.

There was one last item of business to wrap up.

In the employee's lounge, where I punched my time card for the final time, a slender young girl with ratted hair and the features of a Hollywood starlet arrived for duty. I had worshipped her since Day 1.

As I hyperventilated myself into a state of delirium, she smoothed out her uniform, put on lipstick, and teased her brunette hair into a thick hive with hairspray, spit, and an enormous, red plastic comb. In later years, I came to reevaluate her as a cheap, lower-middle class, gum-smacking trumpet, but in my fevered adolescence I considered her a paragon of beauty, the personification of charm, the very essence of chic. Though she jabbered constantly about her various dates and boyfriends (I pictured them as sullen, swaggering guys who held their shoulders back when they walked and laid rubber when they drove off) I remained madly in love, holding out a rather ludicrous hope that she would note my intelligence, my future handsomeness, my career potential. She was, I believed, my lone link to happiness. Her name was the Biblical Sharon, and, in her starched white Handy-Andy blouse and blue serge skirt, she was like the Rose of, mentioned in that famous tome.

I hovered there uncertainly, queuing up the courage to speak to her. Anybody who is familiar with rejection understands the hesitancy involved in this act. I was intimately familiar with all the varieties of rejection.

"Hi, Sharon," I said, boldly, determinedly, grimly— seizing the moment like a pelican seizes a flounder on a swoop to the surf. After a second or two, Sharon glanced my way, watching her fingernails dry. They were painted an extravagantly vivid shade of chartreuse, which, in my libido-driven madness, I failed to recognize as an important warning signal.

"Oh," she said, off-handedly. "Hi." She wiggled her fingers slightly, to speed up the drying process. (Nails and hair were, I suppose, critical aspects of her persona. Looking back, I'd wager she didn't have a persona without her hair and nails.) After the nails dried, she hitched up her skirt, pulling tight her flesh-colored panti-hose with a swift, sure, unself-conscious motion, while I watched, fascinated and excruciatingly horny.

I decided then to be reckless, to charge forward into the fray, to lay it all on the line—my ego, my superego, my ability to have children, all future cares and aspirations. I moved closer to her in one clumsy but debonair shuffle step.

"Sharon," I said, like Romeo, except to the backdrop of corrugated cardboard boxes and canned goods.

"Yes?" she said. She glanced at me inquisitively, but impatiently, shifting from one saddle-oxforded foot to the other.

"I'm leaving," I said.

"See ya," she said. Obviously, she didn't fathom the far-reaching significance of this piece of information. I filled her in.

"I've had it here," I said. "My talents aren't appreciated. It's time to move on." I interpreted her slightly knitted eyebrows and pinched expression as an indicator that she was surprised, sympathetic—moved, perhaps. The fact that she glanced away conspicuously to check the wall clock I disregarded strategically.

"Well," she said, really pouring out the emotion. "Goodbye, then. See you around." She held out limp fingers for an all-too-polite shake.

"Goodbye," I croaked, my entire future receding monstrously like an ebb tide in a hurricane. My words reverberated among the crates and wood pallets and cases of canned corn stacked along the walls.

"Look," she said, with a flutter of her fingernails for

emphasis, "I'd better be going, I guess. My shift starts in five minutes."

"OK," I said, but stalling, searching frantically for options. "But there's something I need to tell you." Sure, I could understand, objectively, why she wouldn't be interested in me, a lowly sacker—a former lowly sacker, now. But a former sacker with brains, flair, a robust sense of humor, the capacity for analyzing human relationships instantly and accurately. A plan began to develop in my mind—I would dazzle her with my knowledge, my creativity, the wide range of my intelligence.

"What is it?" she said, tapping her toes on the concrete floor.

"Can I go forward when my heart is here?" I said, quoting succinctly from "Romeo and Juliet." I guessed she wouldn't know the passage. "Turn back, dull earth, and find thy centre out." She stared at me blankly, as if I had asked her perhaps to sing an aria from a Wagner opera (which, by the way, I could). She wiggled her fingers, checking them another time, one at a time. She laughed. She didn't know why she laughed, I am certain—surely it was some kind of nervous reflex—but I felt heartened by her reaction. In retrospect, I recognized this as a dangerous laugh, frightened, sarcastic, possibly litigious.

"You're crazy," she said, with that skittish, hardened expression females sometimes put on when they feel somebody is coming on too heavy.

"I know," I said, pressing forward pluckily. "Crazy about you." She raised her eyelids in a mocking salute. Undeterred, with nothing to lose, really, except perhaps in a legal action, I picked her up in a dance move, sliding her across the floor in a kind of clumsy country two-step.

"Hey," she demurred, "You're messing up my blouse."

"You're beautiful!" I pleaded.

"My makeup's getting smeared," she protested. My chances dissipating, I threw all caution to the wind.

"I'm in love with you," I said, before launching into Shakespeare again. "O she doth teach the torches to burn bright!/It seems she hangs upon the cheek of night . . ." And then it came—the slap. Flat against my cheek, it stung almost to the marrow of my bones. It stung spiritually and morally, as well as physically. It seemed to knock me back somehow through the years, into a remembered litany of my most embarrassing childhood moments. I understood a slap.

"Let go of me," she said, then. I let go of her. I was panting like an overheated bloodhound. My white shirt was wrinkled and my tie askew. My hair hung in my eyes. My poor sacker's psyche lay in shreds, crushed on the floor.

"Will you go out with me?" I asked plaintively, ridiculously, in some demented, desperate, final, ill-fated effort. (This wouldn't be the last time in my life I believed the sheer force of my emotion would overcome whatever obstacles stood in the way.)

"Are you out of your mind?" she said. She didn't actually spit, but there was a mental spit, no doubt about it. "I've never gone out with a sacker. I'd never go out with a sacker. And you're not even a sacker, anymore. You're less than a sacker. You're a failed sacker."

I had no answer. This was, I understood now, a social issue, a clash of classes, a case of Aristocracy v. Common

Man. I gave up. It was over. As part of the recovery process, I immediately began downgrading her in my mind.

I trudged slowly to the store entrance, feeling as heavy and tired as a lame pack horse. As the glass doors glided open automatically, I cupped my hands around my mouth.

"So long, suckers!" I yelled. "See you all some day—when I'm running a major international corporation with a multi-million dollar payroll and 500 employees bending over daily to kiss my ass!"

The doors closed behind me then and I never looked back. My tie I flung high into the air, therapeutically. A stray shopping cart I rode briefly across the parking lot, whooping like a cowboy. My sacking career was finished. Life began anew.

Kingston: the Lizard, the Man

When my college-student son informed me that his mother (we're divorced five years now) had bought him a baby iguana, I wrote it off as a young man's fancy fueled by his mother's new-age, middle-age reshaping of her life mode. She had herself recently purchased an iguana for her home, and everything new that she did she enthusiastically promoted to others as the answer to the riddle of a happy and fulfilling existence. (Not a bad trait, necessarily, but not part of my personality.) Besides, I was a dog man from way back—a dogged dog man, you might say—and the notion of a lizard as a pet left me, excuse the easy reptilian metaphor, cold.

When I visited David one winter evening at the house he shared with several other stalwart young gentlemen, idealistic but sensible and passing to a new stage of life all, he showed me "Kingston," as he had named his lizard, for the capital of Jamaica, where iguanas ran free. (Or stared free, as the case may be. They spend a lot of time crouched in one position, staring into space. They don't really run much.) As David took Kingston from his cage, my first surprise impression was that of a cute little green guy with a sweet, sensitive face and a kind of cool intelligence that seemed to suggest a secret, that he was holding something back. I could tell my son was proud of him.

"Want to hold him?" David asked. I felt a strong, sudden stab of worry.

"I don't know," I said. "What will he do?"

"Just relax and he'll be all right," David said. "He'll just sort of sit on your hand."

"OK," I said, not believing entirely, but wanting to please my son. I stuck my hand out flat, fingers together, thumb in. I was anything but relaxed.

That next summer, David's house lease expired and his friends dispersed and he moved back in with me on a temporary basis. Kingston, with his clear plexi-glass cage, moved with him, installed in a small living room off the entrance hallway to my house.

Left alone frequently, Kingston and I began to become acquainted on a one-to-one basis. It fell on old dad to feed and water him and to keep his cage filled with clean white straw. One day I put his overhead light on an automatic timer that David said gave a healthy regularity to Kingston's nights and days. I chopped up tiny platefuls of yellow squash and green beans and other vegetables (variety in diet is good for lizards) and placed them carefully in a bowl on the floor of his cage. In short, I found myself taking a regular shine to little Kingston, sweet, noble little Kingston, gentle, poetic Kingston.

"What would happen if Kingston got out of his cage?" I asked David one day.

"We'd never see him again," David said. I waited until David left the house to check the seams on Kingston's cage. Sure enough, one joint needed to be taped.

I didn't hold Kingston much (I feared he would squirm away), but I watched him often—constantly, in fact. He was shy but very calm, almost yogi-like in his self-possession. If I entered the room while he was poised over his food plate, he stopped still, with his mouth open, refusing to move until I left. He didn't want anybody to see him eat. He probably didn't want anybody to know his religious preferences, either. He liked to keep some things secret.

As a 21-year-old young man living at home with his father, David was 99% agreeable and charming, but there were occasional, understandable spells of non-communication or discontent. He wanted to be out pursuing his dreams. He wanted to carve out his own niche. But it was a sure-fire positive whenever I mentioned old Kingston. Kingston drew us together in a common bond of lizard admiration. But it was more than that, really. It was a sharing of beliefs, a similar outlook, an intergenerational crossing. Like our mutual enjoyment of organized sports, it was an oblique but effective way for us to communicate as two mature gentlemen living in this world that contained both paradise and thorns.

"Look where Kingston is today!" I said, pointing to the cage where Kingston might be crouched with one delicate webbed foot splayed out over a leaf. "Kingston climbed up his branch." "Kingston is suspended from the roof." When David came home with a new floor heater for the cage, we were both excited as Kingston seemed pleased, standing on the heater for hours, motionless, content, soaking in the invisible rays.

We joked that Kingston was an intellectual, a sage, a guru, withdrawn into himself while mulling over difficult questions of metaphysics and cybergenics. We said that Kingston was a fan of reggae music and late night comedy shows, some on the raunchy side.

Life went on. The Christmas season was hectic and fast-paced. My daughter Kate returned home for a month-long stay from a college on the East Coast, filling the household with her cheerful and chatty personality and a steady stream of polite and congenial friends, girls and boys both. There was music in the air. As all this activity swirled around me, I felt comforted, contented, joyful almost, coming to grips at last with all the recent changes in my life, able now to look, at least tentatively, to the future. A future. My future.

One night, just after New Year's, I stopped short as I walked through Kingston's room, something catching my eye. I rushed over to the cage, lifted the lid, thrust my hand inside. Kingston was motionless as always, but there was something about the quality of his motionlessness that concerned me. I touched him with a sense of foreboding. His body was stiff and withered and lifeless. His eyes reflected nothingness. He was gone from this earthly realm, no more cognizant than the straw that lined his cage. He was dead.

A huge, terrible sense of loss floated up from my body as I stood by Kingston's cage, wishing, praying that this awful thing wasn't true. "Damn it all," I blustered. "Damn it all." I paced for hours in a restless, feverish state, waiting for David to return home so I could tell him the news. My voice was barely under control as I led him to the cage where Kingston lay still. I couldn't move him yet. I had to wait for David to see him first.

"I don't know what could have happened," I lamented. "I don't know what I could have done different." David looked at me as if to provide guidance and counsel. He shook his head.

"Kingston was really small to begin with, Dad," David said. "He probably had some kind of congenital problem." We shared a moment of sadness and grieving as two strong men and then began the attempt to move forward, as the living must do.

The next morning, at David's suggestion, I buried Kingston's little body in our back yard beside our Chihuahua Chelsea in what I might now call a family pet burial plot. It was a peaceful place, at the top of a gentle slope angling down to a patio at the edge of the house. Standing there, shovel resting on the ground, I realized that Kingston represented many important things to me—David choosing to move back home, albeit temporarily, and that I could provide a safe, secure place for him; my loving him through this pet he had first loved; even the fact that his mother had bought Kingston for him held significance for me, reminding me of our long lost love, those early, dizzy days of romance, the difficult but rewarding years of child-raising, the plans and career moves and next steps. The moments that David and I shared discussing Kingston, the humor, the good-natured intellectual hypothesizing were priceless to me, a healing balm on my soul, a way for me to know that I could relate to someone that I loved.

A few weeks later David moved out again, as someone his age should want to do, but just before he left his mother and he bought a new iguana to keep at my house until, supposedly, David could afford a deposit to keep it with him. They were really just doing it for me.

Skipper and Ken Visit Barbie's Pad

As befitting her exalted station in life, Barbie (yes, that one!) lived in an upscale apartment complex in Northwest Hills, with a panoramic view of the lowlanders in the city proper. Ken was but a few blocks away in a different but equally high-end complex, in which upcoming young doctors and attorneys and your more presentable drug dealers were prominent. Mercedes and BMW's parked in the white-lined parking slots outside the doors, a pair of kidney-shaped swimming pools, tennis courts painted a rich forest green.

Skipper, wouldn't you know it, lived in not quite so opulent a pad, without the French doors to the patio, the deep-pile carpet, the Pfister-Price fixtures in the bathroom and kitchen. Skipper was a nice kid, a little too skinny, but her background was not nearly as unblemished as Barbie's. There were no elaborate skiing vacations in her past and there was even the hint she might have come from a broken home. Sure, she dined on Sushi now and knew her wine list, of course, but still . . .

Presently, Skipper knocked on the door, dressed in a mustard-colored culotte suit with a subdued floral design.

Barbie thought it was the wrong thing to wear for the occasion, but held her opinion.

"How do I look?" asked Skipper, striking a model's pose in the doorway.

"Just great," lied Barbie. Actually, she thought the outfit made Skipper look bloated and ponderous. And an overload of makeup made her seem almost in costume. "You look wonderful."

Skipper smiled and fussed with her hair. Obviously familiar with Barbie's apartment, she sat pertly on the armrest of a muted-white couch.

"Okay, so who is this dude you've got me hooked up with tonight, anyway?" asked Skipper with a false nonchalance which was transparent. "Have you seen him?"

"All I know is he's some friend of Ken's," Barbie said. "From his softball team. He's supposed to be athletic, good-looking. But Ken's never had him over before."

"God," said Skipper, crossing her right leg deliberately over her left. "I hope he's not like that guy Ken knew from work—the computer programmer. That guy really came on strong."

Barbie stopped in the kitchen doorway with hands on hips.

"I didn't think he was all that bad, really," Barbie said. She didn't enjoy Ken's friend selection impugned. "He seemed a little wild maybe. That's all."

"Well," said Skipper, a trifle miffed. "You didn't have to deal with him alone, after we got back. He practically raped me."

She uncrossed her right leg and crossed the left. Sometimes Barbie made her feel so—inferior.

"You're kidding," Barbie said. "I didn't know about that." But she felt certain Skipper was exaggerating.

The doorbell rang and Barbie laid down the pearl-handled hairbrush she had been holding and straightened her dress.

"That must be them," said Barbie, like some chiming musical instrument. Skipper arranged herself ladylike on the sofa. She prepared to smile upon meeting her date.

"Hey, hey, hey," Ken said as he bustled inside, taking Barbie's hand over his head like a swing dancer, then—while she stood tilted backward—giving her a big wet smack on the lips. "How's my party girl?"

"Ken!" said Barbie, wiping her mouth with the back of her hand. "You've been drinking!"

"What, me drink?" said Ken, releasing Barbie and assuming an angelic posture. His lips formed into an exaggerated pout as he held his thumb and index finger .5 centimeters apart. "Maybe a little teeny nip now and then, but nothing I wouldn't tell my own mother about. Just a wee insy bitsy bit."

"I think you're drunk," said Barbie defiantly, as Ken searched for a spark of humor in her eyes.

"Not a chance," he blustered, standing now like an explorer surveying his domain. "Not old Ken. Not me."

Skipper's date, meanwhile, stood uncertainly in the doorway, desperately, delicately maintaining a large, ponderous smile like a gigantic boulder on his back. A scrubbed and clean-shaven young man with the overbulked physique of a football lineman, he stood with hands on hips, balanced all to one side. He looked as though he were about to topple over a fallen defender on the line of scrimmage.

"Well, Mr. Not Drunk," chimed Barbie, "How about introducing your friend?"

The friend stood straighter, his soft, wide, unlined face changing to the color of a new-born baby. Heavy-lidded, boyish, he appeared a bit unsavvy and slow-talking to be Skipper's type—not that anybody had really determined what Skipper's type was. Skipper seemed to lose patience with guys very quickly. The most long-term relationship she ever had was with an aspiring writer type who was sharp and witty and considerate but with very little future, fiscally speaking, and he drove a campy, screwed-up old Volvo sedan that issued exhaust trails like an industrial plant. Embarrassed, Skipper dumped him. Never mind that he caused her to laugh, think deeply, explore life with a fresh, open mind—in the final analysis, those things didn't matter a whole lot to her.

"Bill!" sang Ken, hands cupped around his mouth like a Bavarian yodeler, "Yo, B-i-i-i-l! Oh, there you are, right where I left you, Silly Boy. Impressive specimen, isn't he? Played defensive tackle for the Texas Longhorns from '99 – 2001. Would've made All-America, too, if it weren't for a broken ankle suffered during a grueling panty raid during his sophomore year. Excuse me, during an extremely brutal scrimmage."

Barbie and Skipper tried to act impressed.

"Anyway," Ken continued. "Bill—this this is Skipper

and this is Barbie. Skipper and Barbie—this is Bill." They all shook hands politely.

After the intros were completed, Barbie planted her hand on Ken's chest and propelled him forcefully toward the kitchen.

"Say," Barbie said, "Why don't you two sit on the couch and get acquainted? I need to talk to Ken for a minute. Privately." She took Ken and dragged him through a swinging door and over to the maple dinette.

"Okay, Hot Shot," hissed Barbie, three inches from Ken's face. "What's the big idea of showing up here looped? You know I don't like it one bit."

"No big deal," slurred Ken. "I just love ya, Honey. I love ya a lot. You're the girl of my dreams. Marry me!"

"You know we've discussed the matter previously, Kenneth," said Barbie, in a sharp, injunctive tone. "And you realize it's just not possible right now. Not while I'm still trying to—"

But Ken had lunged forward, pinning Barbie with his outstretched arms against the pine-paneled kitchen cabinet which drew envious raves from female visitors. Grinning, he breathed beer fumes over Barbie's ideal face, causing her to contort her mouth as though she had just sucked a lemon. He closed his arms around her back and tried valiantly to kiss her, but she wouldn't have anything to do with it.

"Ken!" said Barbie, squirming her face out of the path of Ken's jabbing lips, "Just what do you think you're doing?"

"Come on, Babe?" said Ken, in a deep, Lothario voice, eyes pleading. "I'm horny as a mule."

Barbie wriggled free from his hand and popped Ken across the cheekbone. He relaxed his grip in an instant.

"Jeez, Kid," Ken said, tracing the blow with the tip of a finger. "When did you get so darn demure?"

"What kind of example do you think you're setting for your friend?" lashed out Barbie. "He probably thinks he's got the A-Okay to move right in on poor Skipper."

"Skipper'll probably ask him for his bank balance before she even speaks to him," Ken said, with a small, sardonic smile, a mere lopsidedness in his face. "After that there'll be the requisite check of MasterCard limits."

"That's not nice," Barbie said, but not without a glimmer of perverse satisfaction. When you're the Golden Girl, everybody is a potential rival.

Skipper and her date sat stiffly on the sofa, separated by a demilitarized zone of eight, maybe eight and one-quarter inches. They didn't speak, but Bill seemed to be humming under his breath—a buzzing sound reminiscent of locusts. A TV show was on, some summer re-run with a laugh track, and they both focused intently on that. Skipper concentrated all of her willpower and sneaked a tentative little peek in Bill's direction.

"Well," she said blithely, after a deep, cleansing breath and shifting a tad to face him obliquely. "So you played football for UT, huh?"

"Yes, ma'am," said Bill, blushing fiercely. Skipper was several years older than Bill, and being called "ma'am" made her feel absolutely ancient. She was already sensitive about reaching her late twenties still unmarried. What did this guy take her for—an old maid?

"Gosh," continued Skipper, deflated but forging ahead with feigned enthusiasm. "That's so exciting. I mean, the crowds and all, the cheerleaders, the media. What was it like playing in that huge stadium with all the spectators, the band cranking out the fight song, the big drum pounding? It must have been some thrill."

"Well," said Bill slowly, tweaking the tip of his rather fleshy proboscis in a meek, self-effacing fashion, "I didn't play all that much, really. I got hurt early in my sophomore year and never rose above second string after that." Bill glanced wistfully at the ceiling. "You know, I mighta been one whale of a ballplayer if not for that old hamstring flare-up."

This retrospective seemed to trigger some deep-seated romantic impulse in Bill, as he scooted his big old lineman's butt across the couch and looped his arm loosely around Skipper's narrow upper lumbar section. His fingertips rested lightly on her far shoulder blade.

"Oh, God," sighed Skipper, beneath her breath, though undoubtedly all that Bill intended, with Barbie and Ken snuggled up next door in the kitchen, was a little innocent make-out action. "You get out of your teens and everybody assumes you're ready for sex the minute you say hello."

She screwed up her shoulders and tightened into a fetal shell. They sat locked in silence for the next five minutes, while Bill queued up courage for a direct frontal assault. But he decided that a bit more conversation was in order first.

"Ken tells me you work over at the Capitol, in some

state senator's office," said Bill, in a plagiarism of cosmo-politanese. "That must be awfully exciting."

"Ahhh," said Skipper, picking haphazardly at her bangs with her fingertips, "It's all right. Actually, it's pretty hum-drum except for a for weeks late in the legislative session."

Bill nodded in rabid appreciation. Then there was another long silence.

"After I got out of school," offered Bill, finally, bashfully, as if revealing one of the secrets of the ages, "the Assistant Athletic Director called some guy he knew over at MBank and got me fixed up with a job. I'm Accounts Manager over there now."

"Mmmm," said Skipper, abstractedly, pulling long hairs from the top of her scalp and inspecting each painstakingly. "Sounds utterly divine. Perhaps you could set me up with a payment-free note of ten million dollars?"

Bill required a moment of profound reflection to determine that his leg was being pulled and then he laughed, his puffy little ice-blue eyes hooded in his obelisk-like face. A soft, cautious laugh in its nascence, it ripened into a great, immoderate, locker-room guffaw. Back-slapping time. Skipper rode it out with a firmly noncommittal expression.

Apparently, Bill decided that the onset of this jovial ambiance was an invitation to make a major move. Leaning close to Skipper's face suddenly, he swiveled his head and lowered his lips onto hers. When he did, she reared back and whopped him a good one right across the chops. The women were in a fighting mood tonight. But immediately after, Skipper's face contorted in dread and self-disgust. She lowered her head and covered her face with her hands.

"Oh, God," wailed Skipper. "I'm so sorry. I'm all screwed up. I don't know what's wrong with me."

Bill sat sheepish and uncertain as she sobbed into a latticework of fingers, flagellating herself. A vivid red stripe lay across Bill's square jaw like a road map to a desolate country.

"It's okay," said Bill, hands folded on his knees. "Maybe I was just a tad too forward."

"No," said Skipper, decisively, self-derisively, "It's me. I've got this horrible hang-up about people touching me. It drives me nuts. I need to see a psychiatrist or something."

Bill sat leaning forward, thinking hard. One could almost detect the old cranium bulging outward.
"You know what," said Bill, in a soft, earnest, get-down-to-business manner, "I think you're a real cute little old girl. It bothers a lot of folks to have somebody come up and just grab 'em."

Skipper shrugged, Bill reached gingerly for her hand and held just the tips of her fingers in a soft, passive embrace. Skipper shivered at first, but let it be, the title of her favorite Beatles song.

Barbie stood stock still in the doorway, quivering with amazed excitement.

"Ken," she whispered fiercely, waving like a highway flagman, "You gotta get a load of this. They're holding hands."

"You're kidding," whispered Ken, fingertips on Barbie's slender shoulders. He whistled softly. "My God, Bill was absolutely the last person on earth I figured would get along with Skipper. I racked my brain for other eligible candidates before asking Bill. But a lot of folks have already gotten burned by Skipper."

Barbie's limpid powder-blue eyes sparkled unabashedly and she smiled as she inclined her face upward toward Ken. She wrapped her hand in his.

"Hey," Barbie coaxed. "I was acting kind of snooty in there just now. Now that we've got a little time on our hands, why don't we . . ."

Ah, but just then the doorbell rang and it was Barbie's token Black friend, her token Oriental friend, and her token Hispanic friend, all dressed up to party. Barbie sighed and got with the program.

Jane Fountain

Jane Fountain was just one girl in the history of the world, but I felt like the luckiest guy in the history of the world to know her. It was so much fun hanging around her. She got my jokes, she told good jokes herself. She was quite savvy regarding the visual imagery presented by her name. I loved her name—Jane Fountain.

"Did anybody in school call you Jane Fountainbleau?" I asked.

"Oh, yeah," she replied. "I got Fountainbleau, I got Overflowing Fountain, I got Fountain of Plenty. My name was a never-ending source of amusement for all my friends."

We both laughed. I laughed possibly more than was strictly warranted by the quality of her humor, but I wanted her to be sure that that I found her amusing. She seemed to believe I was amusing, too.

We met during our junior year as fellow staff members on The Daily Texan, the student newspaper at the University of Texas. We were both new additions to the staff, transfers in from out of town colleges. She was a pretty, pouty-lipped, peasant blouse-wearing, would-be photographer from Lubbock, out in the West Texas plains, and I was a skinny, sarcastic, "Peace and Love, Man," secretly-romantic, romantically-deprived, insecure, would-be features writer from San Antonio.

Goofing around the copy desk late at night, we developed a friendship and a rapport. During breaks in production, we hopped over to a back booth in the Orange Bull coffee shop across Guadalupe Street from the newspaper office, where we teased each other and criticized the hell out of everybody else.

Her feet, folded nonchalantly beneath the table, pointed toward me, pointed significantly, I believed, pointed with emotional and emphatic purpose. I felt that her feet at that moment personified her feelings toward me—alert, unfettered, impressed, open to new adventures. It's hard to explain, but with Jane my poor self image melted away, leaving me sharp, entertaining, honest, in control. This was my real self, I hoped, or at least an authentic alternate self that could rise to the fore occasionally.

"So when you're a hot-shot writer on The New Yorker you'll still be afraid to call up girls," Jane said, shooting off one of her usual lines of repartee.

"I might call you sometimes," I shot back. "I might even give you an assignment. If you're lucky."

We had a shoot and shoot back kind of relationship. I liked to compliment her, she liked to tease me. I wanted to think that her teasing meant that she liked me. Though I understood that there was nothing sexual, nothing serious.

For one thing, she was taken. Jane said that she had a boyfriend back home in Lubbock, an intern at a hospital there, a doctor-to-be, and the plan was for them to marry as soon as Jane completed college. I had a girlfriend from a formerly Soviet-bloc country in Eastern Europe, I said, a discus thrower for their national team—and we planned to marry as soon as the Olympics were over and the steroids had washed out of her system. Jane laughed, covering my hand briefly with hers. As she did, my gaze took in our two hands as if they were some freshly-hewn natural wonder. My heart leaped like a gazelle in the African veldt. It was all I could do to keep from leaping into her arms.

Her father was an oil company executive, Jane said, her mother a realtor, one of those dress-to-kill to show you around types. Both her parents were politically conservative, solidly square. My parents sold turquoise jewelry in a city square, I said. Sitting on blankets. With a large, panting dog chained behind them. Jane laughed again, swinging her legs delicately, and deliciously, around the table legs alongside mine on the concrete floor, and a huge shock of excitement engulfed me, like a tidal wave. I felt pleased to be near her, happy to be with her, honored to exist in her presence. She spoke, and her melodious West Texas voice, more lilt than twang, propelled me forward in a rush of absolute joy. God, how I loved that voice! God, how I loved her sensibleness. God, how I loved her teasing me. God, how I loved—I couldn't tell her, of course, but God, how I loved her.

"No. Really," she said, rapping a red-painted fingernail sharply on the table top. She had a few carry-overs from her Lubbock upbringing—she wore makeup, for instance, and perfume, a delightfully girlish scent that when it wafted into my nostrils let me know she was near. Many girls when they arrived in Austin immediately shed all that. I was happy that she didn't. "What does your father do?" Her eyes focused on me narrowly—penetrating, serious. Searching for humor there I found none. Despite her superior sense of play, she could be dryly matter-of-fact when wanting something, when prying for additional information. I admired this quality in her. Of course, I admired all of her qualities.

"My father. Really," I said, "is an accountant. He's like head accountant for this office supplies firm in San Antonio. The biggest office supplies firm there." Jane nodded, the animated centers of those deep, dark brown eyes twinkling again, like diamonds, truly, or stars in the sky, and I felt another powerful surge of emotion. Now it was her time to joke.

"So how does he account for you?" she said. This was a low-rent joke, I suppose, objectively speaking, but coming from her it seemed an absolute howler. I laughed again, delighted by her quick mind and racing wit, elated that she would deign to spend her time making me laugh. I guess that was it, really—that she would want to laugh made me swell with pride.

"Mrs. Dr. Fountain," I said, in a starched, formal tone, reaching out to take her hand in mine.

"Mr. Husband of National Team Discus Thrower," she said. We looked at each other and laughed. Then we shook hands decorously, like white-mittened art gallery doyens. Our hands lingered for an additional moment, though, and I swear that my heart migrated to a new position on the exterior of my chest. I hoped that she couldn't tell—or perhaps I hoped that she could.

That night, I went home singing Frank Sinatra tunes, campy love songs that made Jane feel somehow closer and more real to me. Other nights, when she ignored me or flirted with somebody else on the news desk, I went home in hell.

One day, late in the spring semester, Managing Editor Nick LaMacchia assigned us two to cover a story together in Kyle, 30 miles down interstate 35 toward San Antonio. Our assignment—photograph and interview Kyle residents for a feature article depicting "small town life." Silently I blessed the Managing Editor, a pompous prig empire-builder who treated staff members with imperious disdain. Today, he was my best friend.

We split from campus in my car, Jane and I, a Nissan Sentra I had cleared out for today by tossing everything into the trunk. Jane held her Pentax camera on her shapely blue-jeaned lap and my spiral notebook lay in the drink-well between the bucket seats. It was a pleasant afternoon, weather-wise, a sunny, soft, warm, lush spring afternoon, with a balmy south breeze blowing sweet scents and the shadows long and the daylight-saving-time induce sunshine lasting forever. I was delighted to sit alongside Jane in the secluded bubble of my beat-up old automobile, grateful for the chance to talk to her alone, without interference from others. Jane told me that she had turned her cell phone off—a huge honor—leaving us blissfully oblivious to the rest of the world. Taking advantage, we talked non-stop on the drive down, full of information, filled with energy, cooler than thou, above it all, smarter than anybody else. Damn, that felt good! Damn, that felt fine.

We parked on a short, shady street perpendicular to Kyle's old-style town square and set out to walk. I took notes and nodded, Jane snapped pictures, we smiled at one another, and all was copasetic. Within an hour or two, we had interviewed the owners of a woodworking shop, a pair of back-to-nature boys emigrated from Chicago; the foreman of the Longhorn Cement Works, a short, wiry man with a Fu Manchu mustache and a shaved head that lent him an intimidating air; and a radical Catholic priest, a throwback to the days of liberation theology. I ached with pride and longing as Jane shuffled along beside me in her white peasant blouse and jeans and open-toed shoes that kept slipping off her feet. We brushed against each other as we walked, and I was happy to tentatively, tenuously, temporarily call her mine.

The shadows were long now, the sun beginning to slide down behind the aging wood facades facing the town square. We had one stop left, a tall, peaked, Victorian-style house on a wide corner lot surrounded by a freshly-painted white picket fence.

"A To Kill A Mockingbird House," Jane said.

"It sure is," I said. "I hope Boo Radley isn't there."

Boo Radey wasn't there. Instead, there was a manic software salesman who had moved to Kyle for the unpolluted air and placid pace-of-life, trading the grinding 55-minute rush-hour commute to downtown Austin for peace and quiet when he arrived home here. Clad in tan seersucker suit and tie with loosened knot and filled with a convert's zeal, Neil Bennett squired us proudly around the perimeter of the town square, pointing out landmarks and historical markers in his adopted home. He surprised us, this man, a good, solid, decent, sharp-minded fellow in his 40's, forward-thinking, observant, analytical, making us realize that we need not become ossified or locked in obsolescence, even though allied to the Establishment. We felt enlarged, uplifted, transcendent even. We had learned some things today—about ourselves, about other people, about the world in general. It had been a satisfying day. We knew we had a blockbuster feature story on our hands. I could see the headline in *The Texan*: "Small Town Life— Not What You Think."

Waving good-bye to our new friend Neil, we turned back toward my car, strolling past an old-fashioned food mart and a row of antique stores on Center Street. We felt like conquering heroes. Always one to take things one step farther, Jane decided we should race to my car, a long block away. Laughing, I pulled ahead early but let Jane catch me in the end. We slapped the car door as we finished. Afterwards, we stood with rear ends propped against the hood, breathing heavily.

"My camera weighed me down," Jane gasped out.

"Yeah, but I had a broken leg," I said.

"Yeah, right," Jane said. I pretended to punch her on the arm. We wrestled briefly. We both laughed. Jane sighed.

"Guess we'd better get back," she said. "I need to get these pictures developed and you need to write your story."

"Guess we'd better get back," I said. Reluctantly, I

unlocked the car doors and we climbed inside.

As I started the car and pulled away, Jane checked her cell phone for messages. She held the phone to her left ear, frowning.

"What's going on?" I said, uncertainly.

"Oh, nothing," she said. "It's just Charles."

"Charles?" I said.

"Charles," she said. "The Doctor. He makes me so mad. He's such an ass sometimes."

"What did he do?" I said.

"Oh, nothing," she said. "He always does this to me. He promised he would take off and spend the first two weeks of summer with me here in Austin. I should have known it would never happen. He tells me now he's going on a trip to California with his parents." I sat with my hands on the steering wheel, appearing bummed out.

"That's too bad," I said.

"What a jerk," Jane said.

"That's too bad," I said again. I hit the heels of my hands against the steering wheel. Jane clicked the cover of her cell phone closed. She looked over at me, in a way that seemed to assign a portion of blame for belonging to that vile species, "Men." I tried to show by my demeanor that I would never do anything like the Doctor did. She turned away.

"Let's drive a little bit," she said.

"Drive back home?" I said.

"No, just drive," Jane said. "Let's see where this road takes us. I don't feel like going back to the newsroom yet."

"Sure thing," I said.

And so I drove, away from the town square and along shady streets lined with historical old homes and then the clusters of fast food restaurants and chain hotels on the edge of town and onto some winding two-lane blacktop road slicing through the green, wooded countryside. Neither of us spoke. I focused on the road.

"Hey, why don't you pull in there for a minute?" Jane said, noting a billboard advertising "Hays County Park, ½ Mile." "Let's just sit."

"Whatever you'd like to do," I said.

"Let's sit," Jane said.

I crunched along down a gravel driveway into the parking lot and stopped, picnic tables and barbecue pits facing us across a barbed-wire fence. The sun was sliding down to our left behind a stand of live-oak trees, a stupendous orange ball shooting off 93-million mile long tendrils of light. The field before us lay in shade, a deep, restful green. My heart was beating fast. I turned off the engine, hand shaking. The silence seemed immense. I sat staring straight ahead. Jane broke the silence with an exclamation.

"That was fun!" she said.

"It sure was," I said.

"That computer guy was wild!" she said.

"He really was," I said. "He was wild." Jane shook her head of dark hair so that it tumbled luxuriantly around her shoulders. She shook her head of dark hair incredibly well. We looked at each other and laughed. I laughed myself into a coughing fit.

"You okay?" Jane said, leaning toward me. She clapped me on the back.

"I'm okay," I said.

"You sure?" Jane said. She clapped again.

"I'm sure," I said.

Jane settled back on her side of the car and shook her head.

"Man!" she said.

"Man!" I said.

We both fell silent then, lost in our own thoughts. At least I was lost in mine. I e-x-h-a-l-e-d slowly, more as an activity than anything else. I explored a gap in my back teeth with my tongue. I held the steering wheel as though driving. I glanced at Jane covertly. Hand over head, she held a plastic barrette not in her hand but in her mouth, very casually, I thought, very efficiently. She was very efficient, I thought, at just about everything that she did. A peaceful feeling came over me then. It felt good that she accepted me, just sitting there beside her. I almost didn't mind that she had the Doctor. I was almost happy that she did. Amused, delighted, overwhelmed by her presence, I laughed at her, a weird, convulsive snort. She took the barrette in one hand and stuck out her tongue.

"Don't swallow that thing," I said.

"Don't you worry," she said, pretending to throw the barrette at me. I pretended to punch her on the arm with a volley of right jabs. She pretended to shoo me away. I felt emboldened suddenly, energized by her presence, alive in a way that I could hardly remember feeling before. I felt that I could almost say the things I wanted to say. I wanted to reach out and grab her hand, her hair—or some other part of her physical anatomy. I wanted to hold her close to me. I could hardly stop myself.

"You look awfully cute like that," I said instead. "You look like a movie star."

"Really?" Jane said. "Which one?"

"I can't remember her name," I said. "She's pretty, though."

"Well, that's good," Jane said. "Cool!" But with an oddly curious cast to her eyes, I believed, an alert, strained, questioning gaze. She was on to me, perhaps. I had gone one step too far. I had blown my cover. Whatever she said next, though, was unintelligible, as she had reinserted the barrette into her mouth, her lovely lips distended in determination as she clamped down with her teeth. Distended lips made no difference to me.

A giant groundswell of emotion rolled through me then, a swoon of desire and despair that rendered me virtually helpless. Jane looked so cute and sexy, she was so funny, she made me feel so comfortable that I knew there would never be anyone else like her in my life again. Hardly anyone made me feel comfortable. I was nervous around practically everybody. I wanted to do something. I wondered if I should say something. I turned toward her to try to decide if I should make some crazy declaration or confession—when she leaned forward to kiss me on the lips.

"I love you, Ben," Jane said. My mind reeled. Was she talking to me? Was she saying she loved me? I thought fast.

"You, too," I said. "I love you, Jane Fountain." We kissed again.

"I'm so glad I found you," Jane said.

"I'm so glad I found you," I said.

"I didn't know I could ever feel so happy," she said.

"I didn't know I ever could," I said.

We kissed again, eyes hard shut, holding each other tight. I didn't want to move. I didn't want to leave. I wanted to stay right there forever.

The Plumber: A Tragi-comedy

My kitchen sink is clogged, filled with a thick, disgusting sludge. Divorced, my children grown, I must face this existential crisis, this apotheosis of angst, alone, unsupported, forlorn. After repeated, failed attempts at plunging—the plunger suction cup becoming disconnected from the handle—I call a plumber, my voice reedy and thin, quivering on the verge of breakdown. This is an all-purpose service company, actually, handling a wide range of household breakdowns. They recognize me from my telephone number, providing a huge surge of acceptance. They know me! I am known. I'm not just a number—I'm a number with a name and address and a credit card on file.

"We have an opening now—we'll send a technician right out," the receptionist says. A rough, untutored girl, by her voice, but beautiful in soul, pure in spirit.

"Right now?" I say.

"Right now," the receptionist says. "He's already on his way."

"He's already on his way!" I repeat blindly, blissfully. In my living room I wait pacing, having e-mailed my supervisor of my plight.

"I'll work from home until I get in," I write. He offers standard words of corporate encouragement: "See you when you get here. Cheers."

The technician, the plumber, arrives—always a moment of truth, a huge pregnant moment of hope and fear and stark recognition. This is reality. This is happening. There is no turning back. We greet each other in the entrance doorway, shake hands heartily, exchange names. His name is Nate. Clad neatly in black slacks and white uniform shirt, he is young, in his late 20s, a ruggedly handsome fellow in a fair-skinned, blond, Austrian-Swedish-Norwegian sort of way, with a phlegmatic but generally congenial manner, picture Rolf in "The Sound of Music" before he turns Nazi. Nate can understand instantly that I cannot perform any kind of home repair function beyond replacing a light bulb. It must be some sort of subliminal vibe that our kind put out, a pheromone that travels the airwaves. It's like a horse knowing that I cannot ride.

"So you have a sink that won't drain?" Nate says, legs spread, knees bent, ready to fire out.

"Yeah," I say, trying to nonchalant it, in the parlance of a baseball player. "It's been getting worse and worse for about a week now. It won't drain at all." I fight off tears welling in my eyes.

He nods, striding purposefully forward as I direct him to the kitchen, equipment bag dangling in his right hand. He carefully inspects the sink. He pulls the cabinet door open and peers in underneath, crouching on the balls of his feet. Some subtle signal from him commands me to move back.

Thus alerted, I stand apart as he settles in, like a surgeon donning mask and gloves, giving him room to operate. I make myself appear receptive to information exchange. He does not provide information. He is silent. He is a veritable Buddha.

"How's it looking?" I throw out timidly.

"Can't tell yet," he says, biting off the words like somebody chewing a tough piece of meat. As if I should know this. As if I am, in fact, an idiot. I am an idiot, of course, a person bereft of common sense or general knowledge. Rebuffed, reduced in status, I now pretend that I am disinterested in his little ongoing procedure. I pretend that I have other things to do—important things, high-level, college-educated office-type things.

"Let me know if you need anything," I toss out haphazardly. Head inside the cabinet, he does not answer.

I repair to my living room, adjacent to the kitchen but protected by a wall. I sit quietly at the computer there, shoulders hunched, face scrunched, checking e-mails and cruising the internet. I watch a YouTube of a Monty Python skit involving famous philosophers playing soccer. High-level stuff. Anxiety builds in my chest like a spreading virus.

Finally, Nate speaks, accosting me as he stands just beyond the living room wall.

"There's a lot of grease," he says accusingly, almost angrily. I have no response to this. Yes, there is grease. There is grease that must be caused by my slovenly behavior, my sordid life-style, my role as single parent to two recent college grads. I think of excuses. "I had a party and people dumped grease down the drain." "I leased the house to a band of gypsies." The excuses are all lame. Like a wraith, Nate disappears back beyond the wall.

He spends the ensuing half hour tromping back and forth to his van, taking equipment out, lugging equipment in, while I sit staring at the computer screen with a pretend happy face.

I see that Nate has brought in "the snake," technically a motorized augur that is designed to slice through sludge and tree roots and other stubborn objects. It is a dangerous and powerful tool. Used unskillfully, an augur could damage plumbing and cause injury to the user himself. As Nate settles into the grueling procedure, I tiptoe in to briefly observe. He stands low near the kitchen counter, pulling the snake like a tug-of-war participant, breathing hard, grunting savagely. I feel that I have brought him to this. I am filled with remorse. I am a bad person. There is no salvation for me. His breathing and grunting rise to a grand crescendo, a staccato huh-huh-huh that makes me cringe with anguish and despair. It is as if he is grappling for his very soul, and by extension, my soul as well. I return to the computer where I Google "Prayers for Serenity."

At last, the horrible whirring and clanging end. Nate's heavy breathing subsides. The house is suddenly as silent as a mountain valley at sunrise. I sit quietly, hands resting on the computer keyboard. My heart flutters spasmodically. After a moment, Nate emerges from beyond the wall like an angry ninja warrior. His shirt is sweat-stained and his hair is matted to his head. His eyes are wild.

"I found the clog," he says, as if he tracked down a

dangerous criminal. "It was in the grease trap. Somebody might have thrown some leftover rice down there or it could have been egg shells or shrimp peels. Rice expands in water. I pushed it out."

"You pushed it out?" I say.

"Yeah," he says, "I pushed it out. It's gone."

It was as if he had told me my blood tests were clear. It was as if he had told me I was accepted to my first choice of college.

"That's fantastic," I say. "That's incredible." Nate nods tightly, the modest hero accepting post-game praise and adulation.

"Yeah," he says quietly, "Yeah, it is."

As Nate copies down my credit card information for payment I begin to tell him details of my personal life. I'm not sure why. I tell him about the divorce from my wife of 18 years, my two children in their early twenties, their dogs I keep occasionally, the bankruptcy I had filed nearly a decade before, my search for a woman to love, my fear of growing older, my transfer at work to a new position I did not enjoy. Nate listens with scarce acknowledgement, writing out my bill with a small, inscrutable smile. When he is finished, he hands me a clipboard with bill attached. I sign without scrutiny. What's another $452.81 in the credit card debit sheet?

As Nate prepares to leave, we shake hands again in a spasm of strong emotion. I move to hug him but refrain. When he leaves, closing the front door softly behind him, it feels like closing a chapter in my life story. I stand by the window, spying through venetian blinds as I wait for his van to drive away. Warily, then, I return to the kitchen to run the tap. Water runs down the drain unfettered. I run the tap wantonly, promiscuously, effulgently. Life is good. Life is good again.

Paterfamilias for the New Millenium

In recent years, my role as paterfamilias has devolved into one simplified, streamlined process—buying things. The former, multifaceted roles I had once played--companion, mentor, guide, protector, fall guy, comic relief--have become vestigial appendages, like tonsils or the appendix. Now, I'm just a money machine. (With a low daily withdrawal limit, at that.)

"Daughter," I proclaim to my 13-year-old daughter, attempting to be conversational, humorous, contemporary, with it--qualities I consider preeminent in myself and invaluable in my role. Meagan is a sweet, beautiful young thing transforming with frightening rapidity into a woman, bursting out of her former shape and style, like a rose captured in time-lapse photography.

"What, Dad?" says she, imbuing the "what" with a certain sarcastic impatience, a tone all parents everywhere can recognize instantly. The "what" of the princess and the pauper alike. But a small swift smile crosses my face as I purposefully maintain my dignity and decorum. One must take the high road, here.

"Nothing, Daughter Dearest," I say, punching her lightly on the upper arm, which, in earlier days, might spawn a spot of roughhousing, as dear Dad would be required to extricate himself (cheerfully) from a hammerlock or a piggyback ride. Now, for this budding adolescent, it leads only to a shrug and a smug, put-out exhalation of air. "I wish merely to partake of your esteemed presence in a game of . . . something."

"I'm busy, Dad," she says. "Why don't you do something with Brian?" Brian is her brother, my son, a 16-year-old who is off driving around, for heaven's sake, going out with a girl. Talk about having little use for your old man.

"He's not here right now," I persevere. "Why don't you and I go hit some volleyballs, or play Scrabble, or cards, or Bingo, or something."

"Bingo?" She acts as though I have demeaned her utterly. "I've got homework to do right now. Maybe we can do something later." Later, she lays prone on her bed with a telephone attached to her ear, sharing the news of the day with some peer group person of anonymous gender.

She comes to me next evening as I read the sports section of the newspaper, unwinding from the daily grind.

"D-a-a-d," she croons, in a voice that is as dulcet and sweet as confectioner's sugar. I am pleased and happy, though I recognize her tone as manipulative, conniving, a sure-fire solicitation. I'll take manipulation and connivance if that's the only attention I can get. I sit at rigid attention, arranging my features and my faculties for a round of intense negotiations.

"Yo, Darling Dearest," I say, laying it on thickly in a

dramatic overtone, somewhere between a British butler and a Mongolian goatherd. She inspires me. I cannot help myself. "What is it thou desireth?" She rolls her eyes again, but with a glint of sly, playful humor--she makes a mental note to remain genial until she gets what she wants, at least.

"God," she says. She understands that I am partially nuts, but I think she secretly appreciates it. At least I deceive myself that she does. ("You wouldn't want a dull dad, would you?" I ask.)

I ask questions rapid-fire.

"Are you...?" "Is that..." "Do you wish..." Among other faults, I ask too many questions, she believes.

"'I need some new clothes," she interrupts.

"Raiments for the princess?" I respond. But then the archetypal penurious father in me leaps out. "Just to satisfy my curiosity, didn't we get you a whole bunch of new clothes when school started--like, three weeks ago?"

She appears unfazed, unchastened by this pointed fiduciary remark--kids never are, in these days of unlimited credit card spending. She's ready with an answer. Kids are always ready with an answer.

"Yes, but I can't wear a lot of that stuff any more, already," she says. "Now that the weather's getting cooler I need another pair of jeans. I only have one. And for this dance coming up next weekend everybody's going to wear a dress."

"A dress?" I feel skeptical, amused, justified. "You said you didn't want any dresses this year. Nobody's wearing any dresses, you said."

"I know I did," she says, "But everybody's wearing a dress to the dance."

"OK," I relent, all too easily. I want her to like me. "You can get another pair of jeans. Or if they're not that expensive, two. And a dress for the dance, if you think you really need one."

"Thank you, Daddy," she says. "I do." I think she is going to kiss me and present myself for a kiss, but receive only an awkward hug, instead.

Minutes later, we pile into my red Nissan Sentra (utilitarian, but with a certain, low-key flair) for the short drive over to Highland Mall, strategically located near a two-highway interchange, and seated like a milky-white palace, majestic, grand, exalted. It is the Taj Mahal of the "spend-spend-spend" society.

There are strict, unyielding requirements, here. I must be invisible, walking thirty paces behind, minimum. I must not speak, unless absolutely necessary. I must never intimate that there is any sort of connection between the two of us, any relationship. We're just sort of there together, co-existing in a confined space, but separately, unilaterally, coincidentally, perhaps, by destiny, two sets of electrons orbiting in a shell together.

Inside Dillard's Department Store we locate the Junior's section, then I am summarily dismissed--Meagan's expression reads, "Scram!" Dad on the lam, I prowl haphazardly through the crowded and colorful mall corridors, settling in finally to a Barnes & Noble book store, where I partake of selections from the Self-Help area, wishing for sudden revelation.

I return to Dillard's, as instructed, in thirty minutes. There, folded neatly on a counter top, lies a color little pile of garments--a well-dressed, attractive young sales clerk hovers nearby. Meagan takes my hand in hers and squeezes, slightly. Oh, she can pull the heart strings!

"Dad, can I get this sweater, too?" she says, anxious, breathless. (Anxious and breathless being the standard modus operandi of the American female teenager.) "It goes with this pair of slacks I already have. And I needed some stockings with the dress. Oh, and this blouse is only $11.00. It was on sale." I hesitate only fleetingly as my heart melts.

"OK, Sweetheart," I say. "As long as you think you really need them." I grimace, at first, as I mentally calculate my VISA balance. But then I think, "Hang the cost." I'm happy because she's happy.

When I present my card for payment the sales clerk smiles knowingly, like somebody's big sister--but I'm not sure she understands the nuances of my situation. She is young, herself. She considers me a money machine, too. Wallowing in wealth. With his life in order. All of his problems solved. The rough edges smoothed over.

She has no real understanding yet of the rhythms of life beyond 20-something. She certainly has no inkling of this feeling of separation that is beginning to occur, this distancing from the members of my own family, this ever-growing sense of detachment, yes, alienation. She cannot see through to the pain inside, albeit pain mingled with pride, as one's offspring grow and change and develop and want to get away. She is still an offspring herself. She cannot possibly know that life is a continuum, that one is always searching for answers, that (logically and conversely) there can be as much to live for at eighty as at eight.

We drive home giddy with the power of our purchases (such a sweet potion buying is), then Meagan races inside and dumps the Dillard's sack on the bed and turns on the TV. I ask her a question and she shrugs--she has retreated back into herself. The telephone rings, and she pounces like a desperado on the run.

I read the newspaper quietly, waiting for my son, my wife, somebody to come home. My wife is out there somewhere, learning to be fulfilled. She has her own life, these days. Everybody seems to have his or her own life. I grab the TV scanner which Meagan has abandoned and surf through the channels, searching for something of interest. And waiting. Waiting for the next phase of life to begin.

The Saturday Morning Fun Club

My family had just moved into a house we had built in one of the newer subdivisions on the outskirts of San Antonio, Texas, called Inspiration Hills. All the streets had "view" in their names. Our street was Highview, the next street over was Clearview, the street at the top of the hill was Broadview. There was a view of downtown San Antonio, a glimpse, really, of skyscrapers nestled majestically in a wide shallow valley a dozen or so miles away. Scoured from caliche and oak covered hills, the neighborhood was very 1960s suburban, with wide sidewalks bordering both sides of the sloping streets and light poles that resembled Roaring 20s gas lamps. Our house had a pink brick façade and a concrete patio in back and a fenced backyard the size of a small South Texas ranchette. The inside smelled of fresh plaster and wood paneling, giving it an unfinished, under-construction feel. Everybody in the neighborhood seemed to have just moved there, still whipping their 4BR 3BA split-levels into prime condition. Down the street, green lizards scampered around an overgrown vacant lot with a For Sale sign leaning against a lone oak tree.

You can never know all the variables. You can never control all the variables. The new house was my parents' dream come true—additional space, an upscale new neighborhood, prestige, a secure future—but I didn't want to move. I didn't want to change schools. I was operating under protest, my tender ego and fledgling libido under siege. I was 11 years old, an insecure and tentative 11 in my new life, starting sixth grade in a new school, a school where I was an unknown, a non-entity, and I could feel my old, successful life slipping away, gone forever. I was a has-been at age 11.

My younger siblings, not as entrenched in the old neighborhood and the old school, seemed fine with the move, oblivious. They didn't understand the pain and the burden that I carried. At the old school I was a baseball star, a "smart" kid, an established figure. People looked to me for advice and counsel. There was a flirtation with a cute, smart girl. In fourth grade my teacher Sister Dolores (I attended St. Paul Catholic School) pulled a classmate and me aside to request that we help a newcomer to the school feel welcome and comfortable. I felt like that kid now. I had to prove myself all over again. I had to explain myself. I had to show that I could hit the ball, field the grounder, catch the pass, make the tackle, deliver the joke. On the playground, in the classroom, in the hallways, in the restroom I had to go the extra step to show them what a cool and savvy guy I actually was. I spent fitful nights tossing and turning in bed, thinking up snappy ripostes, searching for security and happiness.

My mother fretted over me, but dad had little sympathy for my plight. A salesman for an office supplies firm, he dropped my siblings and me off at the new school each morning with a gruff admonition to basically suck it up.

"Be a man," he said, as parting words of wisdom.

At night, he sat imperiously in his easy chair in the wood-paneled den, his wood-paneled den, we all understood, sending off beams of aggression and hostility, like a petty dictator. My mother flitted around performing supporting activities, holding the household together with her smarts and feminine wiles. You wondered how they originally got together, because my father mostly grunted or barked responding to my mother's gentle entreaties. He treated her like she was an incompetent boob, speaking over her, for her, around her. She continued on her daily duties seemingly unaffected.

I learned later that mom was a sort of secret revolutionary. Picking up on the vibes of the changing times, she was plotting her escape from the monochrome mid-1960s suburban culture. She remained a housewife, but a housewife with a plan for fulfillment. Now that all the kids were in school, she was starting to get out a little, taking classes at the community center, playing some friendly tennis in the mornings with other mothers in the neighborhood, joining a book club. It was modest, but it was a forward step.

My first, early friend at the new school, St. Luke's School, was a chubby kid with a severe buzz hair-cut named Bobby Hubachek, who lived the next block over on Clearview. We shared some traits in common, perhaps. He was overweight and ridiculed and outcast. I was new and ridiculed and outcast. His parents were second-generation Czech-Americans, and they seemed even lamer and more old-fashioned than my own parents. They seemed determined to replicate the old country in their home and in their lives. There was a shrine to Our Lady of Victory in Prague perched on a table in their living room. The sprightly sounds of polka permeated from a large portable radio placed on a kitchen counter. They played Bingo in the church cafeteria on Wednesday nights. They spoke Czech sometimes, in asides among themselves, or in instructions to Bobby or his younger sister that they must not want me to understand. (For the record, having just two children in a Catholic family was considered slightly suspect, debauched, pagan.)

Bobby's mom was a lively, red-haired person who seemed afflicted with a variety of fears and paranoias. She alternated between trying to shield Bobby from the pervasive dangers of the modern world and hectoring him with demands to "clean your room," "comb your hair," "pull your pants up straight." "What are you up to?" she said, with a look that seemed to suggest he was involved in some sinister and illicit plot she had to stop in its tracks. Bobby's father was a short, squat gentleman with a buzz cut strikingly similar to his son's. He was a man of few words and gestures. Thumbs hooked into coveralls, he stood observing his wife and children with a bemused, uncertain expression, as though questioning what sort of life-long predicament he had gotten himself into. Sometimes after school or on Saturdays I would go to Bobby's house and hang out, playing board games and watching horror movies on TV. Bobby (and his mother and sister) cackled like hyenas at all the hokey parts.

"The mummy's coming out!" Bobby said, pointing. All the while I was there I was thinking, "This isn't where I want to be, this isn't what I want to do with my life." But it was all I had, the only friendship in my new, reduced existence.

One morning at school a pair of seventh graders, austere and giggling at the same time, were ushered into our classroom for some sort of public service announcement. They were there to announce the revival of the school's Saturday Morning Fun Club, which had become moribund apparently due to lack of interest. The Saturday Morning Fun Club was a loosely-knit two-year program of sixth- and seventh-grade boys that met (as the name suggested) on Saturday mornings in one of the empty classrooms at the school. (By grade 8, apparently, everybody had moved on to girls and drugs.) I immediately accepted, filling out a form with my "interests" and "likes" that was never to be referenced again. Bobby Hubachek joined also, despite my sending out fervent prayers that he did not. Even with Bobby, I thought the Saturday Morning Fun Club might be my ticket to acceptance and success.

Bobby's mom picked up me up for the club's first meeting dressed in a flowered housecoat and slippers, and with her hair in a curler net. She and Bobby were engaged in some sort of dispute about the shirt he was wearing and the chores he was scheduled to do later on. Bobby gave me a self-effacing smile and a shrug as I climbed into the back seat of the car beside him. It made for an unnerving ride to the school.

"Don't forget to comb your hair!" Mrs. Hubacheck shouted, turning her head to the back seat as we arrived. Bobby shrugged and pulled up his pants. I walked quickly, hoping to separate myself from them.

A slouching seventh grader guided us to an empty classroom, the rows of desks and chairs appearing forlorn and forsaken. We sat near the front, in a small, nervous cluster. The meeting was called to order. We stood for a quick, mumbled prayer, obviously de rigueur. The seventh grader leading the prayer smiled cryptically the entire time.

A seventh grader named David Weathersby served as president (or head something) of the club. He was tall for his age (though he stopped growing at age 14 and eventually I passed him up), with a crop of curly blond hair and a peach fuzz mustache and a permanent smirk on his pale, oblong face. He had an intimidating mean streak, calling out club members for their physical and mental attributes, keeping us all in line. His sidekick was a stocky, silent, offensive guard type named Rick Bosky, who stood beside Weathersby laughing at his jokes but glaring out at the crowd when necessary. Occasionally he shared a fleeting, conspiratorial smile with us peons out in the desk chairs.

It was a loosely-structured operation, as far as theme and objective. There were no goals or merit badges involved. Usually we began with some tales from the seventh-grade world—a sophisticated, savvy, mysterious world containing a cryptic combination of macho posturing, potty humor, and girls. Sometimes we watched a Saturday morning cartoon show on a TV wheeled in on a stand from a utility room somewhere. If the weather was cold or crummy, we headed to the gym where we played basketball or dodge ball or just ran over and under the bleachers. If the weather was good, we went outside on the athletic fields to play baseball or football or soccer, depending on the season.

There was a dry creek running through some undeveloped wooded land on the back side of the school property, meandering for a mile or so before disappearing into a tunnel under a city street. It was a forbidden land, filled with tropical plants and wildlife and bird calls and bugs, reminding us of another forbidden land, a land on the far side of the world where our country was waging war—Vietnam. This was before public sentiment had turned against the war effort there and it was perhaps inevitable that red-blooded American 11- and 12-year-old boys would turn to war games when left to their own devices.

We'd divide into squadrons and fan out into the jungle canopy, talking softly, crouching low to avoid detection, searching for Viet Cong. Along the way we'd gather dirt clods and spear grass for weapons. Sometimes we'd try to ambush the other group by sneaking in behind them. Other times we'd have pitched battles on opposite sides of the creek bed, dirt clods landing and splattering like thudding missiles. Our hearts thumped madly in the throes of glorious battle, the euphoria of war with low-stakes consequences. We arrived home dusty and sweaty, our clothes and our grime-streaked faces a testament to our virile heroism.

One day we had ranged deep into the bush when our squad leader, the illustrious David Weathersby, hit upon a brilliant strategy for smoking out the enemy. He called us over, waving urgently with a cupped hand. We gathered around him, squatting on our haunches or on one knee. With a grimy finger, he draw a game plan in the dirt. Unfortunately, his strategy involved a human sacrifice.

"I know how we can smoke them out," Weathersby said, his trademark smirk morphed into a sly smile.

"How?" someone asked.

"How?" Weathersby said, placing a sardonic hand on the boy's slim shoulder. "Elementary, my dear Watson. One of our esteemed squadron members walks down the center of the creek pretending to have a gun and speaking on a walky-talky. When they fire on him we'll know their position and take them out. Of course, the esteemed squadron member will be dead. Literally, perhaps."

Some brazen desire to become a hero—albeit a fallen hero—moved me to volunteer. I threw up my hand in a nano-second.

"I can do it," I said. "I'll do it." Weathersby looked at me skeptically. Perhaps I didn't seem like I had the stuff to walk down the center of a creek in a war, even a pretend war. He stroked his cheek pensively.

"You sure, man?" he said. "You've got to do it right. You can't turn back or start running."

"I can do it right," I said. He placed his hand on my shoulder now. I felt like I had received a blessing from a holy man.

"OK then," Weathersby said. "Here's what we're gonna do."

Minutes later, outfitted with a ceremonial bazooka that was actually a log, I started my solitary stroll down St.

Luke's creek. I felt isolated, alone, yet my senses seemed engaged and almost preternaturally aware. At first, it seemed deathly silent in the brush above me as I walked, the lips of the creek walls looming high above, unassailable, insurmountable, like the cliffs of Normandy. Then I began to pick out bird calls and crickets buzzing in the trees. The occasional car horn or revving motorcycle engine punctuated the otherwise pristine sounds of nature. I had walked almost the length of the creek when I heard rustling in the brush to the right ahead of me, like a large animal crashing through. Then all hell broke loose. It was like Godzilla himself had emerged from the brush.

There was the other squadron, looming above me on the cliffs like gladiators of ancient Rome, arms cocked and off-hands loaded with a cache of hard, ugly dirt clods. I was a sitting duck.

"There he is!"

"Get him!"

"Let him have it!"

They opened fire, dirt clods raining down like mortal shells. All I could do was duck and cover my eyes and my head. The fusillade went on for a good thirty seconds.

"We got him," they said. "He's dead." Their entire squadron stood gloating on the creek bank, cheering and shaking their fists.

My team emerged then—finally—and began firing their own dirt clod missiles over the top of the ditch and over my head. The other team was out of ammo, and after a few futile throws of spear grass and weeds, they fled into the bush. The final tally somehow seemed weighted in their favor. I had done my part, nonetheless. I was dead. Nobody seemed too concerned about it, though, as we began walking slowly back toward the school grounds in wrap-up mode. It was time to get picked up.

When I got home Dad was there, sitting not in his evening chair but at the kitchen table. This seemed strange because Dad worked Saturday mornings at the office, going over accounts and cleaning up invoices and so forth. We were used to him being home in the evenings but this seemed intrusive somehow. He was taking up too much space, sucking up the psychic oxygen from my mother and the rest of us. It was tough to operate when he was there. There was tension. There were instructions and commands. There were looks exchanged between my mother and him, looks that were ominous and mysterious and freighted with innuendo.

I shot a quick nod to Dad before heading for my room to clean up and change. I didn't want to hang around and invite commentary.

"Steve," Dad said, calling me back. He said my name in a certain, unique way that induced fear and uncertainty.

Trapped, I stood by the kitchen table, squirming and trembling like a soldier up for officer's review. I thought he was going to dress me down for some unknown reason—my appearance; my grades; something he had found in my room. I tried to remember what contraband items I might be currently keeping in my room.

"Your father has something to tell you," Mom said.

I nodded, waiting—waiting for the boom to fall. Dad flexed his hand, as if in a preliminary gesture to speaking, but said nothing. I glanced back and forth between Mom and Dad, uncertain, unknowing, pulse rising as I pondered possibilities. Dad stayed silent. Mom spoke up finally, softly, steadily.

"You remember Daddy's nephew Paul Gallagher?" she said. "You met him, from Dallas. He was here for Christmas one year with Aunt Janey and Uncle Bill and he met us at Six Flags when we went up there." She paused, for a breath or to gather her composure, or both, perhaps. "He was killed in Vietnam yesterday. Daddy found out late last night."

I couldn't think of anything to say. There didn't seem to be much of anything to say. Anything I said seemed like it would be rash and meaningless, so I just stood there silent, nodding. And breathing. And listening to my heartbeat. The sounds of life. I was alive. It was strange to think about, surreal and philosophical and terribly, terribly adult, cruel. Paul was dead. Gone. I remembered him as a lanky lefthander who showed me how to throw a knuckleball and hit a golf ball through the windmill on a putt-putt course.

"He was in a jeep," Mom said, "and they hit a mine in the road. The jeep blew up. Everyone inside was killed."

I could only shake my head numbly. It didn't seem real, and yet it was all too real. It seemed like something that happened to other people. I wasn't sure what to do. It seemed beyond the grasp of my 11-year-old self to absorb and comprehend. Dad wasn't the kind of guy you could hug. I don't think he wanted a hug.

"Wow," I said finally. "Wow." Dad waved his hand at me, which seemed like a signal to leave. I went into the kitchen and made myself a sandwich to eat, as I had planned to do, though I wasn't hungry anymore and the food tasted flat. Then I went to my room where I lay on my back in bed, contemplating life and death, and my new school, and the Saturday Morning Fun Club. The future seemed sort of hazy right now. The future didn't seem like it was there at all.

To Paris at 2:00 A.M.

They made love all afternoon in his Manhattan penthouse and then he had to catch a red-eye to Paris at 2:00 am. But before that he was going to need to bump off a man in Philadelphia and drink a beer with Johannson, who would already be drunk. There would, of course, be a sumptuous five-course dinner at Sardi's, with a table facing the park. And they wanted to watch a DVR'd episode of "30 Rock," which they never missed, except when he was watching it with his other girlfriend in Buenos Aires or his pal Hank in New Orleans. He really needed to work on his taxes. And he should call his wife to let her know he'd be late—and then gone for three weeks.

"Is there something wrong?" Natalie said, in a troubled tone, cocking her head to question him with her eyes. "You seem distracted. You seem tense."

He shook his head dolefully. He constructed a smile. He didn't want to ruin her afternoon by cluing her in on everything that was going on in his life. She believed he was an investments advisor for a Fortune 500 Wall Street firm. She was such a trusting thing, so free and open, like the girls he knew in college, wanting to change the world and help her fellow man and interested in organic foods and recycling to save precious energy resources and all that. He didn't want to shatter her innocence. He didn't want to let her see what the world was really like.

"It's just the Yankees," he said. "They can't seem to get their starting rotation set. Jeter's too old now. A-Rod's washed up. Mariano Rivera can't go on forever. Who knows whether he can really come back from that injury?"

"Poor Yankees," Natalie said. "I wish I could make them good for you. I wish I could have helped them sign Cliff Lee. I wish they could be like they were in the late 1990s."

He pulled her close, kissing the top of her head where the roots parted, moved by this exuberant display of genuine empathy. She actually does love him, he thought. Forget his obligations, he wanted to just stay here with her forever.

"Marry me, Natalie," he said. "Marry me today."

"I will, Alex aka Ala'n aka Federico," Natalie said. "But aren't you married already?"

"I am," he said, "But that can be rectified—in a hurry."

Natalie looked troubled again. Perhaps she was remembering that she really was at heart just a college girl who wanted to change the world for the better. And the practical daughter of a tax attorney.

"Maybe you'd better get that taken care of first," she said.

He nodded, formulating a plan. Another thing to do, another thing to put on the list.

"When I see you in three weeks I won't be married

anymore," he said. "I've got a place in the country, up the Hudson River from here. Let's go there."

"OK," she said.

He kissed her on the mouth. And then, in that moment of joy and connection, of two human beings bonding together, he began to back off mentally from what he had just said. He couldn't make that commitment to Natalie. He couldn't commit to anything. He remembered the words of Sister Doloretta, the Irish nun who taught him in seventh grade: "You flit from one thing to another like a hummingbird on the wing." And he knew then, after leaving later that day, he would never see Natalie again.

Quality Photos

The summer of our wedding my bride Claudia VanderMeer and I leased a split-level duplex on a dead-end street in a close-in gentrifying area of south central Austin, a quiet, in-transition neighborhood of young families and senior citizens and dogs. The opposite side of the duplex was occupied by the owner/landlord, a white-haired University of Texas professor who we figured was gay. We were fine with him being gay (perhaps we even wanted him to be gay), both for philosophical reasons and as a counterpoint to our conspicuously heterosexual, pre-children, pre-jaded bliss.

We exchanged vows at 3:00 PM on a hot summer Saturday in a big, ceremonial Catholic high Mass, but marriage wasn't the only new thing in my life. I had recently accepted a position as assistant editor for an architectural design magazine, a glossy magazine in a glitzy downtown high-rise, the ground floor lobby a bank, ornate and open and airy at the same time, giant glass panes opened effulgently to an ever-changing street view. Claudia remained working for the tax attorney's office where we had first met. She was the receptionist, I was a file clerk—

basically, I did whatever they told me to do. I always seemed to fall for the receptionist. Laughing at my jokes or listening to my stories as I passed by, they seemed to trigger in me some deep, inchoate desire to please.

This new job was a big deal, a giant step up. It was actually my first job "in my field" of journalism, and such jobs were never easy to come by for recent college grads. I had been lucky enough to have been recommended for this particular opening by a former features writing professor, an elfin man whose chin whiskers and suspenders made him look something like Ben Franklin. After a final formal interview with a cadre of over-dressed, self-impressed 30-something blowhards around an imposing glass-top conference table, I was offered a position as Assistant Editor. We all shook hands and drank a toast.

As the new guy, one of my tasks was to deliver film (they still used film then) for the magazine's visuals to a photo shop for processing. Nobody else wanted this task, but I enjoyed getting out of the regimented office system and into the colorful, hipster-inhabited milieu that was the streets of central Austin. Driving along with my neatly-sealed package beside me, I felt both rakish and debonaire, protective of my company's material but also a man on an adventure.

Quality Photos was a high-end professional photo shop, for magazines and glossy advertising circulars and wedding photographers, located on a busy corner of MLK and Lavaca Streets, just south of the University of Texas campus. The adjacent streets buzzing with co-eds in shorts and guys walking with backpacks over their shoulders created in me a strong nostalgia for my college years. Which, in many ways, was where I would rather be. I found the working world to be both stressful and mundane, a low-security prison of sorts, impinging on my freedom and sapping my energy. The magazine editor, my supervisor, was a complete stuffed shirt. At 30 he acted 60, gliding around with a surfeit of pomposity and grandeur, as if emulating Miss Manners. A few weeks after my hire the editor looked on me rather skeptically, I feared, with a good deal of buyer's remorse.

A neon sign over Quality Photo's threshold read, "Serving Your Photographic Needs Since 1970." The lawn out front was small and brown and bare, the unwatered grass beaten down into dirt. The building itself was a former residence, white clapboard, with a high bay window providing a kind of stage for the activities inside. The counter clerk there was a young woman of about my own age, a recent college grad herself, short, buxom, attentive, chatty, with her straight brunette hair turned up in a flip at the shoulders in a quite attractive pageboy look. There was a splash of freckles on her fresh, fair-skinned face. Her name was Anne, Anne Sommers, in fact. This being summer, she wore flip-flops and Mexican peasant blouses, scooped at the breast and pleasantly revealing. She always had something interesting to say, something sharp and witty, and I tried hard to say something sharp and witty back. Feeling guilty (because of my new wife), I nevertheless looked forward to our conversations, our easy banter, our jokes. She laughed at my jokes. I laughed at hers. One day, we both declared our desires to move to New York, me to be a writer, her to be an actress. But I told her I didn't think I'd make it there now.

"How come?" she said.

"Oh well, you know," I said.

"Your wife?" she said.

"Uh-huh," I said. I fell into a dark, indicative silence.

"So you're an actress?" I said, changing the subject. "What have you been in?"

She took a small, theatrical bow.

"I played Emily Webb in *Our Town* and Ophelia in *Hamlet* and Elaine in *The Last of the Red Hot Lovers*," she said. "Oh--and Stella in *A Streetcar Named Desire*."

"I'm impressed," I said.

"I'm actually in rehearsals for a play at Zachary Scott right now," she said. "It's this Sam Shepherd production, very avante garde. You'll have to come see me sometime."

"I will," I said. "I sure will." Honored and pleased, I smiled, and we stood facing each other across the counter for a long time. Then touching her arm I said goodbye.

It was easy being with her. It was fun. At first, our conversations lasted only as long as it took to drop off the photos or pick them up. Later, I would linger, sometimes keeping the words flowing through other customers, linger until she was called to the back.

One day, she reached across the counter to place her hand on my wrist--and left it there while ringing up my receipt. She laughed. We continued on with our banter. She removed her hand when the bell over the door clanged indicating another customer was coming in.

I guess I didn't talk about my marriage much, but

maybe she could pick up the vibes. Six weeks in, and I was already uncertain whether I wanted it to work out. Claudia and I really didn't know each other all that well. We didn't like many of the same things. Her sense of humor was different from mine. She had standards for organization and comportment that I was unable to meet. I found out very quickly that she didn't want me going out with my friends at all, that after work was over I was supposed to stay put with her and only her. I missed hanging out with my friends. I didn't want them to disappear from my life. Furthermore, she remained angry for days after a the slightest argument, withholding sex, smiles, a sense of security. None of these were things one wanted to find out after a marriage started.

Some days I stormed off to work fuming, convinced that we were going nowhere and that my life was in ruins. One morning there was a giant flare-up when I asked Claudia (softly, in the nicest tones possible) if she could iron my shirt since I was running late—and got chewed out royally. I never figured out why exactly, but apparently this request triggered an intense emotional reaction based on some incident from her childhood or an experience with an earlier boyfriend. I rarely asked Claudia to do anything for me again.

Shirt wrinkled, I walked out trembling, stepping on my own shoelace and spilling coffee on my dress slacks. I turned back to make some vengeful remark but Claudia breezed right past me to her car and drove away, tires squealing. Squealing her tires was yet another aspect of

Claudia's personality that I hadn't known about before we were married.

That afternoon I drove over to Quality Photos to deliver some film. I didn't really need to go that day, but unable to focus on work I convinced myself that fresh air and a change of scenery would revitalize me. Even with Anne, my conversation seemed stilted, forced. I was pressing too hard. I couldn't think of the right things to say. Leaving, I felt even more depressed, empty, incomplete, locked in a prison of solitude and angst. A cloud of doom trailed over my head. My life was a sham. My future was a wreck. But as I started the engine to drive away, Anne ran out to the car after me. It was the first time since I had been making my visits that she had left the building.

"Wait!" she called, waving wildly. I eased the car to a stop alongside the curb. I smiled, uncertainly. She opened the passenger door and slid inside.

"What's up?" I said.

"You forgot something," she said.

"Really?" I said. I patted around between the seats reflexively. I smiled again. "What did I forget?"

"Some of your finished photos," she said. "I'll go back and get them."

"Oh, don't worry," I said. If I left something this would give me another trip back in the near future. I found myself delighted to have her near me in the car, her face, her voice, her hair, her fragrance, her ample breasts. She had really ample breasts. "I'll get them next time."

She drew in a breath and looked at me in a way I had

failed to observe in my previous visits. It was almost—well, in that one instant I almost thought it was a look of love.

"Oh, what the hell," she said. "Life is too damn short."

"What do you mean?" I said.

And then she leaned across the gap between the seats to kiss me smack on the lips. I turned into a bowl of Jell-o. I didn't invite the kiss (I told myself in my sin-wracked Catholic school mind), I didn't encourage it, but there it was, the sweetest, softest, most fantastic kiss I had ever received. I was trembling afterwards. I wanted more.

"Oh Lord I'm married," I said, more a declaration to the cosmos than a real attempt to repel her advances.

"I know," she said. "I know you are." She pulled me to her for another kiss, and this one was even better than the one before. I acquiesced with a sense of inescapable inevitability. God, did I ever acquiesce. I was squeezing her back, I was stroking her hair, I was caressing her neck. This was all in bright broad daylight, parked in front of her place of employment.

Finally, Anne pushed me away. She sat up straight on her side and began to straighten her hair and her clothes. I was beyond doing that. I was like a smoking ruin.

"I guess I'd better get back in," she said.

"Okay," I said.

"I'm sorry," she said. "I'm just so attracted to you. We have so much in common. We talk about so many different things. You make me laugh."

"Oh, God, I know," I said. "You make me laugh so hard sometimes. I love to hear you laugh."

She sat strangely still for a moment, looking away. Then

she turned back to me. Her mouth seemed almost quivering.

"Hey, I need to tell you," she said. "I'm going to New York."

"New York?" I said. "A trip? A vacation?"

"It's more than a trip," she said. "I'm going there to live."

My jaw dropped. My heart skipped a beat.

"When are you going?" I said.

"Tomorrow," she said. "This is my last day here."

"Tomorrow," I said. The word was like a life sentence imposed by a judge. My heart was sinking now. It was dropping like a chunk of steel to the bottom of a deep, dark lake.

She nodded.

"I was hoping you would come by today so I could tell you," she said. "It came up all of a sudden. I have an opportunity for a part in an off-Broadway play. They've got the audition all set up. I'm flying out in the morning."

"Oh my God," I said. "Oh my heavens." I hardly knew this woman, but I had never felt so desolate, so devastated in my entire life. I took both of her hands in mine and held them tight. All bets were off just then in terms of sin and depravation. I didn't care what happened to my eternal soul.

"Will I ever see you again?" I said.

"I don't know," she said. She seemed to ponder something for a few moments.

"Would you to want to come with me? Would you want to come to New York?"

"Come with you?" I said. "To New York?"

She nodded.

"We could rent a place together. We could live together."

"I don't know," I said. "I just got married."

"I know," she said. "But maybe this would be the best time to break it off, before you really get established and get a lot of baggage. If it's not going to work out why prolong it. You want to be happy, after all."

"You're right," I said. "I do want to be happy." I paused, considering. But there just wasn't enough time to make a proper decision. I didn't see how I could just pick up and leave. There were family considerations, career considerations, gifts received and used. I sat for a long time quietly holding her hands, not wanting to move, wishing we could just stay like this forever.

"I better get in," she said finally. She started to pull away.

"I'll write you," I called desperately. This was before the days of email and the internet, of web sites and cell phones and text messaging. Communication was slow and laborious. There was the land-line, of course, there were pay phones, but getting in touch with somebody then was not so simple or neat.

"I don't know my address yet," she said.

"I'll write down mine," I said. I scribbled my address hastily on a used envelope lying between the car seats. "Here's my telephone number at work, too. You could call me there."

"Okay," she said. "I'll call you there."

I knew it wouldn't happen. Once she left the car I

would lose all hope for future happiness. She leaned in for one final kiss, and then she was out the door, bounding across the lawn in her girlish way, breasts bouncing, hair tossing. She stopped to wave one last time before disappearing inside. I was thankful for that. At least I had that.

Christmas Eve

Christmas Eve is when everything is going to be all right. You're going to do this, accomplish that. You're going on a fabulous trip. You're going to meet a wonderful girl, and marry her. The girl you are going with now will be wonderful in the future. No more arguments, sex all the time. Everything's going to change. Everything's going to be all right. Everything's going to be great! You'll be moving into a big new house, a house with a luxurious lawn and blooming flowers and gregarious (but respectful of your privacy) neighbors who will host lawn parties on long-shadowed, verdant summer afternoons. You're going to get the promotion. You won't have to use your credit cards for anything. If you do, you'll pay them off right away. You'll write a best seller. You'll paint a classic picture. You'll tell the boss off—and he'll admit you're right, giving you the raise and the promotion you've always deserved. You'll be the office hero. You'll do something noble and life-changing. You'll be known as a selfless, giving guy, a guy who would do anything for anybody. You'll get up early and exercise. You'll exercise at night, one of those enviable individuals you see striding purposefully along the roadway at dusk, looking loose and limber and free. You'll be neat and orderly. You won't lose patience and snap at family members and friends. Yes—Christmas Eve!

It's Christmas Eve in suburban San Antonio, Texas, sometime in the latter half of the 20th Century. I live in a raw new shade-less subdivision with the quixotic name, Inspiration Hills. Our house has a broad, sloping front lawn with a view of the skyscrapers in downtown San Antonio, ten miles away. My father is a corporate attorney, my mother a stay-at-home mom with an inventor's mind and a wise-cracking comedian's style. She's Erma Bombeck with a girdle and a menthol cigarette in one hand. I am nine years old.

My prize gift this year is a dark brown Rawlings baseball glove, stiff and smelling of fresh calves' leather from Mexico. Playing with this glove I am assured of being an all -star third baseman next spring. (And a big league player a decade or so hence.) I sleep with the glove, a shiny new baseball tucked into the pocket, forming the pocket, molding it. There is nothing like a new fielder's glove and a new hard ball. Sweet dreams tonight!

As a pimply, lovelorn adolescent, I receive shirts and CD's and a video game system which I proclaim as "awesome!" but which I relegate immediately to the outcast land of unused gifts. It is, lamentably, the wrong system, an outdated system, the product of poor communication and bargain shopping.

That evening, I slouch about in our sunken living room, tossing my long, greasy hair debonairly and foolishly, almost tauntingly for my father's benefit. I watch my younger siblings with building envy, observing their carefree antics, their pure joy in the magic of the moment. I am anything but pure. I am a product of bad alchemy, an adulterated mix of chemicals brewed in a contaminated, back-street lab.

My father, the corporate attorney, is a demanding man with impossibly high standards and a temper to avoid, and he seems to think I am a bum, a slacker, a future flop. He wants me to become an attorney like him, but I have no desire to follow in his footsteps. I'm a writer, I tell him, and he turns away as if I have slapped his face. My mother, a creative person herself, is more sanguine on this point.

"Daddy," she says, "Leave him alone. He'll do what he wants to do. He'll be a success." Dad grumbles something that sounds like a curse.

What I really want for Christmas is something my parents cannot provide—an attractive young female who will like me, accept me, talk to me, make me feel like a man. Or at least a human being, not the bizarre outcast creature that I appear to be.

As the night wears on I go through the motions of a happy Christmas, smiling, hugging family members, rough-housing with the dog, uproariously laughing. But I feel alienated from the frivolity, distant, like a spectator in the far upper gallery of a theater. Taking advantage of confusion and a general atmosphere of bonhomie, I mix myself a bourbon and coke and knock it down and then another and yet another and before I go to bed I puke. When my dad wakes me the next morning for Christmas Day Mass, I puke again. Merry Christmas, punk!

At age 21, things are picking up. On Christmas Eve night, I sit in my grandparents' retirement-community condo nursing a bourbon and coke highball that my grandfather has mixed, sanctioning my official entry into adulthood. My father and I sit side-by-side in leather wing chairs, drinking openly together for the first time. Amazingly, all the bitterness and rancor of my adolescent years seems to have washed away in a 90 proof river. We sit chatting amiably, like old office mates, discussing political and sociological topics of the day. I am more artful now in my responses to him. I dance away from controversial answers. I refuse to be baited. I concur gracefully on some of his more dubious opinions.

I have a girlfriend now, a girl I am heading over to pick up in a few minutes. I am proud of this girl. I am happy to be with her. She is a short, attractive, well-put-together, raven-haired young woman with a trace, just the slightest trace, of a Southern accent learned from spending her first ten years in rural Alabama. We live together secretly back in our college town, Austin, and we have sex together on a regular basis. Oh my God—sex! They were right about sex, that it's the greatest elixir there is, a miracle, a magic potion bottled up in our own bodies. No wonder they don't want anybody to know about it too soon. It's dangerous stuff. I turn to my father, clad in a starched dress shirt and striped tie, like his father before him, and blurt out some sentimental, bourbon-induced bromide.

"I think everything's going to be okay," I say, referencing pretty much our entire history up to this point. "Everything's going to be all right." Leaning over, I embrace him, awkwardly, his light lawyer's hand forming a practiced circle around my back, as though I am a client. It is our first embrace since early childhood. My mother I observe watching us with a combination of indulgence and amused skepticism.

Driving through a montage of city lights to pick up my girlfriend Sandy, I bask in the afterglow of the highballs and my rapprochement with my father. Life can be good. The earth is a good place. Sandy is ready for me when I arrive. She wants to go. She wants to go with me. But first, we embrace. We kiss. In the soft bath of yellow light beside her doorway, Sandy appears ravishing in a tight black dress and platform heels and her hair pulled into ringlets—a wedding guest look. Emotion welling in my chest, I kiss her ravenously, ravishingly, one last time, and afterwards she buries her head of brunette hair in my shoulder. I don't want to move. I don't want to leave. For the moment, I am happy, about as happy as a human being can be. I am content. I am content to be *me*.

"Your breath smells good," she tells me.

"It does?" I say. "Really?"

"Uh-huh," she says. "It smells like whiskey. Whiskey is good."

I accept her testimonial with poise and equanimity.

"That's good," I say. "That's good to hear."

She is mine. Everything is going to be okay, after all. My God, everything is going to be okay.

In my late thirties now, I am married (though not to Sandy), with two lovely blond-haired kids, a girl aged 9 and a boy aged 6. The girl is smart and sassy, the boy a future techie nerd, determined and undeterred by outside social forces. I work for a large international conglomerate with a field office in San Antonio. Our facility is a long rectangular one-story mirror-glass building located near a freeway interchange in the outer layer of suburbs. I sit in a cube. I edit documents on a computer screen. If I stand up out of my desk and walk a few paces into a kind of cube corridor, I can see daylight outside. I can tell when it's raining by the crescendo of sound on the gravel roof. My wife Sara is an art instructor for a private school, a smart, gregarious woman who accumulates friends as she strolls smiling through life. Unfortunately, I don't believe I am one of them.

We're spending Christmas Eve at my parents' house, the same house where I grew up. Dad is retired from his law firm now, and Mom, afflicted with emphysema and osteoporosis, is hooked to an oxygen tank, wheeling it around like a miniature grocery cart. She is cheerful still, still brimming with jokes, but there is an underlying sadness now, a foreshadowing of mortality. I try to keep her laughing with my observations and ready wit. Her laugh emerges in a wheeze. Sara is free and easy with my parents, sometimes too much so, blithe, almost callous. She says things to my parents like, "Come on, Dad, you can do it."

I sit leaning forward on a couch, and Sara sits across from me on the carpeted floor, legs crossed, arms folded across her chest. It is a posture that seems designed to repel my overtures. I try catching her attention, but she flips her hair and stares steadfastly away. I cough. I wave, even. She takes a call with her cell phone—one of her cadre of friends, no doubt, checking on her Christmas Eve activities. Can't they leave her alone even tonight? She is talking and laughing easily with her caller. I wish she would laugh with me.

My spirit droops. My heart aches. The fact strikes me like a bludgeon to the chest—Sara enjoys being with her friends more than she does with me. Sometimes it seems that we live separate lives, lives that intersect for only a few brief moments each day. We go to work in the daytime then she goes off to hang out with her friends at night. It's an arrangement that has become established over time.

Here at my parents' house, watching the children play, we seem terribly, tragically distant from one another, mismatched, like different chess pieces, a rook and a bishop, perhaps. I am edgy. I am unfocused. I won't admit this to anyone, but we have come to that stage in our marriage where everything seems stale and brittle, ready to crack. I want to try something new. I think Sara does, too.

That night, on our drive home across town, all the pressure bubbles to the surface and we erupt in a terrible argument, yelling at each other, hurling insults. The kids shrink back silently in the back seat, suffering silently. Finally, our daughter, the take-charge older one, says, "Do you two even like each other?"

"Sure we do, Honey," Sara says. "We just get mad at each other sometimes. Everybody does."

We hush then, but later Sara locks herself in our

bedroom, shutting me out. I sleep on a hard couch in the living room beside the Christmas tree, amid wrapped presents and symbols of joy, turning fitfully every few minutes, my life turning over like a body in a centrifuge.

Next morning the children rouse me early, filling the early dawn with their shouts of surprise and delight. I pretend I am interested. I pretend there is a reason to go on. Sara sits stone-faced across the room, her fresh-ground coffee cradled harshly in both hands.

I am 45 now, this Christmas Eve, divorced, a single dad. I send vague and amorphous prayers heavenward, hoping that any second something good will happen with my life. Actually, the kids are holding me together. They keep me from falling off of a very steep cliff. I don't know what the future holds. I don't know where I'll be next year—or next week. I walk a tight line, hoping that I'll be able to hold things together, hoping that I won't fall apart. Everything is a giant pendulum swing.

This one day, this one night, I feel relatively happy and secure, both kids hanging out with me, not out running around or with their mother. Watching a video of "Scrooged!" with Bill Murray, we huddle together in a ring on the floor of my parents' house, touching feet like Cub Scout campers, connected by physical proximity and a sudden, satisfying synergy. I feel connected. Tomorrow and the day after, who knows? I make no plans. Nobody would follow my plans anyway. I hope for the best.

Christmas Eve is when everything is going to be all right. It will be all right.

Grime

Forcing open a balky window pane on my 18th floor room in the Pickwick Arts Hotel in mid-town Manhattan, I inhaled deeply, satisfyingly. The quality of the air was like leaning over the brim of an apartment house dumpster. It was grimy, confusion-laced, filled with a babble of sounds, a bad orchestra of sounds, emanating from deep in the heart of the five boroughs, deep in the universe itself, it seemed. I reveled in the griminess. (In reveling, I coughed.) I felt like Balboa topping the crest of a ridge to sight the Pacific. All the human drama you could possibly want—and I wanted a lot. Focusing in, above the background hum of traffic and voices I ascertained the sounds of a discussion in some fast-paced foreign tongue, Middle Eastern in origin, wafting up through the narrow utility shaft between the hotel façade and the adjacent building. This was delightful. It was all delightful. I breathed it all in. I inhaled it like a big, aroma-tic cigar, a big fat stogie. And coughed again. On the verge of hyperventilation, I willed away my excitement.

This was my first night alone in the city, the first, I was convinced, of a long, successful run of nights, days and nights of drama and passion and fulfilled dreams. Oh, there were loose ends, of course, some nagging loose ends that lingered just beneath the surface of my joy, like a sore tooth. There was a girlfriend back home in Texas, a hostage to my self-promoting dreams of glory and adventure. Amanda had returned to Austin just this evening on a night flight from JFK Airport, which seemed a million miles from anywhere. A sad, sweet parting it was, at hopelessly unromantic Delta Terminal G, a fast, final kiss as we leaned clumsily between red-plastic waiting room chairs, fixed to the floor, announcements blaring. Then I watched Amanda walk bravely down the boarding ramp, with her long blond hair and flowered shift dress and sandals, and she turned and waved one last time, and then again one more time, tears glistening on her cheeks, tears glistening on mine, as I jockeyed for a better view, before disappearing through the entry doors, her boarding pass taken brusquely by a no-nonsense female attendant. I rode a bus and then the subway on the long, long trip back to my Manhattan hotel, feeling both liberated and lost.

I was on my own. I was free. I could do any damn thing I wanted to. Freedom is powerful. Freedom is a drug. I sat staring out the window, a small, desktop TV blank. I switched it on and flipped through the channels distractedly, mainly to see what TV was like here. It was exhilarating—at first. It was the same as TV back home—news, sports, sitcoms, political talk shows, reality shows, ads, weather. Nonetheless, I watched for several spellbound minutes, pondering the astounding reality that I was watching TV in a hotel room in NYC, the Big Apple, city of my dreams,

1,500 miles from home, isolated from family and friends, isolated from anyone I ever know or associated with. I cut off that line of thinking quickly. I switched off the TV. Freedom was wonderful, all right, but what was freedom if you couldn't do anything with it? What was freedom if you were sitting on your ass in a drab and dingy hotel room, doing nothing? I decided I must act. I must do something.

I slipped on shoes and buttoned up my shirt and rode the creaky, cranky elevator to ground level, where it stopped a half-floor short. Dressed in jeans and polo shirt, I passed myself off as a savvy New York native as I strolled through the ornate lobby with plastic chandeliers and threadbare carpet in interlocking geometric patterns, past an Indian family, mother, grandmother, child, women dressed in saris, father tall and hawk-nosed, garbed in mis-matched Western-style shirt and slacks, and onto the street. Discreetly, I checked the 12 oz. aerosol spray can of liquid mace (recommended by the guidebook, *New York on $150 A Day*), tucked into my right front pants pocket, tapping twice. I smiled strangely at a passerby who caught me tapping.

"It's not a gun," I said, even more strangely. Avoiding eye contact, the passerby made a jab step and pushed by quickly.

Berating myself for my un-New Yorkerish demeanor, I shuffled along cautiously, using peripheral vision to scan my surroundings. I walked an ever-expanding counter-clockwise perimeter around the hotel site, each step an experiment, each step forward a new, successful venture. I passed a homeless man sleeping on the ground. I bought a lemonade from a street vendor. I observed two young people stealing a kiss on a street corner; she was holding her skirt down with one hand. Street lights were coming on. Storefront lights blinked on and off, like jazz music. Moving more confidently, I eased onto the southern edge of Central Park, at 59th Street near the retention pond. Music wafted in from the band shell, a quarter-mile away. A horse-drawn carriage clumped past, its occupants a family of four, father, mother, daughter, son. The girl was dressed like a princess. I smelled cotton candy and roasting peanuts. The city was magic. My life was exploding with sensory perceptions, with metaphysical clarifications. There was a dance in my gait.

Then the trouble began—I discovered I was being followed. I suspected I was being followed. I felt certain I was being followed. Using peripheral vision, I determined there was a group of Goth-looking teenagers following me, a mixed-race, mixed-gender gang laughing and jostling each other, black hair glistening, long chains clanking at their sides. They were their when I left Central Park, turning onto 7th Avenue. They were there when I crossed 57th Street. They were there when I turned left onto W. 57th and crossed over the Avenue of the Americas. They were there when I turned past the outdoor skating rink at Rockefeller Center. When I crossed W. 52nd Street, they were still there, edging closer, closing in on me, moving in for . . .the kill.

I stood still briefly, taking stock on my bearings. I stood at the corner of 52nd and Madison Avenue, approximately (by my measure) 12 blocks from my hotel. I lingered briefly near a pretzel vendor, who was packing up his food truck for the night.

I had one advantage—my pursuers didn't know where I was going. I concocted a plan. I would zig-zag my way back to the hotel, keeping it between them and me at all times and a running lane open for a final dash to safety. I tested my legs, bouncing on the balls of my feet. I felt good. I was young and healthy. I played tennis twice a week. (Who would play tennis with me here, I thought?) I imagined myself running down a ball behind the baseline, whacking it back cross-court with a savage backhand. I could make a run of it if need be.

Fortified momentarily, I strode powerfully, purposefully forward. The blocks glided by, like interval markers on a race course. Finally, turning left onto W. 49th Street, I saw the hotel looming just a short side block in front of me, a veritable gleaming Taj Mahal. Outside stood a security guard garbed like a British gendarme. Flags from many nations flew from angled stanchions along a second-floor balustrade. A small crowd milled outside the entrance lobby, people waiting for cabs, getting directions, making plans, saying goodbyes. I was alone in the world. Nobody knew the pickle I was in. I exhaled, ready for the final push. I would soon be back in my room, safe and sound. But then suddenly there they were, moving toward me, blocking the sidewalk. They had circled around me, out-maneuvered me. They were making eye contact now, looming, menacing, bleating some weird gnostic chant. They were ready to pounce. I had to move now. I veered left, into the street. A yellow cab zoomed by, honking. I felt its hot exhaust on my back.

Somebody shouted something. It may have been, "Get him!" One of them made a motion at me in the street—or I thought they made a motion. One of their chains was twirling. A hand reached out for me. My own hand reached inside my pants pocket for the tear gas canister I had secured there. It exploded inside, soiling my pocket and stinging my hand. The group laughed, jeered, jumped back, providing an opening.

"Hey man, what's going on?" somebody said.

"What's he got?" somebody else said.

I moved swiftly then, like a halfback shooting through a hole in the line, arm pinned to my side, shielding my ruined pocket with a numb and throbbing hand. I did this while attempting to appear like a perfectly normal person on a leisurely jaunt back to his hotel room. At the hotel entrance, I flashed my room card to the security guard and slipped inside. In the lobby, I glanced back once to ensure the coast was clear, then dashed for the elevator. Inside, the other passengers averted their eyes and stood away, the odor from the exploded tear gas canister casting a sinister and uncertain tone.

The elevator lurched to a stop and the doors creaked open on my floor—above my floor. The exit was blocked by some sort of athletic team, a swim team, perhaps, ruddy-faced adolescents males and females both, wearing tee shirts and warm-ups and lugging sports bags with team logos. I wiggled past them, now like a basketball forward looking to establish a post-up position.

Entering my room, I locked chain and deadbolt both. Heart pounding, back against the door, I stood still, listening. I held my injured hand aloft. The cell phone in my left pocket rang. Oh no, they had found me! I saw the number—it was my girlfriend Amanda calling. Thank God. Thank God in heaven.

"Amanda!" I cried out. My voice sounded like someone who had just spent all night in the house of the Amityville Horrors.

"I'm back," Amanda said.

"You're back?" I said. What was she talking about. This made no sense.

"I'm back in Austin," she said. "My flight just landed. I'm in the airport."

This seemed implausible, impossible, that through some space-time warp in the universe she had re-materialized 1,500 miles away back in our college town, Austin. A vision of Austin flashed through my mind, its wide river cutting through the center of town, the green hills out west, the university area, rowdy crowds milling along Sixth Street. It didn't seem real.

"That's great," I said. I was silent for a moment, gears clicking, wheels turning in my head. I began to pace about the room, touching items obsessively as I walked—the windowsill, the TV top, the headboard of the bed.

"What's the weather there?" I said. I was killing time, trying to regroup, trying to formulate a plan.

"Hot," she said. "It's hot like when we left. You could tell as soon as you got on the ramp. A blast of hot air hit you right in the face."

"It's pretty cool here," I said. "I think it's like 75."

"I know," she said. "I was just there."

"I miss the heat."

"There's plenty of it back here," she said. She started to say something else but I jumped in.

"Guess what?" I said.

"What?"

"I'm coming back."

"You're coming back? What do you mean? When?"

"Soon. Tomorrow if I can. As soon as I can get a flight back. I don't want to stay here. I want to be there with you."

"Give it a try," she said. "You just barely got there. You've only been alone for like three hours."

"I don't like it here," I said. "I was wrong. It was a mistake."

There was a long, awkward silence on her end. I waited in agony for her next words.

"Don't come back," she said.

"Why not?" I said. Alarm was in my voice, panic in my heart.

"I don't want you to come back," she said. "I've been waiting for this to happen, I've been waiting for you to leave for a long time. I need a new life. I need a fresh start."

"But I love you," I said. "We love each other."

Another awkward silence.

"I'm not sure if I love you anymore," she said. "It seems like we were just marking time these last few months. I need some time to think. I need some time alone."

I held the cell phone hard to my ear, legs shaking, heart pounding. The room reeled.

"How can you do this, Amanda?" I said—it was a plea, a prayer, a supplication. "Why didn't you tell me? I didn't know."

"I think you knew," she said. "That's part of the reason you wanted to get away. You're the one who wanted to leave, remember? You wanted to follow your dreams."

My own words seemed to mock me now.

"I didn't know," I said, stubbornly.

Silence.

"My shuttle's here," Amanda said. "I've got to go."

"Amanda . . ."

"You'll be OK," she said firmly. "You'll be fine. Stick with your plan. Do what you were going to do. It'll be your great adventure. Get your new life started."

"I don't want a new life," I said. The phone went dead. I pressed CallBack but the call went into voice mail. I tried again. Voice mail.

I turned on the TV. The local news was on. There was one feature about a man with 26 cats in his apartment and one about a family that was split apart because of an immigration matter. It was just like home. Just like back home.

Exploding
Astrodome Scoreboard

My family home was a 1960s-era pink-brick mock Colonial that sat stolidly high atop a broad corner lot with a sweeping view of downtown San Antonio, in a subdivision with the elegiac name Inspiration Hills. The view made me long for something I couldn't name, something in my past, something I never had. The fresh-cut grass and blooming crepe myrtle made me imagine eternity. An automatic sprinkler system shot skeins of water in pulsing arcs across the verdant lawn. Inside, the A/C blew drafts of refrigerated air from a 3.5 BTU central unit like mythological messengers of joy.

I was back home that summer, back home after dropping out of grad school, back home from another life. My college girlfriend had broken up with me. I was fragile. I was broke. I was broken. Back home, it was as if I had leaped from a high parapet into a courtyard below, family members shuffling along as fast as they could with a fireman's canvas safety net. I didn't know where I was going or what would be happening next. It was summer 1976, the Bicentennial Year. Fireplugs and mailboxes were painted red, white, and blue. The American Basketball Association played with a red, white, and blue ball. Jimmy Carter was running for president. Tall ships sailed across New York harbor and Boston harbor on the 4th of July. Bjorn Borg beat Ilie Nastase at Wimbledon, beginning a five-year run. The Montreal Olympics were on TV. Charlie's Angels debuted on ABC. African-Americans grew giant, puffy Afros that seemed a badge of honor, a breakthrough of self-respect and good-natured defiance, a symbol of their emerging role in society. A lot of breakthroughs had occurred during the past decade.

My father walked in from work, dressed like the exploding Astrodome scoreboard after a home team home run. His outfit consisted of a blue polyester leisure suit, robin's egg blue, striped tie, white patent leather shoes, and red plastic belt—fashion-wise, he was 70s all the way. He wore his sideburns jaw-length and puffy, almost Elvis-y, and his dark moussed hair fell over his earlobes and was combed to a V over his forehead. He was an accountant for one of San Antonio's leading office supplies firms. He was 54.

He had arrived home early from work, surprising us— my two brothers, my sister, and me. We all lay sprawled on a long, tan sectional couch, unmoving, like various forms of inert matter. We were watching TV. The Olympics were on in real time. Our sunken living room was like a cave, a cool, pine-paneled, dimly-lit cave with A/C cranked down to a frosty 73 degrees. You could almost see shafts of icy air blowing from the ceiling vents. It was difficult to rouse ourselves from our lethargy, having spent a difficult, energy-sapping day playing miniature golf in the morning, watching a movie matinee, then swimming at the neighborhood association pool in the high heat of a Texas summer afternoon. I felt like a cool, smart, slightly smart-ass camp counselor to my younger siblings, sophisticated and savvy in the ways of the world.

My father stood in the entrance foyer, briefcase in hand, essaying the situation. He was watching us as if we were some exotic hybrid species just discovered. Through years of hands-on experience, we understood exactly what he thought and how he operated. Standing there, he was appalled and fascinated by us, his own offspring, and by the times, by the world, by what everything and everybody had become. A decade ago, everything was clean and clear-cut. You got a job, you bought a house, you raised your kids, you went on vacation trips, you retired to sit on the patio steps in overalls and a baseball cap. Now, he felt like somebody standing atop a steep, narrow slope, the earth eroding around him, blowing into the air. People doing things and smoking things and having fun in ways that had never even occurred to him, it all seemed so debauched and sinful. His character was formed first as a child in the Depression era and then in World War II, where he was deployed to the Philippines as part of an occupation unit at the tail end of the war.

He switched on an overhead ceiling light, causing us to shield our eyes and groan. Slowly, painfully, we roused ourselves from our torpor to wave and say hello. We squinted in the sudden unwanted bath of hard electric light. As the oldest, and leader of the group, I pulled myself into an upright, answering position. The role of oldest child was a heavy burden at times.

"Hey Dad," I said. "How's work?"

"Work's OK," he said, though his OK sounded more like not so hot, crappy, actually really terrible. He had served in his position as chief accountant at the store for more than 25 years.

"How's Ms. Bricken?" I said, searching for some sort of connection, some thin thread for conversation. I remembered Ms. Bricken fondly/amusedly from a short stint I had working for the store one summer. She was a strong, straight -backed single woman with steel-gray hair that seemed held together with super glue, purple lips, and wide, formidable hips. In her striped, ankle-length pedal pushers and sleeveless blouse she looked capable of fending off a block from an offensive lineman with one hand and sacking the quarterback with the other.

"Ms. Bricken's OK," Dad said. "She was out for six weeks with a hysterectomy but she's back now, going strong as ever. She's on a vegetarian kick. What are you guys doing?"

"Nothing much," I said. The others stared at the TV screen, assiduously avoiding eye contact. "Just catching some of the Olympics on TV. They're doing swimming now."

Dad looked at me sharply.

"Weren't you supposed to call Paul Dudley?" Dad said. His briefcase swung upward, a punctuation mark.

"Oh yeah," I said. "I will. I didn't get a chance today."

"I gave him your name," Dad said. "He seemed interested."

"I'll call him," I said, rushing the words. I was sweaty and flushed suddenly, overheated, entering into the early stages of hyperventilation. It depressed and embarrassed me talking about this humdrum, career-related detail with my siblings nearby. We were on a different track—play, swim, relax. "Tomorrow."

"Tomorrow's Saturday."

"Monday then," I said. "I'll call him first thing Monday."

"You better."

"I will." His briefcase swung like the Sword of Damocles.

Thankfully, he moved on, trudging off to the kitchen where he seemed to perform some sort of exploratory food surveillance, then to the bedroom, muttering under his breath. There was no dinner ready. There was nothing for him to eat. Mom was out working now, working part-time at a J. C. Penney's department store, working outside the house for the first time since I was born, twenty-something years before. It wasn't the money, it was blow-drying her hair and pulling on panti-hose and a dress and high-heeled shoes and presenting herself to the world, a world that was changing rapidly and unstoppably. She wanted to explore the world before it was too late. She wanted to escape this cave.

Dad reappeared, necktie removed, suit jacket draped over one shoulder.

"What time does your mother get home?" he said.

"Usually about six."

"Six?" he said, raising his eyebrows. "She told me five."

"Sometimes it's five," I said. "It depends."

"Depends on what?" he said.

"I don't know," I said. "I guess on what times she gets off."

Dad nodded tersely, uncertain what to do next. Home early, he really had nothing to do here, no place to go, no assigned duties to perform. He was as out of place here as a panhandler at a princess's wedding.

"Want to watch the Olympics, Dad?" I said. The question seemed to startle him—and my siblings, too. It was hard to imagine him coming over to the couch and climbing aboard with the rest of us.

"I don't think so," he said. "I think I'll go outside and trim some limbs."

"OK," I said. One of my siblings turned slightly to rearrange his view and to prop his chin under one hand.

Dad turned to go then turned back again.

"Isn't anybody going to ask me why I'm home early?" he said.

"Oh yeah," I said. "Why are you home early?"

"The store is going out of business," Dad said. "Pretty soon I won't have a job anymore."

"Wow, Dad," I said. I focused in on the start of the 400 IM relay. They had a new camera that showed the swimmers underwater. The horn to start the race sounded. "Wow. That's big news."

Dad stood transfixed, as if waiting for some exegesis

of the situation, some definitive explanation. He liked explanations. His entire past and future seemed to coalesce there in that moment. Everything was in flux. Life was not what they told him it was going to be. Tossing his jacket over a chair, he went outside to trim limbs.

Back Home with Alex and Alexis

Spatula in one hand and TV controller in the other, I whipped up a weekday evening dinner for my son, Alex. Recent college grad, reluctant career seeker, and surveyor of the universe, Alex was speaking on the telephone with his girlfriend Alexis, still in undergrad out in California. Alex had moved back home recently, back to Austin, back to his familiar old corner bedroom with the sports posters and the writing desk and the waterbed. I heard the bed sloshing back and forth as Alex and Alexis conversed, the rhythm of Alex's words seeming to flow with the movement of the bed. Divorced, alone, I was happy to have my son back in the fold, if only temporarily. The plan was for Alex to move in with Alexis in Berkeley, but something had happened to delay this, something I couldn't know or ask about. So I picked up where I had left off years before, cooking dinners, handing out spending money, providing succor and support and sage advice as needed. Alex left hand-written notes by the front door to tell me where he would be when he went out for the evening. I did the same for him.

I fancied myself as something of a high-level amateur

cook, with some reliable old standards but willing to venture out occasionally with advanced and innovative dishes (gleaned from internet sites). Tonight's offering was an old standard.

"How does spaghetti tonight sound?" I shouted out, pushing open the bedroom door a crack. Alex looked up from the telephone just long enough to answer.

"Sounds good, Dad!" he said. He gave a thumbs-up signal that I returned. My spirits lifted. A sense of worth returned. From his answer and demeanor, I conjectured that Alex was having a good night, emanating positive vibes from his interaction with Alexis. Sometimes afterwards he emerged hangdog and defeated, eating silently as he stared at the TV set. I wanted Alex to be happy. It made me happy. It was about all I had directly in front of me now, all I had on a day-to-day basis. My ex-wife Angie had remarried and moved on, my daughter Kelly was off to college herself, a sophomore now at the University of Chicago. Kelly and I exchanged texts and emails, the occasional call, there were trips home at holidays, but the long gaps in between felt like the gaps between stars in a galaxy. Gaps filled inadequately by work and sports events and extended family and friends, friends who didn't understand or really care. It was a life, I guess, though barely a life, a life with the pace and pulse of a slug. I never knew what was coming next. It was like waiting behind a closed door to be released from captivity.

A short while later Alex emerged from the room and loaded up his plate for dinner. There was no pause for discussion. He shook Parmesan cheese onto his mound of spaghetti with meatballs and filled a water glass from the tap.

He sat down on the couch facing the TV and grabbed the controller, changing stations deftly with his free hand.

"How's it going?" I said. I spoke hovering inelegantly in the entranceway of the kitchen.

"Good," Alex said. He shook his head definitively, once. "Going good."

"That's good," I said. "Alexis doing well?" I sounded like a character from some 19th Century British comedy of manners, a savvy but subdued butler who sublimates his buoyant personality for the sake of the household.

"Alexis is doing well," he said. He nodded again.

"How was work today?" I said. Alex worked part-time as an orderly in the state psychiatric hospital several miles north of the University of Texas campus. An English major in college, he aspired to write but first wanted to do things to support humanity. He said he was not yet ready for a real career. After a shower, he dragged himself off in the morning with a sweet roll and a take-out cup of coffee. (Old dad was down seven coffee cups to this point.) I went off to work shortly after that. I think Alex slept most of the afternoon before coming alive for his nightly phone call to Alexis.

"Work was fine," Alex said. He shrugged. "Nothing remarkable. Northing earth shattering."

"That's good," I said. I searched my mind for something else to say, some way to expand our relationship, to move forward. We seemed to have hit a kind of ceiling, repeating the same themes over and over. Alex was running through the channel guide quickly now, focusing somewhere in the reality show spectrum. I recalled a topic that I thought might engage him.

"Hey, did that habitual liar guy come up with any new stories today?" There was a guy on the hospital staff, another orderly, who claimed all kinds of amazing talents and experiences. He had played halfback on the University of Texas football team. He had known Obama as a community organizer. He could high jump seven feet. He had met Brooke Shields in a campus-area coffee shop one day. Any one claim by itself seemed possible, but put all together they painted a picture of a con man and a trickster. Alex laughed lightly, nodding again.

"Naw, not today," he said. "I don't think he was even there today. I think it was his day off."

I nodded reflectively. I was one of the great reflective nodders of all time.

"How's the chow?" I said.

"Good!" Alex said. "Really good!" He took a big bite, rolling up strands of spaghetti on his fork then stabbing a meatball, as if to demonstrate his gusto. He smiled, mugging for my benefit. Then he focused his attention on the TV. I was out of the picture. I stood frozen for a few indeterminate moments before receding back into the kitchen. I considered my options. I was trying to figure out what to do for the rest of the night, for the rest of my life. It all seemed pretty much a blank.

After dinner, I sat at the computer checking email and surfing the internet, while Alex watched TV. I feared the day that Alex moved out again. The house would be empty and hollow, coming home a nothingness, the kitchen a place to exit quickly after microwave meals that required little preparation or clean-up. Sometimes now Alex's friends came by to hang out in the evenings. Alex came alive then, talking and laughing. This was an Alex I loved to see, smart, witty, erudite, open-minded, handsome, slender, in-shape, his eyes flashing intelligence and good humor. I was proud of him. It felt good having raised him. I stood with him, near him, a quasi-member of his group. We might watch a football game or some stupid reality show, drinking beer and poking fun at the participants. Alex enjoyed having me around, I think. I think he was rather proud of me, too, that I was hip and debonair for an old geezer, able to transcend the generations to provide value-added to his group. During these moments, I felt whole for a little while, at least mostly whole with a wedge out of one side.

Every now and then Alex would try to prod me into thinking about dating again. I was flattered, but I couldn't seem to think about that too much. The best I could do was think about hypothetical women, idealized women, fantasy women who would hone in on my strengths and accept my weaknesses, no questions asked. After the breakup of my marriage, I went into a relationship shell, holing up with work and the internet and my own jagged thoughts. The kids kept me from a total breakdown, from falling off the edge of a very steep cliff. It seemed that starting a new relationship would be like building a house from the foundation up, hand by hand, brick by brick. And I couldn't build a damn thing. It would be too difficult. I was the worst builder in the world.

"Hey Dad," Alex said encouragingly. "Have you ever thought of getting on match.com?"

"I've thought about it," I said. "It just seems like it would be too much work. Mom and I were married a long time. I don't know how it would be starting over with somebody new."

"You could do it. Mom did it."

"I know. I don't know."

One night I returned home from work to find a note from Alex lying on the floor—he was out for the evening at a comedy show with friends. He wouldn't be home until after 11. The house was still. I had peace and quiet. This would be the opportunity I had been waiting for. Well, there was a woman in the picture now. It had happened suddenly. She was someone in my office, a blond, 40ish divorcée who had moved in from out of state. Her name was Amy Schroeder. I saw her in the break room one morning, looking perplexed. Introducing myself, I showed her the ropes on the coffee and supplies and where everything was located. The next morning I saw her there again and we had coffee together, standing at the break room tables. She was not too much younger than me, maybe five or six years, and we had some things in common. We both liked coffee! We liked the writer Walker Percy. She had a pair of daughters, one in high school and the other in middle school, both blond like her. She was smart and funny and pretty in an offbeat, unconventional, counter-cultural sort of way, like hippie women of 40 years ago, and her voice was smart and quick and cultured. We talked freely and easily, sometimes touching, brushing up against each other, by "accident," of course. She held her necklace up as we talked—a sign, I had read, of interest or attraction. I walked her back to her cube, where she touched me on the wrist as she told me bye. In the following days, she seemed to enjoy me stopping by her cube after coffee, never cutting me short or running me off with some fabricated excuse. It was all very preliminary, all ambiguous, but there seemed some real possibilities there. She seemed to brighten when she saw me. I brightened when I saw her. She sought me out for advice on office matters. If she saw me at a distance, she waved hello. She went out of her way one day to find me in the break room.

"There you are!" she said. "I've been looking for you!"

One afternoon I stopped by her cube to tell her goodbye for the day. She swiveled in her chair, thanking me for coming by. She smiled.

"Look at this," she said. She pointed me to something she was looking at on her computer. I leaned over her shoulder, grazing her with my chest. The sensation made me shiver.

"Have a good evening," she said.

"I will," I said.

"Call me sometime if you want to," she said.

"I will," I said.

"My cell number's on my email," she said.

"I'll look it up," I said.

I tidied the room, clearing space around the telephone desk. For optimum clarity, I wanted to call on the landline. I brushed my teeth and combed my hair. I cranked out 20 jumping jacks, wanting to feel lean and quick-witted and agile. I brewed a pot of coffee, pouring a cup for energy and moral support. (In moments like these, I wished I hadn't quit smoking, years before.) I tried to clear my mind, focusing in on the task at hand, reviewing potential topics of conversation. I jotted some of these in a notebook I had laid by the telephone. I reached for the phone several times before pulling back. Finally, my hand punched the number and I heard the call going through. It was too late now. I dug in, preparing for the consequences. It was a moment of existential angst, a turning point for my entire future. Maybe she wouldn't be there. Maybe I had dialed the wrong number! Then I heard Amy's voice on the other end and I knew I would be doomed . . . or exalted.

"Hello?" she said.

"Hello!" I said. "Amy, it's me, Dave. Dave McKirk!" I sounded overly excited, unhinged. I took a sip of coffee. I told myself to settle down.

"Oh—hi," she said. "How are you?" She sounded surprised, uncertain, vague, caught off-guard. Even though she had suggested that I call. Her voice sounded different here, small, modulated through a filter of home and family.

"Pretty good," I said. "Great."Now I thought I sounded flat and uninterested. I tried to recalibrate. It seemed that the preambles were taking forever. I wanted to get down to business. I needed to get down to business. My attention span for this sort of thing was very brief. "What do you know?" Too nebulous, too stock, too open-ended.

"Oh, not too much," she said. "Just putting things up from dinner. Natalie and Nicole are starting their homework."

"Oh—" I said. "Is this a bad time?" My spirits lifted.

Maybe this could just be a placeholder and I could call again another time. Next time I'd get drunk first.

"No, it's OK," she said. I could almost see her looking away from the phone to where her daughters were. "The girls are pretty good about working on their own."

"That's good," I said. "I bet they are!" Flat and unhinged in consecutive sentences.

I picked up the notebook, walking around the room. I checked my notes. "Ask about her supervisor Jay Huggins," one said.

"Hey," I said. "What's it like working for Jay Huggins? I don't know all that much about him." I did, really, but I thought that this question might open her up. I loved to hear her talk.

"Jay's a good guy," she said. "He leaves me alone, pretty much."

"That's good," I said. That seemed the end of that topic, a short, dry, two-sentence response.

I asked another question from my notes—How different was it here from her home state of Virginia?

"It's not that different," she said. "People are pretty much the same everywhere."

That wasn't exactly the answer I had been hoping for, either. The conversation floundered around from there, touching on topics ranging from work to politics to home life. It came close, but never quite coalesced into the sparkling banter of our workplace conversations. Her voice seemed somehow muffled, modulated, edited in this new context. We laughed, but the laughs seemed stilted, theatrical. I felt like we were saying the same things over and over again.

"Hold on," she said. "Natalie's calling me." Natalie was the older one (I thought), a teenager, a high school sophomore, precocious and pretty but shy and self-effacing, in Amy's telling, still unsettled after being uprooted from her friends back home in Alexandria. I waited patiently, pacing with the phone held to my left ear. I took a sip of coffee. I heard Amy say something to Natalie. Finally, Amy returned.

"I guess I need to go," she said. "Natalie needs some help with her geometry."

"Sure thing," I said. "Good luck on the geometry!"

"Thanks," she said. After a pause: "Good talking to you."

"Good talking to you," I said. I think I muttered something else then that even I couldn't understand, something I hoped she didn't even hear, before I laid the phone lightly in its cradle. Doing so seemed to seal the conversation for all eternity. I wanted instantly to call her back for a do-over.

I wasn't sure if it was good, really. I wasn't sure if the conversation had moved our relationship forward. I wasn't sure if perhaps it hadn't changed things in a negative way, so that our relationship at work would now be different and more awkward and less spontaneous. I paced around the room again, feeling empty and uncertain. Everything had been so easy-going and stress-free. Every day had seemed an adventure of discovery and exploration. Maybe this arc or progress would be strained now. Tomorrow at work we would have to acknowledge the call. I tried rehabbing myself. Maybe this really was a necessary next step. Maybe it would propel us forward, after all. I couldn't be sure. I couldn't be sure of anything anymore. I sat down at the computer and Googled, "Phone call to woman from work?" The answers were not all that conclusive or satisfactory.

I lay asleep on the couch when Alex returned home, close to midnight. The TV was on a cable news report. He roused me, grabbing my shoulder.

"Hey," I said. "What's up?" I sat up. Alex stood in the semi-darkness, hands wrapped around his chest. It seemed strange for him to be standing there. Normally he would have roused me and moved on, already in the bedroom or bathroom, preparing for sleep. He shrugged, but oddly, I thought, inexplicable, unprovoked. His face seemed somehow imploring.

"Nothing much," he said. But he didn't move. He looked like he was holding something back.

"What's wrong?" I said. "Is something wrong?" My stomach flipped. My heart raced. It was like when Alex was 11 and in junior high and he failed to make the A team basketball. It was a terrible feeling. It put everything on hold.

"She broke up with me," Alex said. He could hardly talk. "Alexis broke up with me."

"What?" I said. "Crap. No." Though the announcement was no surprise, it was still a terrible shock. I stood on shaky legs.

Alex nodded yes. He said down heavily on the couch, head in hands. I stood over him, touching the top of his head.

"Why?" I said. "What did she say?" It was a stupid thing to ask, of course. Why does anybody break up with anybody? The relationship wasn't working anymore. She was no longer interested. She wasn't having fun. She had met somebody new. It wasn't worth the effort, with her living 1,500 miles away and interacting daily with a completely different group of friends. The harsh facts that you never want to hear or accept. I knew the feeling. I knew all about it. There was no solution. There was no talking anybody out of it, once the decision had been made.

"I'm not gonna make it, Dad," Alex said.

"You're gonna make it," I said. "It'll all be OK."

Alex rolled over on the couch, head buried in the cushions. I knelt beside him, patting him on the back. He was like a little boy again. I was like a young dad, soothing and supporting, feeling his emptiness and his pain. I stayed there for a long time, waiting until he fell asleep. I had something to hold onto for now. I had something for a little while.

Civilization Was Crumbling

Civilization was crumbling. The world as we knew it was coming to an end. The social compact had disintegrated into small fragmented tribes, isolated and self-serving. We considered everything in a socio-political light, reflecting the harsh glare of current events and technological advances and philosophical dichotomies. The tired old rules of human nature weren't going to apply to us. We were immune to greed, envy, boredom, violence, and bad relationships. We would make love when we wanted, where we wanted, how we wanted, without regard to public opinion or parental influence. In short, we were like every generation on the cusp of adulthood, believing that we, unlike all those who came before us, understood the secret to the human condition, and held the key to happiness and contentment.

The year was 1968. The place was San Antonio, TX, in a new suburban neighborhood with the idyllic name, Inspiration Hills. It was a former Parade of Homes subdivision bulldozed from oak-covered hills in northwest San Antonio, with a glimpse of downtown skyscrapers in a wide shallow valley ten or so miles away. All the streets in our neighborhood ended in "view." My street was Highview. The next street over was Clearview. The street at the top of the hill was Broadview. The view made me long for something I couldn't name, something in my past I never had. Fresh-cut grass and blooming crepe myrtle made me imagine eternity. On warm spring evenings, the tch-tch-tch of oscillating lawn sprinklers and the shouts of children playing outdoors ricocheted like the voices of a Greek chorus through the winding, wooded streets of the neighborhood.

Like every place back then, San Antonio was booming and changing, part of the great cultural revolution occurring nationwide. Like underground resistance fighters, enclaves of hippies had sprung up around town with their head shops and bongs and communal-style living, a different kind of living, peaceful and free, with cooperation rather than competition their guiding light. Blacks and Hispanics were breaking free of their historical bonds of repression, developing their own identities, their distinct styles. Relatives and friend were drafted into the Vietnam War, triggering protests at local colleges. HemisFair '68 attracted visitors from around the world. The Riverwalk became a destination for tourists and locals alike. There were nightclubs for teenagers, with names like Teen Canteen, where we went to hang out and listen to live music and stare longingly at girls* in mini-skirts and low-slung jeans. We smoked pot in back rooms and alleyways and dreamed of running away to San Francisco, where we would live wanton and carefree.

Mystical, mythical creatures made even more so because I attended an all-boy's Catholic school. I saw them only at quick forays to the girl's school after class or at heavily-chaperoned school dances.

People looked different now. People didn't look the same in 1968 as they did in 1962. Their posture, their hair, their accoutrements, the very shape of their physical bodies seemed different, evolved. It was a new world, an altered world. There were the Beatles and the British Invasion; Haight-Ashbury; the Vietnam War; political assassinations and race riots; the Apollo space mission; and more, much, much more.

Civilization was crumbling.

My home was a pink brick Colonial at the bottom of the hill, though my stop-overs at home were furtive and quick. Waving Hi, I would rumble through (hoping to avoid criticism for my hair and clothes), grabbing a dinner plate before retreating to the safety and security of my back bedroom, equipped with a small black-and-white TV and large writing desk. As the oldest of five siblings, I held myself aloof and austere, far from the madding crowd watching "My Three Sons" and "The Beverly Hillbillies" in the wood-paneled living room. Sometimes my mother peeked in the door, hoping sweetly, desperately for interaction, some sign of faded familial recognition. Sadly, all I could dredge up was a tight, nervous smile.

Sadly, I say, because my mother was an honorable, upright individual, someone I hoped to be able to save in the time of the revolution. A short, peppy brunette, she was moving forward with the times, growing out of a dreary past of paternalistic depredation. She had grown her hair out, stopped using hair spray, tossed away her girdle, enrolled for a yoga class at the community college. A decade earlier she would never have been able to do that. My father remained unmoved, tethered defiantly to an Antediluvian 1950s past. A salesman for a local office supplies firm, his reaction to the changing world was to deny it, oppose it, grouse about it, retreat further into his hard shell of Cold War certitude.

I had a friend's house where I went to escape. My friend Jon Donovan Jr., lived atop the hill, in a track-lighted, architect-designed split-level that had been the model home in the Parade of Homes exhibition. It had everything—remote-controlled garage doors, an intercom system, an early-stage microwave, a trash compactor, a wine cellar, even. We all understood that Jon was a privileged byproduct of the evil capitalistic system, but we tried to deal with that in a cheerful and optimistic way. It was a burden we all had to bear.

Not only was Jon's house large and luxurious, it was easy and free, open for young people to come and go as they pleased. Nobody kept tabs there. Nobody even knew you were there. Many nights we hung out there, Jon and me and Jon's younger brother Edward, in the privacy of a detached guest house across a lighted flagstone walkway near the swimming pool, talking and planning and cooking up idealized versions of our future lives. We wore love beads around our necks, bell bottoms on our legs, shirts of checked flannel around our backs. We drank beer, purloined from Mr. Donovan's stash in the main-house refrigerator. We played records, stereo records on a portable turntable. We watched TV.

My friend Jon was tall and strapping and Adonis-like, with tousled blond hair and a salesman's smile and a weightlifter's chest. He had the first-born's sense of privilege and power, a touch of noblesse oblige. It was Friday night, no school tomorrow. Johnny Carson was on TV, a large— by those day's standards—27" color console model. Johnny's scheduled guests were Neil Simon, Godfrey Cambridge, and Tallulah Bankhead. Jon sat facing the TV in a director's chair with a Budweiser can in his left hand and a cigarette in his right. Younger brother Edward sat hunched up in a corner, feet on a coffee table, a blanket over his legs, an expression of disdain and derision on his face. He was a nihilist, a negative individual who never wasted an opportunity to belittle or criticize. I feared him, in a way. I never knew what he might say, which direction he go with his remarks or ridicule. He liked to put me in my place, as a visitor, an interlocutor. Jon took a sip of beer and a puff of cigarette. He seemed to be pondering something, which made me nervous. The rich think they can do pretty much anything they can dream up.

"We need to go to California," he said.

"Yeah," I said. "We ought to go sometime. That'd be a fun trip."

"I mean, let's move there. Get out of here. I'm tired of San Antonio. Everything's cool out in California."

"Really?" I said. "You mean it?" Running away to California made perfect sense to me, because I had a lame family and shitty future prospects and I was an ugly duckling with a big nose and crooked teeth who wore my hair long not so much as a political statement (though it doubled as that), but to compensate for my physical flaws. Jon was rich and talented and handsome, with a fabulous future in front of him.

"I mean it," Jon said. "It's my only option. Dad expects me to go to UT and then become a lawyer, just like him. I don't want to be a lawyer. I want to make a difference in the world."

"Lawyers can make a difference," I said. "Your dad makes a difference."

"I know," Jon said. "I know he does. But I want to do something different. I want my life to be different."

I nodded, anxious and enthusiastic at the same time. In California everything would be perfect. All my problems and insecurities would melt away. Girls would like me. Friends would flock to me. Every day would be an adventure. Still—that would be a mind-blowing change. I'd be giving up everything I'd ever known. "What the hell," I thought, making a snap decision. "Why not?" You only live once, after all. I felt liberated and free.

"Let's go," I said. "When do you want to go?"

Jon shrugged and took a drag off his cigarette. He glanced over at Edward, hunched up in the corner, turning down his nose at us.

"I don't know," Jon said. "Sometime. Sometime soon."

"Sounds good," I said. Whew—off the hook for now. "Let's go sometime."

"Chicken shit," Edward said. "You won't ever go. You won't ever go anywhere."

"We'll go," Jon said. "Don't worry about it."

"You never will," Edward said.

"Like you will," Jon said.

"I will," Edward said. "I really will go."

"Yeah—you'll go to hell," Jon said. Edward snorted,

moving his feet slightly beneath the blanket. He shot the finger casually, like it was just as normal as scratching his nose. Jon shot the finger back.

"Why don't you get some friends of your own," Jon said. "Why do you have to hang out with us all the time?"

"Why don't you get better friends?" Edward said. "Maybe you could think about getting a girlfriend some-time. Oh—I forgot—you're queer."

"*You're queer.*"

"*You* are."

Jon stood up, slamming the legs of the director's chair into the floor.

"Why don't you just get the hell out?" Jon said.

"Why don't you make me?" Edward said.

"You want to see if I can make you?" Jon said. He tensed, biceps flexing. He lifted weights and his pectoral muscles were large and well-defined. I wouldn't want to take him on.

Edward stood, flicking a French fry, a stale French fry that had been lying in a pool of ketchup for two days. It hit the director's chair and fell to the floor. Edward turned to leave but Jon grabbed him by the arm and swung him down on the floor. Edward was fairly strong himself, but Jon made quick work of him tonight. After a brief struggle Jon sat squatting on Edward's rear end, holding his right arm behind his back. When Edward squirmed, Jon jerked his arm tight.

"Bastard," Edward said.

Jon jerked his arm tight.

"Son of a bitch," Edward said.

Jon jerked his arm tight.

"Are you ever going to call me queer again?" Jon said.

"Yes," Edward said. Jon jerked his arm tight.

"No." After a final jerk, Jon released Edward's arm. Jon stood up.

"Watch what you say," he said.

"Bastard," Edward sat, massaging his tender arm. "Queer. Pansy."

Then he stood and ducked for the door, shooting the finger savagely on his way out.

"Children at play?" It was our acquaintance Gordon Wood, looming conspicuously by the door.

"Hey Gordon," Jon said.

"What's up, Gordon?" I said.

"Nothing much—just brought some goodies over for you all to try out."

Gordon Wood represented the degenerate wing of the cultural revolution, the drugged-out, decadent wing. He came and went mysteriously, a phantom, an enigma. The only child of a neighborhood ophthalmologist, Gordon was tall and lean, but lean in a pale, ghostly, unhealthy way, like a hooked fish. His jet black hair was trimmed short above the ears, like a business student, and held in place by a heavy dose of Vitalis. Wearing a trench coat and dark glasses, he appeared like the prototype drug dealer as portrayed in movies and on TV. He was, in fact, a drug dealer—and user. He had dropped acid, popped peyote, sniffed coke, and once (he said) mainlined Heroin, which he described as overrated. Concealed in his coat pockets he brought in pot and hashish, sometimes stronger stuff. He took it out in baggies and laid it on a coffee table where we all gathered around, like acolytes at a religious rite. Edward had rejoined the group, leaning in with the rest of us. Gordon provided free samples for on-site consumption, but if we accepted these we felt obligated to purchase some minimum amount. It was like a Tupperware party for adolescents.

"What you got today?" Jon said.

"Panama Red," Gordon said. "Good stuff."

"How much?" Jon said.

"25," Gordon said, "It's really good stuff."

"How about 20?" Jon said.

"I can go 20. Nothing lower."

Jon glanced over at me in consultation, and I shrugged out a provisional yes.

"What the hell, let's go for it," Jon said.

"Good choice," Gordon said.

I pulled a ten from my wallet to chip in and Jon supplied the rest. A delicious thrill of anticipation poured over me, a foreshadowing of future pleasure not unlike being seduced by a woman. Per tradition, Jon rolled a joint from the newly-purchased stash, lit it, inhaled, and passed it around.

"Great stuff," Gordon said, inhaling deeply. He employed a complicated, multi-stage smoking technique which he claimed drew the plant's active ingredients faster and deeper into his system.

"Sure is," Edward said, taking his hit.

"Direct from Panama," I said, after my hit. "Panama Pal. Our pal from Panama." Everybody laughed. I was delighted and surprised by my comedic powers.

Jon wandered over to put some music on the stereo

turntable, the introductory album by Country Joe and the Fish. Titled "Electric Music for the Mind and Body," it featured sharp, reverberating guitar riffs, an electric piano, and poignant, evocative refrains. Each note emerged like a newborn babe and floated across the room, lingering tantalizingly before disappearing down a chute as the next note appeared.

The walls of the room receded, the room expanding to enormous size. The room was a low-ceilinged cave. Jon and Edward and Gordon seemed a million miles away, shrouded by coronas of jagged light. My body felt bathed in bales of soft, fluffy cotton. The four of us seemed aligned in a precise rectangular pattern that seemed somehow pre-ordained since the beginning of time. We were stoned.

"Hey man, let's get out of here," Gordon Wood said. His words emerged as through an echo chamber, sonorous and deep.

"What do you mean?" Jon said.

"I mean, take off, go somewhere else. California. New York. Some place cool. Some place where we can be ourselves. Let's blow this hellhole."

"Yeah, we need to do that sometime," Jon said.

"I mean, right now," Gordon Wood said. "I mean, let's get in the goddamn car and start driving till we reach the west coast. My old man won't miss me. He won't even know I'm gone."

Jon looked over at me. He turned to Edward with a look that said, "Don't say anything. Don't say a goddamn thing." Our plans for escape did not include Gordon Wood.

Jon handled it. He handled it superbly. He handled it like the first-rate barrister he would one day become.

"We've got to finish school," Jon said. "We've got college ahead of us. We've got our careers."

Gordon Wood stood up, hands in his coat pockets.

"You guys are pussies," he said. "All that stuff doesn't matter anymore. If you want to waste your fucking lives in this hell-hole, fine by me."

Jon's father appeared in the doorway then, dressed in slippers and blue silk bathrobe and hoisting a highball. (Wild Turkey and water, no doubt.) His bald head (with toupee removed) made him appear harsh, stern, unforgiving. The hair he did have, pressed against the sides of his head, looked disheveled and disorderly in an effulgent, Patrician sort of way. His bifocals magnified his eyes outlandishly. He wasn't tall, but his shoulders were sloped and bull-like, his hands poised pugnaciously. He looked like a professional wrestler relaxing after hours.

"What's going on here, lads?" Mr. Donovan said. His voice was loud and sloppy and hoarse. The sash on his bathrobe hung loose, revealing a pasty-white gut, thin hairy legs, and red-checked boxer shorts, too large. A fine specimen of 20th Century middle-aged manhood, he was.

"Nothing much," Jon said. He smiled, crunching out the joint stub under his shoe. Smoke floated through the room like an evil genie, pushed by a slowly whirring ceiling fan. The stereo cranked out Country Joe and the Fish. Everyone stood frozen, uncertain, wary. It was as if we had been captured by the police. Mr. Donovan's eyes fell on Gordon Wood, and I could sense an instant revulsion, almost as if he had detected a foul odor. Mr. Donovan was a liberal man politically and open-minded, but he was a member of an earlier generation still, and something about Gordon Wood crossed over even his extremely flexible line of decorum. They represented opposite ends of the cultural spectrum, the staid old guard and the young person from another planet. Mr. Donovan turned suddenly, whipping his head around. There was an odor, of course, the funky, oregano-mingled-with-cat-piss aroma of marijuana in the air.

"What's that smell?" Mr. Donovan said.

"Oh—" Jon said, "It's Ben. He was smoking." Mr. Donovan turned to me with alarm and disapproval. I was always the fall guy in these situations, the gauche, goofball family friend. I nodded yes, patting a soft pack of Viceroy filters in my left shirt pocket.

"That stuff's bad for you, you know," Mr. Donovan said, moving closer to me, placing his hand on my shoulder. "It'll kill you." He sometimes served a sort of in locus parentis role for me, as if my own parents were incapable of performing their required duties in this apocalyptic day and age. Mr. Donovan had a pretty exalted view of his own abilities, at times.

"I know, Mr. D.," I said, "I know it's bad. I'm trying to quit. I try not to overdo it." Mr. Donovan stood holding his hand on my shoulder, staring sharply. His eyes swam. His fingers kneaded my shoulders. His intensity frightened me a little. Finally, he backed away, taking a sip of his highball on the move, so to speak.

"Keep it down a little, boys," he said. "I need to hit

the sack soon. I've got a torts seminar in the morning."

"OK, Dad," Jon said.

"Sure thing, Mr. D," I said. I snapped off an impromptu two-finger salute, an affectionate testimonial to everything our relationship entailed.

Mr. Donovan shot another glance at Gordon Wood, a savage, simmering look of dislike and disapproval. I almost thought he might go over and wrestle him to the ground. He took another sip of his drink, dribbling some down the corner of his mouth, and left.

Gordon Wood sat poker-faced in the corner in his trench coat, emanating intense, strobe-light like counter-cultural vibes.

"We've got to get the hell out of here," he said. This felt like an implicit indictment of Jon's father and everything he stood for. Jon didn't like for other people criticizing his father. Only he could do that.

Jon turned the stereo off. We sat quietly now, saying nothing, each in separate corners of the room.

"Why don't you go, Gordon?" Jon said. "To California, I mean. You ought to go. Then you can come back and tell us what it's like. . ."

"Nah," Gordon Wood said. "What the hell." He stood abruptly, hands in his coat pockets. He was tired of hanging around with us. We weren't exciting enough for him anymore.

"See you mother fuckers around," he said. "I've got to go meet some other people. I've got more business to transact."

"See you, Gordon," Jon said.

"See you, Gordon," I said.

It was quiet now. The three of us sat looking at different sections of the wall. I felt tired suddenly. And hungry! Suddenly I wanted nothing more in life but to get home and raid the refrigerator, raid it magnificently. My house was superior in a few small ways, number one being food supply. My mom kept a cornucopia of leftovers in the refrigerator to feed the starving masses. Jon's refrigerator was filled with beer and stale take-out items. Jon and Edward looked tired, too. Saying my goodbyes, I slipped out for the short walk downhill to my house.

"Ben." I stood frozen in place on the driveway outside Jon's house. This was the voice of Jon's sister Samantha. She was a couple of years older than us, college age, but she didn't go to college. She didn't do much of anything, as far as we could tell. She would pick up the keys to her sleek black Mercedes sedan and peal out in a squeal of car tires, fish-tailing down Broadview Street with the smell of burnt rubber in the air. She always seemed pissed-off when she saw us. She would come into the guest house looking for something or somebody, and say, "What's wrong with you?" The question was directed at Jon, but it seemed to include me, too, in some sort of coven of unworthiness. We never saw her friends or boyfriends, though we did see her talking on the phone sometimes, lying on the sofa with her stockinged feet up on the side rest. She was attractive, if rather unconcerned about her appearance, a sometimes blond/sometimes brunette who wore min-skirts or low-slung jeans and giant sunglasses perched atop her head.

"Hi Samantha," I said. I expected her to be cool with

me but for some reason her voice tonight was different, sweet and melodious.

"Can you help me for a minute, Ben?"

"Sure," I said dutifully, though leery of an ambush, a sudden backlash. My experience with females had left me uncertain and wary. "Watcha need?"

"Can you help me get something out of my car?"

"No problem," I said. "Sure." I followed her to the Mercedes where she opened the door to reveal a large wrapped package on the seat.

"It's a birthday present for my friend Kim," Samantha said. "Would you carry it in for me?"

"Sure," I said. "Absolutely." I leaned inside, hoisted the package carefully, and followed Samantha back to her room in the main house, calibrating my strides like a ballerina. Samantha pointed and I laid the package gently on the bed. I had fulfilled my mission without failure. My life, for this one fleeting moment, was a success.

"Thank you," she said.

"You're welcome," she said. I allowed my heart to flutter briefly as I turned to depart. The air in Samantha's room was like her perfume, scented and overflowing with swift strong sexual currents.

"Would you care to sit down?" Samantha said. I shrugged. My shrug was actually a cover for a shout of joy. She motioned with her hand. I eased down uncertainly onto the edge of the bed, beside the box. My feet I stationed squarely on the blue shag pile carpet, like little soldiers. My hands rested innocently on my thighs.

"Do you like my room?" she asked—sweetly, personably, coquettishly. This was quite possibly the first time she had acknowledged me as a separate male human being, not just her brother's clumsy friend, a being with a heart and a mind and a libido. Boy, did I suddenly have a libido.

"It's nice!" I said. I smiled. I smiled guardedly, still wary, protecting myself. I still thought she might revert to form and sneer at me.

"All the times you've been over at our house, I don't think you've ever been in here," she said.

"No, I don't think so," I said. She took a seat in a leather-covered armchair, walking it over closer to me.

"We should get to know each other better," she said.

"We should," I said.

"Tell me—" she said, "What do you think of my mom and dad?"

"They're nice . . ." I said.

"I mean, really. Don't you think they're a little bit nuts?"

"I don't know. Maybe. I guess so."

"Well, I do," she said. "Sure, everybody thinks it's great being well-off and rich and the daughter of a famous attorney and all that, but really it's a burden sometimes."

"I can imagine."

"What about you? What about your family?"

I shrugged. Nobody here had ever asked me about my family before, at least in a truly interested way. It was just a given they were insignificant, inconsequential. She actually seemed interested.

"They're OK," I said. "They're just average, I guess. My dad's a salesman for an office supplies store. Trying to make a living. He does OK, I guess. I mean, we're not poor." I felt a surge of pride in my family, a sense of self-respect and self-importance I hadn't felt in a long time. I had always felt embarrassed for them here, that I had to apologize for them, cover for them, that we didn't make enough money, didn't go on long trips, couldn't afford to go out to eat at fancy restaurants or drive luxury cars.

Samantha nodded, smiling sweetly. At that point, I let myself go. I let my guard down. And then we were launched on a long, rambling, eye-opening, soul-baring, 100 percent honest conversation, about our families, school, our plans for the future, God, life and death. It was a conversation I had never before had with a girl. With anyone, really. It was liberating. It was exhilarating. It was something I had never even imagined happening. It was quite possibly the highlight of my life to that moment.

When the cuckoo clock in their living room chimed 2:00, I jumped. I stood. I was exhausted, actually. I had perspired onto my shirt. I didn't think I could say anything more. I thought I might take my memory of this encounter and leave now, while there was a happy ending.

"I guess I'd better go," I said.

"Wait," Samantha said. "Wait a second."

"OK," I said.

I stood stock still as she approached me, almost like a soldier at attention. Samantha looked at me, looked me over. Her hands she placed on my shoulders. Then she leaned forward to kiss me, smack on the lips. It was a fantastic kiss—soft, wet, mushy. The top of my head almost blew off. I felt blessed—it felt sanctioned by some higher power, some special, exclusive deal. Whatever it was, I didn't want to stop. I hesitated for a second, then dared to throw my arms around her waist. I pulled her close. The feeling of her breath and her breasts heaving against mine was not just physical, but a spiritual, cultural, and social breakthrough as well. I kissed harder, faster. Recalling something I had heard or read, I rolled my tongue over the surface of her lips, slowly, tantalizingly, and there was her tongue, responsive and ready. I was pretty much clueless as to what should occur next, when Samantha seized my hand and placed it on her left breast. She was wearing some silky white blouse with embroidered flowers and her breasts seemed very prominent, very perky tonight. I massaged her breast slowly, with a circular motion that seemed a reasonably methodology, and she began breathing even harder, muffled panting emanating from her mouth. We collapsed together sitting onto to bed. I pushed the package brusquely onto a corner. Samantha slid her hand up under my un-tucked shirt and onto my tummy. I slid my hand down under the top of her low-cut jeans, as far as it would go. (I may have touched pubic hair, I wasn't sure.) I tried to find a way to take her blue jeans off. My own pants were about to be projected off my body by the force of my exploding libido.

But there was suddenly a slight "chunk" sound of a door closing down the hallway, where Mr. and Mrs. Donovan's bedroom was located. (And a mysterious bedroom it was, too, dark and track-lighted and lined with shelves and shelves of hard-back books.)

"Shhhh!" Samantha said, placing her hand over my mouth.

I tried to stop my heavy breathing. I tried to smooth out my shirt. There was a knock on the door, a soft, tentative, questioning knock. This must be Samantha's mother, Mrs. Donovan, Claire. She was a very private person, the mother, a bit of a loner, an iconoclast. She didn't quite fit in with the rest of the Donovan household, almost like somebody who just stayed there, a boarder, a guest. Hands off as a mother, she let the children—and her husband—fare for themselves. She was pale, almost pasty-white, with worry circles around her eyes and liver splotches on the backs of her thin worn hands. An agnostic in a Catholic family, she spent her free time holed up in her bedroom, reading mysteries and thrillers from mail-order book clubs. She appeared every so often in the living room, ducking through, as it were, like an embarrassed student late to class. She never stayed in a conversation very long.

"What's going on, dear?" Mrs. Donovan said, pushing the door open a crack. Her voice was weary, her patience taut, like the patience of a saint. Samantha turned to me and touched my arm, to signify that she would do the talking.

"Nothing, Mother," Samantha said.

"Is there somebody with you in your room?" Mrs. Donovan said. Samantha shook her head no—though she meant yes.

"It's just Ben," she said. "We've been talking."

There was a pause outside the door, a pause that made me think Mrs. Donovan was running some quick algorithms through her head. Just Ben = Not Capable of Doing Anything Really = Safe, We're Probably OK.

"Oh," Mrs. Donovan said. "OK, then. Hi, Ben."

"Hi, Mrs. D," I said. I said it a little louder and more formally than usual, I think. Another pause.

"Maybe Ben better get going soon," Mrs. Donovan said. "It's getting really late."

"OK, he will," Samantha said, rolling her eyes at her mother. Following Samantha's lead, we separated, scooting carefully across the mattress on our rear ends. "He will soon."

The door opened wider briefly, then closed. We heard Mrs. Donovan's slippered footsteps padding away. When it was quiet again, Samantha said, "You'd better go, I guess."

"I guess I'd better," I said.

Samantha remained sitting. I smoothed out my pants and pulled down my shirt. Leaning over, I reached out my arms to grab hold of her for one last kiss. It was more a lunge, actually, an off-balance, awkward thrust. I could see the points of her nipples pushing hard against the fabric of her silky white blouse. Nevertheless, the kiss was disappointingly tepid. It seemed that she had already turned off her passion meter. I eased away with one final look of forlorn longing. She waved limply as I left the room.

Walking home, I regrouped, putting my disappointment aside and placing the experience into sometime of overall holistic perspective. After a few minutes, I felt pretty good. I felt pretty damn good.

Alas, there was no return engagement. I tried, in the weeks following, to position myself for a reprise, but nothing materialized. Samantha again barely acknowledged my existence. Eventually, I resigned myself to maintaining the memory of that magical encounter, using it to sustain me in times of loneliness or depression.

That was always it, really—wanting to like somebody, wanting to be liked by them. We all grew up, of course, like every generation, seeking security, success, significance, satisfaction. We couldn't escape the immutable laws of nature and of human kind. We married, divorced, raised children of our own, pursued and abandoned careers, pursued new careers. We would be greedy, envious, bored, violent, and prone to bad relationships. It was like a sequence from a Bob Dylan song, "All the people we used to know, they're an illusion to me now. Some are mathematicians, some were carpenter's wives, I don't know how it all got started, I don't know what they do with their lives. Me, I'm still on the road, searching for another joint . . ."

Roadside Restroom

To understand my childhood you should know that my mother looked on the entire world of humanity outside our nuclear family as something akin to a roadside service station restroom—trashed, vile, germ-infested, uncontrolled, and to be avoided except in quick, small doses, fast forays there and back. We operated with cloistered caution, like a convent— or a coven. We prepared for the worst. We expected the worse. We spent more time than anyone I had ever heard of preparing to move to a center room in the event of a tornado. We were masters of the center room move. Our fire alarm batteries were replenished every two weeks and our burglar alarm system was set to catch the movements of butterflies, I do believe. Chickens—oh, my God, in my mother's cosmology chickens were like a species of especially desperate felon. We washed our chickens so thoroughly to avert any possibility of salmonella poisoning, they could probably have been used in a surgery ward. It goes without saying that inside a car my mother launched into full back-seat driver's mode, pointing out potential obstacles with panicky gusto.

This was just my mother's side. On my father's side, we were cheap. My father's family was supposedly from some old German stock that was inherently thrifty and then having lived through the Depression tightened down the fiscal screws another thread or two. My father was an accountant for an office supplies firm and I believe he applied accounting principles to every situation in life— from dating to household management to metaphysics.

Case in point—we owned just a single telephone, located (efficiently, cost-effectively) in a high-traffic area of our living room. I am convinced that the location of this telephone contributed in no small measure to my lack of development with adolescent girls. I could not imagine calling a girl up for a date or simply to converse in our living room with family members eavesdropping while they read or did homework or watched TV. This was before the days of cell phone or portable phones, of course, so I was forced to drive over to out-of-the-way pay phones in shopping malls or convenience stores while making this type of call. These phones never functioned properly, the reception was bad, I was out of my comfort zone, and besides, there was always the squawk of a P.A. system in the background announcing an ongoing sale at Dillard's or a car with its lights on in the parking lot. At the convenience store, the clerk would be speaking loudly in a foreign language.

"Where are you calling from?" a befuddled Girl A (or B, or C) would say. Girl A—innocent, unsuspecting, living in a normal home environment with a telephone in her bedroom or a secluded hallway, at least. There was no way that Girl A (or B, or C) would be able to understand what life was like in my wacked-out household.

"Oh, just over at North Star Mall," I would say, as if this were the most natural thing in the world. As if, actually, I had just been sort of wandering through the mall and the urge had come over me to give her a call. There was inevitably an eerie silence on the other end as Girl A's adolescent brain tried to process this information reasonably and fairly. She probably already thought I was weird, but now she thought I was over the top weird. Most of these conversations never went anywhere. And I never seemed to go anywhere with any of these girls, either.

One phone, one car, also. Yes, we owned just a single car—a tank-sized Pontiac Catalina station wagon with 400-hp and seats in the far back facing the rear. The single car was an economy move, of course, made feasible because my father rode to work with his father, a salesman at the same office supplies firm where my father served as head accountant.

The station wagon sat lodged in our commodious two-car garage like a royal coach. Obtaining permission to use the car required a lengthy series of interview and a background check. Driving off afterwards, I felt cheapened, violated, beaten down, guilty without reason, a suspect in a police interrogation. No wonder that I wandered a bit in college. It's a wonder I didn't run off to live on roots and berries in the desert.

One summer day, as I eased the station wagon into the garage bay my mother emerged from the utility room door to intercept me, holding the car door open as I sat trapped inside like a circus clown. (Though compact, mom could move like a jungle cat when on a mission.) I reviewed my activities for the last few hours, working swiftly to develop an alibi. Sadly, I did not have time to brush my limp, long hair back behind my ears to make it appear shorter—my slicked-back, at home "do" that would allow me to appear like a stalwart citizen in my parents' eyes. In retrospect, I am not certain that this fooled anyone, but it served to provide a workable illusion for my immature psyche.

"Where have you been?" my mother said. Her voice had several textured levels of shrill, moving up and down on the shrillness scale, and this one was near the top. I remained sitting in the car, blocked by my mother. This seemed a huge tactical advantage on her part. Her words were like a baseball bat to my solar plexus.

"At the driving range," I lied. Going to the driving range was one of my standard spiels for obtaining permission to drive the car. I slung my golf clubs into the hatchback of the station wagon and tallied ho, veering off course immediately toward whatever activity I had scheduled for the day—phone calls in the mall, smoking dope with friends, sometimes something even more mesmerizing.

This particular trip I had paid an actual in-home visit to a girl I had met one evening at the high school dance—a sexy little raven-haired siren named Holly, I might add. If you want to know about it, it had not gone well. We mostly stood on the flagstone porch of Holly's red-brick suburban home and exchanged what we knew in real-time were lame, risqué witticisms because we didn't know each other very well and didn't have very much in common. Even then I understood it was not a good sign when somebody you are standing with stares abstractedly over your shoulder while twirling her heavy black tresses. I was forced to leave abruptly when Holly was called into her house. I feel fairly certain that this occurred on a pre-arranged signal between Holly and her mother that kicked in if things were not going well. I drove away from that encounter with a hard lump in my stomach and the feeling that nothing in my life would ever be successful. Already depressed, I drove directly into my mother's welcoming arms.

"You've been gone three hours," my mother said.

"I hit three buckets of balls," I said. I glanced at my hands inadvertently, to see if their un-weathered condition would give me away.

"Your father needed the car to run back down to his office," my mother said.

"I didn't know," I said. "Why didn't he call grandpa?" My mother persisted. She was one of the great persisters of all time, my mother.

"Grandpa wasn't home," she said. "Tell me where you've really been."

She peered through the open car door and through the windows as if expecting to find contraband, hard evidence of my malfeasance. I half expected to find this evidence myself. Could she tell that my golf clubs had not budged since I had loaded them up when leaving? Could she see through to the hole in my heart?

"I told you—the driving range," I said. To those of you who may wonder why I would continue in this sad charade, I can say only that this was another piece of my stinted development. For some deep-rooted psychological reasons, no doubt, I did not want my parents to know the simple, un-sinful truth, that I was visiting a girl at her house. I could not tell them this, I was not sure why. They would misinterpret the situation, no doubt. They would badger me with questions, bombard me with intrusive remarks. I would be stripped of my dignity, reduced metaphorically to a small, sniveling baby boy.

"I know that's not true," my mother said. I felt like a defendant in a trial who is suddenly blindsided by a witness introducing unexpected secret information. I was surprised, confused by this revelation.

"How do you know it's not true?" I said. My mother's face was like a lemon, scrunched-up and tart. Her liver-spotted arm stretched across the gap between door and car like a "Crime Scene—Do Not Disturb" ribbon.

"Sally Peterson saw you driving the car in the Harmony Hills subdivision," she said. "She saw you turning at the entrance off San Pedro." I nodded, as if regrouping for a powerful rebuttal. Unfortunately, I was running out of defenses here.

"There's a driving range out by San Pedro," I said. Thank God I wasn't hooked up to a lie detector machine. "I was cutting through the neighborhood afterward." My mother stomped her foot on the garage floor. Sometimes when angry she actually stomped her foot. It would have been comical if my entire future had not been at stake.

"Why don't you just tell me where you went?" she said. It was a cry from the depths, really, a sharp, penetrating wail. The utility room door opened again and my father entered the scene, standing like a bit character in a play, hands on hips, eyes directed toward the main players on center stage. Faux-Rolex watch gleaming on his hairy wrist, he was undoubtedly calculating number of miles driven=gas used=mileage=wear and tear on vehicle. His eyes seemed to pronounce me "Guilty," of something.

Outwardly defiant as I took on this double-team, I sat with throat, arms, feet, hips, internal organs quivering. My soul mirrored my mind. I wanted to cry. I felt as if the center of my being, the core of my persona, was being challenged, ripped apart by my mother's inquisition. All the years, all the days, all the moments leading up to this one felt like they amounted to nothing. I felt that I was staring up at a very steep, very slippery cliff that I must scale to escape from my bonds of parental control. I felt that I would never be able to do it. I shrugged. I slumped against the steering wheel, burying my head in my hands. I raked my fingers through my hair.

"I'm about ready to give up on you," my mother said. Now this was surely encouraging news. In some ways, I felt that almost everybody else had given up on me already. I was about ready to give up on myself. I picked up my head and sighed.

"I went to see a girl," I said. I snarled this out viciously, almost incoherently.

"Say that again?" my mother said. Her face changed. Her eyes perked up. Her arm on the car handle relaxed. She no longer looked mad. She looked younger, softer, more girlish herself. For a strange, transcendent moment, I could see the young girl in her, happy, high-spirited, hoping to be asked out herself.

"I said I went to see a girl," I said. She touched me on the wrist, a very unusual thing for her to do, totally out of character. It was almost as though another, "regular" human being were touching me, not my mother. This feeling was only temporary.

"What's her name?" my mother said. "What school does she go to? Is she Catholic?" These questions hit me like a nail being knocked home by a hammer. They made me feel even more humiliated, more demeaned. Finally, I made myself move. I disengaged myself from my mother's hand, slid out the door, and pushed past her and my father ignoring all questions, disregarding the chaos of my younger siblings by the phone in the living room, straight to my bedroom where I closed and locked the door. There I lay on my back in bed, staring at a whirling ceiling fan. I was able to find some solace in that activity. I was able to find some peace.

My Double Life

I suppose you could say that I was leading a double life. In my original, baseline life, I was defined by my status as oldest child, an adolescent male in a mundane middle-class neighborhood in suburban San Antonio, Texas. "Loopland," as it was known, lay outside the freeway loop, teeming with strip malls and ranch-style houses and oscillating sprinklers on manicured carpet grass lawns. It was a dull, hum-drum existence. I drove to the Catholic boy's prep school I attended and drove back home again. I worked part time in a grocery store, wearing a uniform shirt with my name "David" on a patch pressed onto my pocket by my steadfast mother.

I'll be frank—it was a harsh, brutal existence, akin to being exiled to a remote gulag in the far reaches of the former Soviet Union. Our family had one telephone only, located smack dab in the center of the pine-paneled living room where family members could overhear my private conversations—if I dared to have any. We owned one car only, a big, clunky Pontiac station wagon, the un-sexiest vehicle alive, which I was required to share with my parents and reserve in advance. Dealing with difficult issues of self-image, wrestling with sexual fantasies, searching for answers to the riddle of my existence through pop culture and punk friends, I kept my household appearances to a bare minimum. I watched TV and ate dinner. I slipped into the restroom and back out again. I holed up in my bedroom, basically, aloof and magisterial, my desk a command post for dreams and wild longings.

My younger siblings, four in number, were decent, wholesome sorts, but they belonged to a different generation, another cohort, a discrete advertising group. I responded to my mother's concerns regarding my future with one-word, monotone answers, revealing little. My father I avoided completely, as if contact with him would force me to acknowledge some ugly, unappealing aspect of myself. A certified public accountant, my father seemed to apply accounting principles to virtually every aspect of life, including child-raising. From me, he seemed to demand a degree of planning and precision that I found impossible to maintain. Our conversations focused inevitably back onto my performance in school, my career goals, future plans and aspirations—all woefully inadequate, half-cocked, flawed, and faulty. I wanted to get these conversations over with as quickly as possible. Afterwards, small and shaken, I felt that my life had already gone up in smoke.

"Son," Dad said, placing a hard, heavy hand on my shoulder. I stood in place, feet locked, eyes downcast, praying that this moment would pass as painlessly as possible.

"Yes, sir?" I said.

"Have you filled out that financial aid form I brought you yet?" Dad said.

"Sort of," I said. "I started it."

"You started it?" Dad's voice assumed a sharp, sarcastic edge that caused me to sink even deeper into depression. "You better get with it. It's due next week."

"I know," I said. "I will." I watched Dad shake his head morosely, regretfully, sorrowfully. He saw no hope for me. Our conversation was over. I shuffled back to my room where I removed a magazine concealed in a desk drawer, opening it to a glossy photo of a voluptuous blond model in skimpy black lingerie. I saw no hope either.

Ah, but in my second life—call me *Mr. Congeniality*! I was a man about town, a comedian *par excellence*, a storyteller nonpareil. I was an emerging intellectual force, a respected commentator on life, a prodigy, almost. This was in my best friend Sean O'Shaughnessy Jr.'s house, where I was welcomed inside with a hearty, extravagant gusto. I flung open the door to their living room and stood inside the entrance like an actor taking the stage. My shirt hung open to the second button, my long hair was flowing.

"Hey, look who's here!" blared out Sean's father Sean Sr., swathed in blue silk bathrobe and slippers and rocking back in his leather recliner chair, holding his trusty Michelob Lite long-neck in his right hand like a toast. Sean Sr. was a high-dollar San Antonio attorney, a plaintiff's lawyer who represented injured and exploited clients on a contingency basis. "It's the Prince!" The Prince they called me because of my hair-style, they said, but also, I liked to think, because they considered me royal material, the stuff of future legends and success.

"Hey, Mr. S.," I said, with a sporty, laid-back demeanor. "Doing good! Doing all right!" I ambled over to Mr. O'Shaughnessy's chair where we clasped hands firmly, two mature men. Joviality reigned like a Bach aria. Smiling confidently, I plopped myself down on a red-velvet wing chair and stretched my blue jeans-clad legs up onto the coffee table. Settling in, I made sure to make them under-stand that I was smart, savvy, clever, stylish, with-it. I proceeded to regale the assembled minions with erudite tales of wild youth, narratives worthy of Dickens or Dostoevsky, my current literary heroes. The minions lapped them up.

My friend Sean lived nearby, up a long, steep hill at the far end of the next block, where a cluster of cubist-inspired homes sat misplaced in our otherwise ordinary 60s-era subdivision with the quixotic name, "Inspiration Hills." Architect-designed, the O'Shaughnessy home sat perched like a compound on a sloping corner lot, back-lit as if by Warner Brothers, shrouded in foliage and commanding a majestic view of downtown San Antonio, ten miles away. The house was a goddamn work of cubist art.

I wanted to live in that house. I wanted to be Sean. I wanted his life, anyway. For Sean had basically everything in life that I thought I should have. He was handsome, handsome like a leading man or a star quarterback, with a broad chest and wavy blond hair and bold blue eyes that seemed to reflect a brash confidence—or the family's net worth. He had money. He had freedom. He moved with autonomy, going where he wanted, when he wanted, without the need for deception or interference from authorities. There was no car-sharing in the O'Shaughnessy home—Sean drove his very own cherry-red Porsche roadster, a present for his 16th birthday. He had an auxiliary vehicle, a Harley-Davidson motorcycle, as well.

Sometimes Sean's sister Samantha entered the scene, pissed off. A slim, sulking, aloof, disdainful brunette, Samantha radiated torrid vibes of rich bitch sultriness. Massive round sunglasses perched atop her poufy hair, she pranced through the living room to pick up her car keys to her Mercedes convertible from an end table and sighed—a sigh that took all of us in, parents, sibling, sibling friends. The sigh seemed to say, "I recognize what you are doing—and it isn't good."

Samantha seemed to resent her family money, as if it sullied her soul, yet she was not one to take an oath of poverty or to take even one tiny step down from her throne of pampered princess. In later life, she would be the one performing community service in a mink stole and designer jeans. Samantha and Sean had a sarcastic relationship, a derisive give-and-take. Sean was possibly the one person in the world who was not afraid of Samantha, with her sharp tongue and her tarted-up face and intimidating sexy curves.

"What is wrong with you?" Samantha said, dark eyes blazing, penciled-in eyebrows arching antagonistically.

"What's wrong with *you?*" Sean said. Samantha shook out her hair as if the answer to the argument was obvious and self-evident.

"I wish you could see yourself," Samantha fired out. "You think you're so *mature.*"

"I wish you could see *yourself*," Sean fired back. "At least I have some friends to be mature with." Samantha gazed out at our little group as if she had stumbled into a den of opium fiends.

"If you mean sitting around drinking beer and watching football games on TV makes you mature, then I guess you are."

"If you mean putting blue eye shadow on and wearing red underwear and teasing your hair with a curling iron makes you mature, then I guess you are, too."

Samantha started to throw her car keys at Sean, but stopped herself short.

"Oh, you!" she said. She stomped her foot. She shook her head. Then she stormed out of the room in a cloud of "Beautiful" perfume, by Faberge. It smelled beautiful, I must say.

As oldest son, Sean had somehow wangled the right to reside in a small, separate guest house secluded from the main residence by a grove of mature live oak trees and a curving flagstone walkway. The guest house was its own self-contained unit. It contained a bathroom, a kitchen nook, a roll-a-way couch, a large screen color TV, chairs and sofas and other accoutrements suitable really for a British hunting lodge, knick-knacks from Mr. O'Shaughnessy's law practice—"Sue the Bastards!" declared one gaunt, cloaked ceramic figure, barrister-like, thrusting a long, gnarled finger into the air—and its own well-stocked wet bar. The only thing missing was a uniformed bartender.

"What'll it be today, sir?"

"A Scotch, please!"

"My pleasure, sir!"

Sean lived in the guest house basically like a college student or a young professional, though he was merely a high school junior, like me. I could relax in the guest house. I could unwind. I could be my own man there, my best self, my true self. Sean and his younger brother George and I spent a great deal of time in the guest house, talking, drinking, smoking pot.

Samantha disapproved.

"This room is a wreck," she would say, appearing in the doorway every now and then, hands on hips, an overblown scowl on her lipsticked face. "Mom and Dad are going to be really pissed." As if she cared what they thought. Everybody stayed still until she left. Then we dissolved into howls of mocking laughter.

Sean and I were camped out in director's chairs in the guest house one summer evening when the TV channel signed off with the Star Spangled Banner and jet fighters taking off from the deck of an aircraft carrier—in those days, TV shut down each night at 2:00 a.m. With the TV showing static, we wandered outside onto the cool carpet grass lawn, damp with dew. It was as if we were crossing the line between very late and very early, and if we just pushed on through, new possibilities, new worlds, might emerge. Frogs and cicadas beat out a cheerful, hectic serenade. Looking up, we saw a shooting star streak across the sky—a sign of future wonders, a harbinger of good things to come, it seemed.

"Man, I'd like to get away," I said suddenly. "I'd like to go far away."

"You would?" Sean said. "Me too, man."

"You would?" I said. "You? You've got all this. You've got it made."

I figured that the reason I would want to get away was understood—a crappy home life, parents who didn't understand me, limited funds. Sean, I didn't get.

"I know," Sean said. "It's just—something's missing. Not everything is there. Everybody expects me to follow in Dad's footsteps and become a lawyer. I don't know if I want to become a lawyer or not. I've never really had a chance to think about it."

"I want to be a writer!" I blurted out. This was the first time I had dared to voice this ambition. It was almost the first time I had dared to think about it. I wanted to be a writer! I wanted to live in New York City, walk the streets of that vast metropolis, describe my background and my experiences and the forces that had shaped my life. Unspoken, underlying my ambition, was the assumption that I would find true love there. I understood for the first time, too, that Sean Jr. was not truly free, that he could not be what he truly wanted to be.

"You'd be a *great* writer," Sean said.

"You think?" I said. I was thrilled by Sean's outburst of affirmation.

"Yeah, man," Sean said. "I always thought you were really funny and creative. You have a way with words."

"I do?" I said. I felt myself grow exponentially in value and self-esteem. "Wow! That sounds cool."

"It is cool, man," Sean said.

"Man, I'd like to go to New York," I said. "I feel like I could really write there."

"Let's go to New York," Sean said.

"You want to?" I said.

"Let's do it," Sean said.

We had been friends but now we were more like brothers. We hugged, like brothers, and then I headed home, spellbound by the stars and the cool night air and the cacophony of night sounds as I strolled down the big steep hill to my house. The stars seemed almost close enough to reach out and touch. Inside, I tiptoed through hallways filled with the sights and sounds and smells of my other life, my soon-to-be-abandoned life. That night I tossed and turned in bed, my mind filled with romanticized visions of the future. I was moving on. I was going places.

Plans changed. (Wise authorial remark here—plans always change.) Downscaled, our runaway trip to New York City morphed into a three-day jaunt to New Orleans, an eight-hour drive away. Sean's dad hooked us up with reservations at the Roosevelt, a genteel old hostelry in downtown New Orleans, across Canal Street from the French Quarter. We weren't running away—we were going on vacation.

Still—I was excited. I had never been to New Orleans before. We left at dawn one glorious late-summer morning in Sean's cherry-red Porsche roadster. As the sun rose before us, driving east, we could see crepe myrtle in full bloom, purples and reds and pinks, the trees were lush and green, the sky a pale robin's egg blue tinged with oranges and reds. What a day! What a day to be alive! We felt revived, revitalized, carried along on a wave of emotion, as if this day truly were the first day in the rest of our lives. The air was soft and clean and fragrant, like fresh folded laundry. I popped a CD into the player and we sang along, cheerful as choir boys.

It was mid-morning—10:00 a.m. or so—when we pulled into a Stuckey's Shoppe near Schulenburg, Texas, for gas and a restroom stop. In today's highway universe, with convenience stores and chain hotels and fast food restaurants dotting the roadside, establishments like Stuckey's have faded away, but back then they were a staple of the traveling experience. Identified by its trademark red rooftop cupola, Stuckey's served travelers with food, drink, restroom facilities, fuel, aisles of cheap, tawdry souvenirs, and space to walk and stretch. Despite its cheerful corporate persona, it was a dim, scuzzy sort of place, with shelves of corny gifts and "Texana" like the postcard of a cowboy riding a giant rabbit or a map of Texas stretching from Mexico to the Canadian border.

The restrooms were located at the far end of a cluttered, dingy corridor and around a corner. The corridor was stacked high with colorful, cellophane-wrapped packages of chocolate praline candy, Stuckey's signature brand. There was a high frosted window, opaque with grime, the type of window that unlatched and slid upward to open. First in line, I went inside, locking the door behind me. The smell was a bracing aroma of stale urine and Pine Sol.

I should mention—Sean's younger brother George had come along with us. A precocious, preening age 15, George had decided that he, too, should partake of the wonders of the Big Easy, inviting himself along. Grudgingly, we accepted. Nevertheless, he didn't seem especially happy to be there. So far, George had lolled back in the right rear seat, earphones in both ears, staring out the window while smoking stinky mini-cigars. He wore long, gray, sweatsuit-fabric shorts and a sleeveless shirt and thick black sports socks pulled up almost to his knees. His dark greasy hair was pushed haphazardly behind his rather prominent ears. An aroma of spoiled brat floated up off of him, like bad beans. I could tell that he was thinking what a superior being he was, so far ahead at this stage of the game, so sharp, so advanced. George combined arrogance regarding the family money with feeling slighted not being the preferred older brother into a seething, sullen package of smart-ass resentment. George and I had a kind of love-hate relationship, with him controlling the terms of engagement. He was insulting, he was demeaning, he liked to make me feel that I was an outsider and a cheapskate. Like Lucy holding out a football for Charlie Brown, he would give me an opening, I would expose myself, he would shoot me down.

After the restroom stop, Sean and I purchased several food items and a newspaper at the checkout counter, then headed back to the car. George was already inside.

"Hey, shithead," Sean said, to his brother. George grunted.

"Hey you, shithead," George said.

Sean settled into the driver's seat, holding a can of Cherry Coke. Staring vacantly into the distance, he jiggled the key into the ignition slot and revived the engine up.

Sean glanced over at me then, and smiled—and for that moment, that one moment, all was well in the world. The newspaper was folded neatly across my lap. I took a swig of coffee—awful stuff, actually, that tasted as though it were brewed with the remnants of the crankcases of the truckers who pulled in here. Possibly this was the coffee's toxic side effect, but it filled me with sublime contentment, making me feel intelligent, forward-thinking, avant-garde. As Sean eased through the crowded parking lot, I fiddled with the CD player, punching numbers. I was filled with renewed energy, a brand-new purpose in life.

"Better get out of here," George said from the back seat.

"Why?" Sean said. We both turned our heads to the rear. "What's up?" There beside George on the back seat lay our answer, a pile of shiny, boxed-up Stuckey's famous praline candies, fifteen boxes at least. George smiled maliciously, pinching his stinky mini-cigar between thumb and index finger. I tried hard to understand the confluence of nature/nurture that had produced this loathsome creature.

"What the shit?" Sean said.

"I threw them out the restroom window," George said.

"Why the hell did you do that?" Sean said.

"I don't know," George said. "I just saw them sitting there. I felt like doing it."

"Did anybody see you?" Sean said.

"I don't know," George said. "I doubt it. Maybe." Sean banged his hands against the steering wheel. He banged his head.

"That's just great," Sean said. "That's fabulous. Yeah, I'd say we'd better get the hell out of here."

Face clenched in condemnation, Sean fish-tailed through the Stuckey's parking lot and out to the two-lane feeder road and then onto IH-10 heading toward Houston, the horizon obscured now by a giant cumulus cloud of trouble. I sat fuming and fumbling in the passenger seat, sipping bad coffee and tearing at the edges of a stale, spongy cinnamon roll. The icing was like candied concrete. I sneezed, sinuses exploding in response to negative stimuli. Since childhood, my sinuses had betrayed me in moments of crisis.

We drove silently, solemnly, the details of George's dastardly deed dancing in our heads like demons from Dante's inferno. The music of Radiohead on the CD player sounded like a dirge. I turned it off. The high overhead sun cast black shadows of doom on the roadway before us. George puffed away in the back seat, the boxes of candy piled up around him like dung from an animal that had crapped in its own den. We shook our heads disdainfully, hating George. It did us good to hate George. George was an ass. George was the biggest ass that had ever lived.

Slowly, imperceptibly, as the miles slipped away, we began to loosen up. We relaxed. All was good again. The candy became a joke. Even I allowed George his little spell of mischief. The bastard.

"What are you going to do with all that candy, George?" I said. George sucked on his stinky cigar.

"Give it to the poor," George said.

"Sure," Sean said. "You've always been big on helping the poor."

"I'll hand it out on the streets of New Orleans," George said. "I'll be the Pied Piper of Bourbon Street."

"Pied Piper of Bourbon Street my ass," Sean said. He shot the finger at George. George shot the finger back. We all laughed.

A few minutes later I saw a look on Sean's face that was like a sharp pang of indigestion.

"What's up?" I said.

"There's a cop," Sean said.

"A cop?" I said. "Where?" Sean motioned with his head.

"Back there," Sean said. "He's hauling ass." I turned to see the flashing top-lights of a police patrol car far away but traveling very swiftly forward.

"Maybe it's not us," I said. "Maybe it's some speeder."

"It ain't no speeder," Sean said. "It's us."

"Shit," I said.

"Shit," Sean said. "George?"

"Shit," George said.

"You're a dumb shit, George," Sean said.

We heard a siren soon after that, and then a voice telling us to pull over from the amplified bullhorn mounted on the police car roof. We pulled to the shoulder and waited. A police car pulled in behind us. George crushed out his mini cigar in a side ashtray. I laid the uneaten portion of my cinnamon roll on the floorboard, beside my feet. We sat silent, facing forward, knowing that we were doomed.

Dad showed up to bail me out the following afternoon. (Sean and George were released to their father's custody that same evening, but by some rule of juvenile law, I must be released to the custody of my own parents.) When I was released from my cell, he was seated on a hard wooden bench in the jail house foyer, appearing awkward and isolated. He was dressed in a pullover Izod shirt, tucked in neatly, blue sans-a-belt slacks, and black loafer shoes, with tassels. The gold band watch on his hairy left wrist gleamed like a diadem. Dad was meticulous in his attire, wary regarding the image he would project.

I couldn't look at him. I slumped in, shoulders drawn, like a sloth. Hands on knees, Dad sat still for a few moments before jumping up suddenly, like an athlete. We didn't normally shake hands, but we shook hands now, in a kind of ritual ceremony. I was cautious, emitting torrid vibes of sullen resentment. Grasping my arm, Dad thanked a balding, somnolent sheriff's officer behind a desk and apologized, as if not only for my recent behavior but for my entire life. The sheriff's officer didn't seem to care. Then we left, Dad pushing me along with his hand on my shoulder. I shrank from his touch. I didn't feel exactly free—I was merely being transferred from one form of custody to another.

Outside, at the far end of the lined and numbered parking lot, Dad's cream-colored Buick LeSabre crouched. Dad felt that a Buick was his station in life—a Cadillac too pompous, a Chevy too low class. Assuming our roles in the driver's and passenger's seats, neither of us said a word. I secured my seatbelt—the snap of the latch resounding like a gun shot in the enclosed space—and closed my eyes briefly, leaning back against the headrest. I wished that I could reset the last two days. I wished that I could reset pretty much my entire life.

Dad crunched out of the parking lot, driving slowly. I hadn't been in the car with Dad driving in a long time. His driving annoyed me. He was both conservative and sloppy, like somebody's old maiden aunt.

The day we had left for New Orleans was bright and sunny and cheerful. Today was a dreary, drippy day, everything gray and bleak and coated with moisture. It was a day where it was hard to see the goodness in anything, hard to see past the mist into the future. It was as if a curtain had come down in the play of my life and all upcoming acts were cancelled. Dad turned the windshield wipers on, then off, then on again. The car tires swished on the pavement.

"Why did you do this?" Dad said, turning on his blinker, entering the highway. "What in the world were you thinking?" It was a demand, an indictment, a damning statement. I shrugged, feeling guilty despite my innocence.

"I didn't do anything, really," I said, weakly. "George did it."

"Why were you a part of it?" he said. "Why didn't you stop it? Why didn't you take the lead?"

"Like I told you on the phone," I said. I hated telling him this. I hated telling him anything. "I didn't do it. I didn't even know about it until we drove away. George put the stupid boxes of candy inside the car while Sean and I were inside Stuckey's."

Dad nodded, unconvinced, unwilling to be convinced.

This was, of course, beyond this one incident now. This was about everything. This was like a jury trial where a chance remark opens up the defendant to evidence from all past transgressions.

"Why don't you like us?" Dad said. "Why don't you want to do things with us? Why don't you want to be a part of the family?"

"I do want to be a part of the family, Dad," I said. "I do." I hit my fist against the glove box, hard. It popped open, spewing Dad's neatly-stacked receipts and car papers onto the floor.

"Crap," I said. I started to say the kinds of things I had always said, things that I didn't really mean, that I would try harder, that I would try to fit in, but something in the situation pushed me beyond that. For the first time in a long time—in a long, long time—I was totally honest.

"Dad," I said, "You really don't understand me or try to understand me. I need to be able to do things on my own. I can't take it much longer. I need freedom. I need space." He started to jump in, to interrupt with his usual line of B.S., but I cut him off. I was angry now, all the pent-up anger of the last few years bubbling up in a geyser of raw emotion. I could see Dad's face redden, his own anger building in response to mine. Dad didn't store anger very well. He was like a tea kettle that whistles as the water inside starts to boil.

"When are you going to find yourself a girlfriend?" Dad said.

"I will, don't worry," I said. "When are you going to stop being such a jerk?"

"Don't sass me, young man," he said. "Your mother and I are starting to be concerned about you. We were talking about sending you to see a psychiatrist."

"I don't need a psychiatrist," I said. "I just need to get the hell out of the house. I know what—I'm just going to move in with the O'Shaughnessy's." Dad's nostrils flared.

"You're sure as hell not going to live with the O'Shaughnessy's," he said.

We were hurting each other now, slamming each other, throwing ugly words back and forth like tennis players with overhead smashes. I don't think either of us knew where this was going. Finally, I snapped.

I screamed—a deep, loud, guttural, strangled sound. The car was silent for a moment as my voice reverberated. "If you don't stop I'm going to jump out of the car."

Dad began to slow, easing the car onto the highway shoulder. His hand reached out reflexively to touch my arm.

"Don't jump out of the car," he said. His voice was small and low and measured, a murmur. My foot was shaking. My entire body was shaking. I realized then how foolish my declaration had been. I felt sorry for Dad then, and stupid, and embarrassed for myself.

"I'm not going to jump out of the car, Dad," I said. "I'm not going to do anything to hurt myself. I don't want to hurt you or Mom, either. But please listen to me. Please try to understand me. I want to be a part of the family. I really do."

Squeezing my arm, Dad eased the car back over to the inside lane and slowly resumed highway speed. For the first time in a long time—in a long, long time—I thought perhaps I had gotten through to him. Moreover, for the first time in a long time, I felt at peace with myself.

"I understand," Dad said. "Your mother and I just want the best for you."

"I know you do, Dad," I said. "And I want the best for you and Mom and everybody else in the family. Trust me. Believe in me a little. Listen to me sometimes. I'm not a bad person. I don't want to be a bad person. I want to be a success."

Dad nodded, one hand on the steering wheel and the other on my arm.

"Maybe we haven't tried hard enough to understand you," he said. "You're our oldest child, maybe we're still learning. Maybe we've blown the whole O'Shaughnessy thing out of proportion. Maybe we put too much pressure on you."

I shrugged, not wanting to commit myself to one side or the other.

"I don't know, Dad," I said. "Maybe so. But I'll be better. I'll try real hard to be better."

We drove on again in silence, boring through the mist with the windshield wipers flapping hypnotically back and forth. Dad removed his hand from my arm and placed it back in his lap. I sat back. I stared out the window. The tension in my chest lightened. I let go of something—what, I wasn't sure. Anger, maybe? Fear? For the first time in a long time, I began to relax with Dad. I had almost forgotten how we were once able to relax together. I think Dad began to relax a little, too. He stuck the car on cruise control and began whistling some ancient show tune, Frank Sinatra or Perry Como or somebody like that. Whistling was Dad's way of showing that he was a cool guy, too.

We were traveling a different route home, taking narrow two-lane highways rather than the interstate. The weather was starting to clear up. The sun was peeking out. We had slowed to pass through a town, one of the numerous small Polish/Czech settlements dotting State Highway 90 between Houston and San Antonio. Red brick businesses with bay windows and Victorian houses with high front porches lined the main drag, a four-lane thoroughfare. Dad glanced inquiringly in my direction.

"Hey, want to stop and get something to eat?" Dad said. I froze. My initial reaction was to say no—I had been telling Dad no for such a long time. But a quick check of Dad's face told me that I should say yes. This was part of the new me, saying yes.

"Sure," I said. "I guess I am kind of hungry."

"Me, too," Dad said. "In fact, I'm starving." He tooled his big old Buick slowly down the main street, scanning for an appropriate eatery.

"This place look sufficient?" Dad said.

"Looks great," I said.

Dad eased into the tree-lined parking lot of an Old West-style restaurant with a striped front awning and a horse carriage anchored out front. The restaurant was called "The Carriage House." Dad liked cheap, but he also liked old-fashioned independent restaurants that served a variety of dishes and served from breakfast straight through to dinner. This place looked like it could be one of those.

Inside, a hearty, big-armed woman in a calico dress greeted us up front and guided us to a back booth by a window facing a square. At this hour, the joint was nearly deserted, and a golden tendril of late-afternoon sun lanced through dancing dust motes to alight on a countertop. On the inside edge of the table sat condiments, a container of saltine crackers, and a juke box player containing Country Western songs, Elvis, some early Beatles. Settling in across from Dad, I put aside my adolescent self to conjure up good times past.

"Remember when we would go to the beach and jump in the waves?" I said. "And remember when we went to Colorado?—and we saw snow in the summertime? Remember how Grandpa Bill and I would sometimes drive down to pick you up after work?"

Dad's face brightened. He sat up straighter. He placed his hands together reflectively, prayerfully almost. He smiled. For this moment, in this pose, he looked somewhere close to content. Hell, he looked positively radiant.

"Yeah," he said, flashing a killer grin. "And remember when we went to Knott's Berry Farm in California where they had a replica of the Liberty Bell. They were doing a re-enactment of the Declaration of Independence, with period costumes and all. The speaker warned, 'This is a great deed we're doing, but it will be fraught with danger. It could mean death for us all.' Bobby grabbed my arm and said, 'Daddy, don't let them sign it. Don't let them sign it.'"

We both laughed.

"Bobby:" I said. "He's still like that."

"I know," Dad said. "I know he is."

A smiling waitress wearing a calico dress appeared beside our booth, holding laminated menus up against her emaciated chest. Her nametag read "Carol." I was relieved that she was not somebody my age, somebody I would have to try to relate to, somebody I would have to try to make understand my situation. She was instead a thin, small, middle-aged woman with an out-of-date beehive hairdo who called us "Hon" and "Dear." I was "Hon" and Dad was "Dear."

"How are you this afternoon, Hon?" Carol said. "How has your day been, Dear?"

"Just fine," Dad said.

"Doing okay," I said. Carol's eyes moved from one to the other of us, sizing up our relationship.

"Take your time now, gentlemen," she said, in a smooth, sweet East Texas twang. She smiled, touching me lightly on the shoulder. It was a touch, it seemed, of acceptance, of recognition, of approval. I smiled gratefully, in return.

Dad and I settled into opposite sides of the booth. We hid behind the laminated menus, popping out to lampoon the waitress and the other diners and the town. Ravenous suddenly, I ordered chicken fried steak with a tossed salad and mashed potatoes.

"What kind of salad dressing for you, Hon?" Carol asked.

"Thousand Island," I said.

"Thousand Island it'll be!" Carol said.

Dad ordered a veal cutlet with salad and green beans.

"Is the House Dressing a vinagrette?" Dad said.

"It sure is," Carol said.

"I'll have that," Dad said.

"Sounds good, ya'll!" Carol said, gathering up the menus and holding them against her chest.

"Where are you guys from?" Carol said.

"We're from San Antonio," Dad said. "I'm Dan, this is my son David."

"Nice to meet you, Dan and David," Carol said. "One of my girlfriends has family in San Antonio. That's a big place!"

"It's a pretty big place these days," Dad said. "We've got the Spurs. We've got Sea World and Fiesta Texas. We're over a million people now."

"A million people!" Carol said. "Hey, we're up to thirteen thousand!"

When Carol left to place our order, Dad and I fell into a laughing fit.

The last leg of the drive back turned into an afternoon of discoveries. I discovered that Dad had wanted to be an artist growing up, and I recalled his exceptional pen and pencil drawings of faces and buildings, sharp and discerning and shaded just so. (If only he had the artistic temperament!) I discovered that growing up in the Depression Era, he had learned the value of sacrifice and hard work. I discovered that my mother had a dramatic side, performing in several high school theatrical productions, her favorite being "Our Town" by Thornton Wilder. She played Emily Webb, the bustling bride to be. In addition, she researched and wrote a detailed family history. Dusk settled in as we approached fifty miles or so from home. The clouds had broken up into light pink pillows, immersing us in a long, soft, slow summer twilight. Elongated shadows chased the car. I discovered myself feeling comfortable, tranquil, happy almost. I was the first to sing a Christmas carol, I believe. Though it was summertime, something in the darkening air or perhaps it was the waitress named Carol that triggered them. Softly, poignantly (I thought), I sang "Silent Night." Dad followed up with "O Come All Ye Faithful," both the English and the Latin verses. Next, we sang "Joy to the World" in chorus, belting it out joyfully, triumphantly, together. Soon, we were singing Christmas carols one after another, trying to remember as many different carols as we could. I think we were up to number forty-five when we pulled into the driveway at home.

Pray Hard, Kick Ass Hard

The high school football team that I played on was the Holy Grace Apaches, though our relationship to Native American tribes of any type was cryptic, to say the least. Far from the grassy prairie or the forest woodland, Holy Grace was an all-boy's Catholic school located near a freeway intersection in suburban San Antonio, Texas, and surrounded by a neon thicket of convenience stores, service stations, a dry cleaner's, and Don's & Ben's Discount Beverages, which served the Holy Grace clientele with an eager capitalistic élan. After pre-season practice in the summer heat, their soft drinks—in metal cases of ice—seemed the coldest in the history of the world. Don, for what it's worth, was a slender Middle Eastern man with a droopy mustache and a tattoo of a serpent coiled on his left forearm. Ben was a short Alabama redneck with a pot belly who dispensed pearls of wisdom from a raised platform behind the check-out counter. They remain today my life-long models for world detente.

Our campus was set back far from the street and concealed behind a line of strategically-placed live oak trees—a long, low, rectangular structure with dark-tinted windows that reflected back the suburban-scape, oscillating sprinklers throwing skeins of fluoridated water into pristine air. We were children of the freeway, the first generation of the shopping mall, progeny of the well-tended carpet-grass lawn.

Our uniforms were deep red, with arrowhead decals on the helmets suggesting a spirited and rampaging (though conscientious and scrupulous) crew of Catholic schoolboys with a winning combination of moral fiber and hell-for-leather tacking ability. Considering our location, a more fitting helmet logo may have been a moping adolescent in a ban-lon shirt—or a family of four in an S.U.V., packed for vacation. We backed off for nobody. We were ready to kick ass. We lived to kick ass, actually. Pray and kick ass. Pray hard, kick ass hard.

Our spiritual leader in the kick ass department was the preeminent Coach Jack "Mule" Henley, whose most salient coaching technique involved standing on the abdomens of players while we performed routine warm-up drills. Supposedly this instilled some sort of character-building traits that would be carried forward through life. I believe it instilled instead a chronic, low-level, simmering rage, a distaste for all authority, and a latent desire to sneer at anyone with even the slightest swagger of command.

Let it hereby be proclaimed that Coach Henley was a first-class—jerk. There was some Bobby Knight in him, some prison guard, some repressed psychopathic cat abuser. Others claimed to find goodness in him, a heart of gold lurking beneath several-hundred hardened layers of gruff, inhumane exterior, but I didn't believe these theories. I believed he was a jerk, through and through. He played favorites, he trampled shaky adolescent egos, he used enlightened psychological techniques emanating directly from medieval torture chambers. He talked about "building character," but then he built only the characters of players he needed. Talented players. Players who could help him win. The rest of us were meat, in his eyes. Maybe not even meat. Maybe vegetables. Some off-brand of boiled pâté.

Me—I couldn't even walk right for Coach.

"Don't shuffle your feet, McBrearty," Coach said.

"Yes, sir," I said. I lifted my feet carefully, walking off down the field like some sort of deranged duck.

"That's better," Coach said.

I didn't know. I had played no organized football before my freshman year. I arrived for the first day of practice with the wide-eyed notion that I would immediately display the exceptional skill set that had made me a star player in my own back yard. I was immediately put in my place. That first day, in fact, was like a walk through a tunnel door into a new dimension. It was my introduction to the veiled, complex adult world of rumor and innuendo, being led by leaders with their own issues and uncertainties, led into situations they didn't understand or know how to control, though they pretended to be in control. I learned that you often pretend things are a certain way, when all the information and your instincts tell you they must be another way. Eventually I learned that I was not as physically gifted as some other people, not as fast or as strong or as shifty. (It was the vision of my superior shiftiness that fell hardest, for some reason. I was enamored with the belief that I could fake out any tackler, any time, any place.) For sure, all my illusions and delusions regarding the glamour and glory of football were shattered. I discovered instead that life on the football field was hell. It was meant to be hell. It was meant to shock forever out of my system the residue of that soft, lazy, hedonistic, summer-in-the-park mentality that permeated my teenage consciousness. It was like a Zen koan that read, "You cannot know the worst, until you are there."

There were speed drills. There were strength drills. We went rolling on a weedy field filled with sticker burrs. Like crazed buccaneers, we wrestled with teammates positioned atop a log, attempting to displace them. We tried to escape from a circle of players, with those on the outside of the circle pushing and popping the pads of the one who was trying to escape. It was all performed under a brutal sun and a heavy aura of intimidation, like a prison camp. There was yelling by the coaching staff, yelling calculated to engender uncertainty and fear. Everybody else on the team was your enemy. Everybody else was a rival for your spot in the lineup. We denigrated the weaker players subtly—and not so subtly. We behaved like characters from Lord of the Flies, only we went home at the end of the day.

We moved rapid-fire from one activity to the next, with never a moment to relax. Toward the end of practice Wind Sprints loomed, dreaded by all. Exhausted, we stood in ragged rows of three to four players, dragging, energy spent, our nascent adolescent wills barely ticking after hours of physical exertion in the blast-house Texas heat. Coach stood imperiously, arms folded across his massive weightlifter's chest, red whistle clenched between puckered lips. His thighs bulged in skin-tight white Rider coach's shorts.

A vein protruded in his neck. A short blast from the whistle and we rumbled forward in unison on a forty-yard dash, knees lifting, lungs burning, hearts beating like a drum riff on a computer simulation, attempting to absorb one extra iota of conditioning to call forth in a game situation. At the finish line, we staggered off to the side. We stood bent over, gasping, dizzy, fighting nausea, grabbing our knees in a dogged, desperate maneuver to regroup. The next group went, then the next. Too soon, it was my group's turn again. We rumbled forward.We stood bent over, gasping, grabbing our knees.

"Don't grab your knees!" the coaches yelled.

We stood up tall, gasping without grabbing our knees. One player stood in place and puked suddenly, like a sick animal. Coach said to ignore him. Two bulky assistants shielded him like gendarmes, ensuring that orders were followed.

Then we were summoned to fall to the ground for yet another round of calisthenics. Lying on scorched summer-baked earth in the grassless field, I strained to touch my left heel with my right fingertips as the sun cart-wheeled through the sky, a tricked-up movie set sun, like at Fatima. I wondered again why I was doing this to myself, why I was willing to forsake the comforts of the swimming pool and the shopping mall to put myself through this torture. Then, just before the breaking point, Coach called practice over. We had survived again. He gathered us around him in a cluster, talking low and level like a preacher or a software salesman in wind-down mode after his main pitch was over.

Finishing up, he made the sign of the cross and led us in prayer.

"Our Father, who art in heaven... ," we began, heads bowed, hands pushed together in a unity circle. We broke with a rebel yell.

"Show them you're men!" Coach said.

"Yeah, like you're a man, you fat bastard!" I shouted in my mind. I visualized taking him on in a boxing match, bringing him down with a flurry of mid-section jabs topped by one final thunderous left hook to the jaw. How sweet that would be.

Then he broke the huddle, clapping his hands loudly, and we jumped up and ran toward the locker room with a synchronized rebel yell. This was possibly the most un-genuine moments in my entire life. We hobbled up the trail like a team of broken horses. Even in the red-painted locker room, however, we were not entirely safe. As we disrobed on benches, preparing for showers, Coach strode through like some preening emperor, snapping off commands that left his frightened subjects scurrying to comply. Nothing set Coach off like failure to comply.

"McPherson," Coach said, stopping to direct a frosty gaze toward Robert McPherson, a giggling, goony, braces-wearing, towel-snapping linebacker. "Get your butt over here."

McPherson failed to move for a tell-tale half second. What's more, he had the remnants of a smirk on his pimply, lantern-jawed face. Everybody saw it. Stupid bastard, everybody thought. Stupid, dumb bastard. You didn't keep a smirk on your face when Coach addressed you. And there could be nothing more like a formal address than this, not an audience with a king or the President or even the Pope. The Pope you could shoot the breeze with compared to Coach. The dressing room fell silent as a chapel after Sunday mass was over.

"What?" McPherson said finally. McPherson was going for broke, it seemed, in a nihilistic, masochistic, apocalyptic mushroom cloud of self-annihilation. He was toast. He was vapor. He would never be able to father children.

Striking like a cobra, Coach grabbed McPherson's right ear and spun him around, a full 180 degrees. McPherson's smirk was gone, overlaid by a grimace. A wiry, tight-chested 6'1", McPherson stood scrunched over to Coach's height, shaking and cowering.

"What did you say, son?" Coach said.

"Nothing," McPherson said.

"I didn't hear you," Coach said.

"I said 'What,'" McPherson said.

"Why did you say that?" Coach said.

"I don't know," McPherson said.

"I don't know what?" Coach said.

"I don't know, sir," McPherson said.

"On the floor," Coach said.

"Yes, sir," McPherson said.

"Make it fast," Coach said.

"Yes, sir," McPherson said.

"Give me twenty," Coach said.

"Yes, sir," McPherson said. Coach released the ear, and McPherson dropped to the concrete floor where he began to crank out push-ups, one, two, three . . . starting strongly, slowing at ten, beginning to wobble at fifteen, and then each one became a tremendous labor after that. We all began to pray, silently, ardently, not knowing what could happen if McPherson did not make the required number. You never knew, Coach might start practice all over gain, make us trot back onto the field and run wind sprints. He was that sort of dictator, that sort of man. All we wanted at this point was to go home and collapse. Home was nirvana, a sanctuary, sacred relief. Home never seemed so good.

When McPherson finished, arms trembling, Coach turned on his heel and walked away. He was at the top of his game. In control. When he disappeared into his office, slamming the red door behind him, we carefully, very carefully, began to come out of our shells, like survivors of a natural disaster. But we were ready to dive for cover.

I began the season by scoring one of my many long touchdown runs, this one on a pitchout down the left sideline, gracefully dancing past defenders as cheerleaders leaped and onlookers observed, "Damn, that kid is good!" Unfortunately, this was all in my mind, watching the game standing on the sidelines with the other non-starters. In truth, I saw game action sparingly, as a blocker on the kickoff return unit where I could cause the least amount of damage, I presume. The remainder of the game I stood holding my helmet, pretending to be excited, pretending that I cared what happened or whether our team won or lost. The sideline unit formed its own little eco-system. Our uniforms remained clean and freshly laundered, unmarked by grass stains or other signs of action. Our minds were dulled from watching, not doing. We carried our hopes and dreams and aspirations within, laboratories brewing hope and despair. We cracked jokes while standing poised, trying to make the coaches see we were ready, prepared to go in, set to deliver at a moment's notice. At the final gun, we trudged back to the bus and took our seats dutifully before the real players arrived, battle-scarred, victorious or glorious in the loss, slapping hands or carrying their long faces like badges of battle. We already on the bus didn't care. We just wanted to get back, get dressed, go home. Dream for another day.

"McBrearty!" I didn't hear my name at first, or it didn't register, like background noise from the grandstand. "McBrearty—hey!"

"Sir!" I broke from my reverie and snapped to attention. It was Coach, motioning from the edge of the sideline.

"Do you want to go in or do you want to just stand on the sideline and play with yourself?" he said.

"I want to go in," I said. I started to pull my helmet on over my head.

"Johnson turned his ankle," Coach said. "I need you to play wingback."

"Yes, sir," I said.

"You know the plays, don't you?"

"Yes, sir," I said.

"I can put Nickerson in if you can't do it."

"I can do it," I said. "I know the plays."

My spirits fell, then rose again as Coach peered at me with a dubious expression, then pushed me out onto the field. I sprinted uncertainly toward the huddle forming in the center of the field. As I neared, several hands motioned me in. I tried to recall down and distance—third and ten, I believed. I leaned in attentively to listen to the quarterback, attempting to appear like an important, knowledgeable cog on the team. (Years later, in the business world, I would display this identical pose in staff meetings.) The sad fact was, I did not know the plays. After not participating in an actual scrimmage play for so long, my familiarity with the playbook had grown rusty. I would have to play it by ear.

"We're gonna run Red 42, Z Formation Right," called our quarterback, Eddie Phillips. I knew that Eddie was not Heisman-caliber, but he had the right demeanor for a quarterback—tall, suave, smart-ass, secure in his own beliefs, no matter how off-base or inane they seemed to others.

Breaking the huddle, I started instinctively to the right side-and my instincts proved wrong. Eddie Phillips pointed me emphatically to the left. Nodding reassuringly, I lined up a few yards outside the left end and one step off the line of scrimmage and peered in toward the center, waiting for everybody else to move before I moved. At the snap, I edged forward tentatively, putting an outrageously large fake on the left outside linebacker for their team. Un-faked, he pushed me with his hands and ran on by. It appeared that we had called a pass play, so I ran a pattern that I felt was appropriate for my position. I didn't know if it was in the playbook or not. I ran about eight yards upfield and curled inside on a button-hook. Then I stood waiting, holding my arms apart to signify that I was "open."

Eddie Phillips had dropped back into the pocket but was quickly flushed out, dodging to his left. He was being rushed hard by big Number 89, their defensive end. Eddie wasn't fast, but he had a good quarterback's knack for picking his way through heavy traffic. He was good at eluding sacks.

In game film, the ensuing sequence appeared like an entirely normal segment of football action and required approximately 10 seconds to complete. But to me, in real time, that moment seemed to be occurring in ultra-slow motion, almost a frame-by-frame slo-mo sequence from an Antonioni film. Eddie Phillips tacked left, pump-faking as he tried to evade persistent Number 89. I took several steps toward the sideline, then stopped and turned abruptly toward the center of the field. Eddie Phillips cocked his arm and launched a throw. It took my mind a moment to register the significance of this throw—the ball was heading to me.

Given my status, this seemed impossible, or perhaps it was some kind of set-up job to humiliate me. I felt uncoordinated. I couldn't seem to lift my arms or do whatever it was with my arms and hands that would be required to catch a ball. I was like a three-year-old taking lob throws from his father, just learning to catch. The ball bored its way toward me, spiraling but wobbling slightly, its trajectory aiming straight at my right shoulder pad, and I seemed powerless to do anything about it. Number 23 from the other team, flashing in from the corner of my vision, dived at the ball just before it reached me, but missed. I was almost hoping that he would hit it, deflect it away, out of my hands, saving me the humiliation of dropping it own my own. Then it was there, on me, like a heat-seeking missile. I was off-balance and out-of-sync. At the last possible second, it seemed, I made a pocket of my arms and caught the ball. It was more like an object sticking to a Velcro web. Somehow, I held onto the ball. Nobody was more surprised than me.

I stood still for a second, twirled (shifty!), and began to run downfield. Amazingly, there was a clear path to the end zone, about forty yards away. I ran as fast as I could but my legs, today not smooth pumping cylinders, seemed to operate in conflict with each other and my legs began to wobble ten yards from the goal. I was about to lose all coordination and fall down ignominiously when someone slammed into me at about the five yard line and I went down in a pile of arms and legs, rolling over and over. When I stood up, I flipped the ball casually to the referee— ten yards over his head.

Recognizing my talents for the first time, my teammates came running up to hug me and smack me on the shoulder pads. Then Damien Johnson tapped me on the shoulder and said he was coming in to take my place in the lineup. His ankle was okay now. That was fine with me. I was done. I was fulfilled. I could not have done anything more.

On the sideline, Coach grasped my face mask and shook it slightly—his congratulatory shake. I stood stolid, waiting for him to finish.

"Way to go, McBrearty," Coach said.

"Thanks, Coach," I said. I didn't want to give him too much credit here. I didn't want to give him any credit. I simply nodded and moved on, nonchalantly taking a cup of Gatorade from an ice chest, edging over to the back of the sideline. Some of my compatriots on the non-starter group came over and we high-fived.

For a while there afterward I felt like the prince of the world. Funny how one little bit of success can produce that result. One afternoon after practice I took a swing over to see old Don & Ben and chatted things up with them for awhile. I felt different now. I was able to talk to them with confidence, a mild swagger, even. I felt important at last.

That was my last season in football. I never caught another ball. But even after the glow faded, I carried the memory of my triumphant moment deep in my soul, a reminder of what life could sometimes be.

After high school, I saw Coach one more time, on a street in downtown San Antonio, when I was in my early twenties. Having graduated from the University of Texas with a journalism degree, I had been hired as associate editor for a statewide architectural magazine. I was engaged to be married. I was returning from lunch when I saw Coach standing on a corner, smoking a cigarette. Portlier now, graying a bit on the sidewalls, he was dressed not in Rider coach's shorts but in a charcoal gray business suit with wing-tip shoes, polished to a shine. The suit though distinguished, seemed too small under the arms, too tight, constricting, out -of-place. (Unlike me, in my free-wheeling editor's duds, an artist on the loose, a cool dude not to be contained.) My first, visceral reaction was to turn tail and run. Don't let him see me. Leave things as they were. My life had moved forward, so had his. But then a back-up emotion kicked in—I wanted to make a connection, close the loop.

I wanted to explain to him exactly what I was doing with my life. I wanted him to know what had happened to me in the years since he had coached me. I wanted him to know, in very clear, emphatic terms, that I was an up-and-coming young magazine editor, engaged to be married, with an office on the twenty-second floor of the glass-walled M-Bank Building overlooking the green hills west of the city. Holy Grace was far behind me. Not that I wanted him to think that he had anything to do with it. I wanted him to think that he had nothing to do with it. I wanted to say, "See, I proved you wrong. I am a success. But I am a success because I decided to become a success, not because of any lessons or wisdom that you imparted to me." I shouted out, "Coach!" I had to shout twice before he glanced up. He looked like he wasn't quite sure who I was. I galloped toward him, hand extended.

"Steve McBrearty," I said, reaching out to shake his hand. His rather befuddled hand.

His reluctant, uncertain hand. "Holy Grace High School, class of 19____. I was on the football team freshman year." Briefly, he looked at me as if I were still vegetables or boiled pâté. But then he seemed to catch himself, reflecting some dim recognition of our changed status.

"Oh, hey!" he said, cranking out an exclamation. "How have you been?"

"Good," I said. The words seemed to just fly out then, years in the making. "I work downtown here. I've got a job at a magazine. I'm their associate editor. I'm getting married in a couple of months."

Coach whistled through his teeth.

"That's a lot happening," he said. "That's good to hear." We both stood silently for a few uncomfortable moments, looking past each other's shoulders. Coach fumbled a Winston soft pack from his shirt pocket and offered me a cigarette.

"I don't smoke," I said. "Go ahead."

"That's good," Coach said. "Not a good thing to get started. Not a good thing to do." He held his cigarette between thumb and index finger, an old-fashioned smoking fiend's style, something you saw from guys with ducktails at car hops in the 50's. We both stood silent again. I tried to think of some topic of mutual interest. I couldn't leave yet. I required more contact than this. I craved it.

"So how have you been?" I tried. "How's coaching?" He took a drag on his cigarette. He nodded. The nod was one that was meant to be followed by an explanation.

"I'm not coaching anymore," he said.

"Really?" I said. "How come? I mean, you were a good coach." (A psychologist could possibly tell me why I said this. I did not know.) He turned his head away slightly, exhaling smoke. I thought he wasn't going to answer. But then he turned to look me square in the eyes, a hard, veiled look, like the Coach of freshman football, long ago.

"You didn't hear?" he said.

"No," I said.

"I thought everybody knew," he said. "It was all in the papers a couple of years ago. I hit a kid. Threw a clipboard at him, actually, hit him in the face. Broke his nose. The parents sued the school. I got fired."

"I'm sorry to hear about that," I said.

"It's okay," he said. "I probably needed it. I've moved on. I sell long-term annuities now."

"Sounds interesting," I said. He shrugged.

"It's a life," he said. "Hey, what time you got?"

"12:55."

"I'm meeting this guy here at 1:00. He should be here any minute now."

I nodded. I shifted my feet. Somehow I felt drawn to him now, this man I had despised, this man who had haunted me for many years, in his weakness, his humanity. I wished I could think of something to say, something to help, something that would put him back where he was before. I wanted him back where he was before. I didn't want to see him humbled. I wanted him to be a big, slap-happy, child-tormenting, egotistical jerk. I wanted him to be Coach.

"I hope everything works out," I said finally. I tried to think of something more.

"Thank you," Coach said.

"You taught me a lot," I said.

"That's good to hear," Coach said. "I appreciate that very much." We stood silently again, facing each other across a gulf of generations and years.

"Well—back to work, I guess," I said. I said this with a shade of embarrassment, as though reveling in my good fortune.

"Go for it," Coach said. "Where did you say you worked?"

"The Texas Society of Architects," I said. "I'm associate

editor of the magazine there. It goes out to all the architects in the state."

"Sounds like good stuff," Coach said. "Sounds like a success story to me."

"Thanks, Coach," I said. "See you around."

"See you around," he said. I turned to go, stopped. I groped for something else to say, some grand final word of closure. I couldn't think of one.

"Good luck with your meeting," I said. He waved his cigarette at me, cigarette smoke in his mouth.

"Thanks," he said, post-exhale. And then, without even knowing I was going to, I leaned into him and we hugged. It was a moving if rather rigid embrace, smelling of suit coat and cigarettes, incorporating somehow our entire histories and intertwining fortunes and differing trajectories for the future. I stepped away quickly after that, beating it back to my office. I felt suffused by emotion, surprised by emotion, surprised by what life can sometimes have to offer.

Back in my office, a neat, pastel-painted oblong of corporate America, I sat and stared out the window and pondered the future and the past. There was an article I should work on, but I couldn't concentrate. I picked up the phone to call my bride-to-be, but realized that she would not understand. Some things nobody else can understand.

Official Publications

We sit with forced fine posture on high-backed wooden chairs in the somber, subdued environment of Official Publications in the university registrar's office, dormer windows high up like something from "Wuthering Heights" providing a fetching glimpse of trees and sky and the universe beyond, huddled in fear. We live in fear. We love our fear, actually, nurture it, coddle it, string it along. It's a presence, something we share, as if encapsulated in a giant bubble, a biosphere dedicated to proper editing marks.

OK—the environment is not all that somber, subdued, maybe. We have just completed a riff of jokes and we are rollicking with laughter, a pencil flying high in the air, someone speaking in a rich, theatrical voice, a risqué epithet mouthed. We are all young and new to the working world and filled with energy and excitement and a desire to excel. We want to show how smart we are. We want to show off. We write copy for the course catalogues that are distributed to faculty and students.

Then it happens, like a curtain rising on stage or a clap of wild thunder. Our Director, the notorious Doris Payne,

60ish, tall and imposing and elephant-legged, has just tromped into the room, dragging her bad leg behind her like a fallen log. The scene hushes abruptly, final words spoken in rushed whispers. We stare grimly at the manuscript pages beneath us, fearful to glance at one another, pencils in hand, deep into editing mode. It is as if we had been performing this same action without break forever, from eternity, no questions asked, no explanations needed. Ms. Payne is a direct descendant of the high school football coaches' school of supervision. She presides through fear and intimidation, as a stickler for useless rules intended to keep her charges in line—and nothing else. She demands neatness, order, a slate as clean as the first fall day of classes.

She has, however, one soft spot that we exploit relentlessly. Childless herself, she considers us her children, unwashed urchins to be guided and nurtured through this crude wide world of grammatically-challenged Bedouins. For our part, we pine to please her, to show her we can do it, that we are qualified to occupy the rarified air of ace editors and stellar wordsmiths.

Suddenly Laine McArthur, boldest and rashest among us, spews out a spontaneous combustion of laughter through closed lips and nostrils. Laine wears all-black clothing and purple-streaked hair, long strands falling loose in front. The rest of us, enablers and peer group junkies, follow suit. There is a long chorus of forbidden release, tension breathing like the change of air pressure before a storm. Ms. Payne scans the room dramatically, gnarled hands on giant hips, lips poised as if to deliver a withering reprimand. We sit poised, half amused, half scared out of our wits. It is an exquisite balance.

Somebody's phone rings then—a giant intrusion. We don't like intrusions here, even from friends, even from loved ones. Friends and loved ones don't understand. There is too much to explain. We're too clannish, too ingrown, there are far too many nuances to convey reliably or with the proper shade of meaning. At 5:00 each workday we say our good-byes and head home and re-assimilate slowly into our regular lives, but for now we're all part of a closed system. We're a unit. We're a team. Nobody can know what we go through but us.

"Yeah!" says Natalie Thompson to her caller, picking up the phone with a certain impatient insouciance. Cool, but understanding that she must move this conversation forward quickly. Cool, but aware that she is one of the few people anywhere who understands the meaning of the word, "insouciance." She shoots a statement with her eyes out to the team: Hey, I know, I'm hurrying here.

"What's going on?" Natalie says to her caller.

Motor-mouthed, the female voice on the other end chirps cheerfully, oblivious to our plight.

"Awesome!" Natalie says, trying to be supportive and preemptive at the same time. "That's really awesome!"

The voice chirps.

"Let's do it!" Natalie says. Looking at us, she forms an expression of mocking irony with her eyes and mouth. She twirls the telephone cord around one hand. "I'll do it."

Chirps. Holding a strand of brunette bangs between two small slender fingers, nails painted chartreuse, Natalie blows air out of her half-closed mouth and falls back on one leg in a posture that is like a flamingo.

"Hey, can I call you back in a little bit?" Natalie says. "We've kind of got a meeting going on here."

"You don't need to call me back!" the voice chirps. "I'll see you later. Be sure to bring your Flaming Lips CD."

"I will," Natalie says. "Talk to you later." She hangs up the phone and smiles, folding her hands across her diminutive chest. She is back in the fold now.

"Hey, let's split for ice cream!" somebody says brazenly, within earshot of Ms. Payne. Ms. Payne sometimes misses things said right under her chin and hears things a mile away. She'll shock you with a recitation of your words from private, offhand conversations with your desk mate from a year before.

"She'll never know!" says someone else.

"How about a movie, too?" I say, representing not just myself but my entire background, my upbringing, my heritage. I am proud of myself. I am a rebel. Hell, she can't fire all of us, can she? And even if she can, is it better to suffer forever in silence or, so to speak, to take arms against a sea of sorrows? We're taking control of our live here. We're on the forefront. We're on the cutting edge.

Ms. Payne stands frozen framed by the doorway of the room, towering like a totem pole. She glowers, she glares, she shakes her head acerbically.

"Could we attempt to maintain some level of decorum in here?" she says.

"Yes, ma'am!" we say in unison, an undercurrent of sarcasm in our tone. Sarcasm is our hallmark, our stock in trade. Sarcasm is our god, almost. Then Ms. Payne clasps her manuscript tightly to her chest—she is never without a manuscript; I think sometimes that her life has been wasted away in manuscripts, in making tiny marks on the margins of printed-out pages, and that the manuscript is a metaphor for her existence—and tromps right on out of the room. The sound of her clumping footsteps is one that will have meaning to my dying day. After a moment of fretful silence, we slap hands and share high-fives all around. The team celebrates.

We never went for ice cream, of course. We didn't see a movie. Our little crew of literary wanna-be's, all precocious, all full of high spirits—gosh, we're full of bull! Like the rest of them, I am a recent college grad, my dreams still intact, not broken and scattered as they become through age and the train wreck of events. My dreams remain gigantic at this stage, giant cumulus clouds billowing 50,000 feet up in a blue summer sky. I see my future as a grand, rollicking amusement park ride or a stroll a stroll along a mountain trail with a view of coastal sunset in the distance. I see girls. I see fame. I see riches.

A sketchy draft of my blockbuster first novel lies tucked away in a desk drawer at home in my ineffably guy's apartment, hidden under socks and underwear, awaiting only a dollop of polishing before hitting the bookstores as a best-seller. Hardly anyone knows about my novel. My roommate Jason doesn't have an inkling, that's for sure. It is too volatile for him, too filled with truths, too close to home. He is too dense, too mentally immature. And he is in it, a thinly-disguised character, depicted without regret or remorse as the hard-driving, unreflective, single-minded law student that he is. The life of his mind is limited to writs, rebuttals, filing injunctions. To my Official Publications workmates I have planted hints and innuendoes, but only Ms. Payne has observed the actual physical product. When I screw up my courage to show her a chapter—I leave an envelope with a sticky note on her desk—she says that it is good. It must be good! My heart races, my spirits soar. Her telling me it is good is almost as sweet as publication itself.

I see others around town here in their 30's, not that far distant in years, chained to their work, their outlook hopeless, their relationships stale, their love lives reduced to "What's for dinner?" and "Did you check out the discounts in the Best Buy ad today?" This won't happen to me, of course. This will never happen to me.

One day, just before semester break, Christmas decorations twinkling over our door frames and on our office tree, Ms. Payne ushers me into her office and surprises me with a rebuke. It is a trifle, some petty, foolish, unimportant thing that she has chosen to scold me on. It almost seems like a traffic cop meeting his monthly ticket quota.

"You shouldn't have told Dr. Grisham that you would change his course description," Ms. Payne says.

"He got his edits in by deadline," I say. For once, I am not meek and accepting. I bristle. I feel demeaned, like a grown-up child feels demeaned when his parents conjure up some unpleasant reminder of his past. I realize that I don't need to take this. I talk back. I depart her office realizing that it is, at last, time to go. I thought I had wanted to stay forever. Now I want to escape in the most desperate way.

The two weeks after I give notice Ms. Payne treats me like a nobody. She bustles past me with work in hand, consults others when she used to consult me, ignores my comments and stares past my witticisms. My co-workers even seem almost like strangers to me now, dupes, malingerers, playing a loser's game, trapped in their own webs of foolish fantasy. "Escape!" I want to tell them. "Escape now!"

My last day at work, I hug them all in a tearful farewell, regaining all of my lost feelings for a final, conclusive moment. Surprising myself, I linger affectionately, touching each desk, cataloguing each item of accouterment in my mind for future recall and reference. I am lost. I don't want to go forward. But I must.

At the very end, just as I am about to slip out the door, Ms. Payne calls me over with a hand gesture. My gloom lifts unexpectedly as I prepare to receive her words of amnesty and reconciliation. Instead, her voice is filled with a tone of condescending warning that I don't care to hear.

"You can't please everybody," she says. "Sometimes you've got to stand your ground." I stand with slumped shoulders, listening stolidly, stoically. I don't want to go yelling out the door. Instead, I sulk off in a state of depression that lingers for a long, long time.

One bright spring morning a few years later I sit slumped in an ergonomic swivel chair in my own private office nook high up in a sleek, snazzy, black-glass skyscraper in downtown Austin. Looking out I see a majestic view of the green hills rimming the western edge of the city and the capitol complex three blocks north. Shadows from clouds prance back and forth over the hills, like gods from mythology. After an interlude of meaningless odd-jobs— driving a bookmobile, running errands for a legal firm—I work now for the publications division of a statewide association for architects, a stuffy, buttoned-down organization, enamored of itself, imbued with showy, self-proclaimed importance. Despite its hard-edged splendor, its picturesque perch, this is a foreign place, a palace without a soul. It's a dictatorship here! Everything is mandated from the top down, organized, regimented, calculated to project a finely-tuned positive image. The cup I must use to drink coffee is color-coordinated with the walls and the window-sills—a muted, pale beige. My desktop I must clear off every night to present a pretend clean slate. Men's shirts are crisp, their pin-striped slacks creased, their neckties swirls of evocative color. Women's garb is chic and trendy--scarves, jackets over sleeveless blouses, brooch pins on lapels. There is a great deal of hearty handshaking, backslapping, and butt -kissing as we proceed throughout our day.

Backtracking momentarily, I should mention that the notorious Ms. Payne has died, leaving her poor husband Howard who doted after her, sweetly and carelessly, like some dashing forlorn lover from the Russian steppes. No one could understand why he doted after her, since she was so crabby and cantankerous and heavy-handed—and who could imagine them having sex?—but he did. They would walk the hallways of Official Publications holding hands.

When they parted, they kissed, pressing their lips together with sweetness and delight. And then he gave her a tender little tap on the ungainly sway of her jumbo-sized rump. Who knows whither love? Perhaps Howard had tapped into Ms. Payne's hidden tender side. Perhaps, beneath her prim, pedantic schoolmarm's cover, she was as gentle as a dreamy Romantic poet and a tiger in bed.

I should mention also, I suppose—I am engaged to be married. The wedding is set for June, a scant two months away. Like great machinery working away in the background, preparations for the wedding are in full swing. Invitations are being addressed, caterers contacted with instructions, tuxedoes fitted, bridesmaid's dresses altered.

Here at work, my hand rests poised on the mouse pad of my desktop computer, my standard pose now. My eyes gaze into a dense scroll of e-mails on the 19" flat screen. My hands move, my eyes scan. While I appear to be working, I am actually engaged in a complicated logarithm trying to determine whether my marriage would be a terrible mistake.

I play out different scenarios in my head, fantasies of married life in the days to come. I go first one way, then the other. One time it is wonderful, the next time terrible. Or it starts out wonderful and morphs into terrible.

Proximity! So much of life is mere proximity. So much of life is a crapshoot. My bride-to-be Sarah Chapman is a smart, pert, pretty waitress at a downtown diner where I stop in for breakfast before reporting to work. She wears a tight black uniform with low-cut bodice and white fish-net hose that accentuate her wobbly, knock-kneed legs. She waits on me with a nervous smile, holding her pen and pad out before her carefully, precisely as taught. I admire this quality in her—she does things as taught. Our relationship develops delicately from biscuits and gravy into passion, romance, amour. Our relationship develops delicately from friendly words in a coffee shop to nakedness and sex.

Oh, Sarah is a fine girl, a sweet, sassy, sexy, fast-talking girl, but she has this one characteristic that is driving me up the wall—she wants to be with me all the time. I can't do anything with my friends. I can't do anything after work. I must report in at all times and in all locations. I can hardly get off to the convenience store by myself without her calling for me to come back soon. At work this is screwing me up. I have a career going. I have to prove myself! I have to show that I am eager, ambitious, ready to rock 'n roll. Kick ass when required. Part of the job requirements here are the shoot the shit with associates, attend social functions after hours, chauffeur visitors here and there with a hearty, upbeat patter. Sarah doesn't like this. She doesn't understand it. She wants to keep me close to home where she knows I cannot wander. With Sarah, I'm beginning to feel already that my horizons are becoming narrow, my dreams are starting to fade, my options disappearing fast. I want my dreams. I want my options.

I sympathize. I try to understand. I realize—of course! —that psychological/ Sociological factors in Sarah's background have helped make her this way. An abusive father, a mother who is borderline alcoholic. Sarah never went to college, and her knowledge of literary forms is limited. She speaks boldly, as if she is strong and certain, but she is a fragile flower, I have ascertained, with emotional scar tissue and hang-ups galore. She ran away from home at age 14. She once tried slitting her wrists. In her late teens, searching for a center, she joined a Southern Baptist youth group that hooked her with Sunday pot-lucks and picnics in the park. They loved her, they said. They prayed for her. They told her she was a good person. They listened when she told them her father was a liar and an adulterer. Their spiritual guidance—while important—was no doubt secondary to their emotional support, as they provided a stable community for her, an extended family, friends who could substitute for real family members who had betrayed or disappointed her.

Because of all this, I feel sometimes that I am on the outside looking in. I fear that I am taking her away from this nurturing environment, that this is what she really needs, not me, not my foolish ambitions and base desires and high-handed, manipulative tactics. But too soon, we had sex, and too soon, I fear, I confided in her my most prized secret—my novel. After sex one night on the couch in her living room, I confessed to her about my novel in a drawer. Holding her in my arms, I told her that I wanted to be a writer, that I planned to quit all this corporate claptrap soon, at the first opportunity, and live the life of an artiste, tucked away in the heart of a great metropolis, perhaps, or back behind a long, lazy beach, with the surf and the stars my only companions.

"That's so wonderful!" she said, after a pause to assess the meaning of my surprising outburst.

"It's what I've always wanted to do," I said.

"That's so wonderful!" she said.

The scenario was set, then, in my mind, at least: me, Writer, great, famous, Writer; her spouse of Writer, beautiful, lascivious, noted for her off-beat, eccentric intelligence. She fell for my line and I fell for her pretense that she cared about any of this, really. Who could blame her after the childhood she had, but she cared more about having a big brick house with green grass where she could throw her keys on the counter and plop her feet on the coffee table and watch rich suburban sunshine stream in. Her defining vision—sitting by her backyard pool in swimsuit and shift, sipping a daiquiri and watching her children play. She wanted to be taken away. She wanted a savior. And she was counting on me to be that person. I had convinced her I could be that person. I can be pretty convincing sometimes, I guess.

The beige phone on my desk rings. It's Sarah again.

"Hi, Honey!" she says.

"Hi, Honey!" I say. She pauses. She draws in a breath. I move the mouse mindlessly, in my imagination watching her ample bosom heave. I know that she is developing her point. She couldn't have much of a point. We last talked just an hour before. Perhaps she feels that our previous conversation was unsatisfactory or inconclusive and that she would not feel right until we talked again. Last time we spoke she told me she thought that we should invite two uncles from her mother's side to the rehearsal dinner.

"That sounds fine," I said then. "Whatever you want to do is fine with me." I guess she thought I was being too blithe, that I should offer additional insight or commentary.

"I mean, I don't like them much, but since we're

inviting Kevin and George from your family, they might feel slighted if we don't."

"Well, sure," I said then. "I think we should invite them."

"But then they always get drunk and start insulting somebody," she said. "They don't like people different from them. My family's so different from yours. I don't want that to happen to your mother or somebody. We really don't want a fight on our hands."

My supervisor Ron Jansen appeared in my office doorway with a scowl and 5 o'clock shadow on his face, waiting for my conversation to end. He was the kind of person who would just keep standing there until you were forced to hang up. I smiled nervously and held up my hand, signaling that I was almost finished. A hot burn of anger—at Sarah, at him, at myself for being such a wimpy twerp—flared up inside my chest.

"Honey," I said, jumping in when Sarah finally reached a stopping point. "I've got to go. I've got a meeting now."

"Oh!" Sarah said, as if she had never considered the concept of a meeting before. "Okay. Just one more thing?"

"I've got to go!"

"I'll call you later, then," she said. "I love you!"

"I love you," I said. I hung up, and Ron Jansen moved in like a predator on the prowl. His dour visage signaled some momentous action in the offing. There is always some momentous action going on around here. Our days are spent in an arc of rising and falling action like an ancient Greek drama. Or maybe a really bad TV sitcom.

Now, a scant hour later, Sarah is back on another tack. It is a topic I had hoped dearly to avoid.

"Honey," Sarah says. "I don't think you should go to that fundraiser thing at the convention center tonight. The weather's supposed to be bad. There's always a lot of strange people downtown. Oh—do you think the weather will be bad for our wedding?"

I pause. I try not to sigh. It's not a good thing to sigh with your bride-to-be on the line.

"I really, really, really need to make an appearance," I say, very nervously, very carefully. I feel like someone stepping barefoot through a field of sticker burrs. "They expect me to. It's important. It's sort of an obligation."

"Well, you've got obligations to me, too," she says.

"I know," I say. "I don't really want to go. It's just— I don't know what I could say. I told them I would go. I can't back out now. They already think I'm kind of lame in the work ethic department."

"Tell them I don't think you ought to go," she says.

"I can't tell them that."

"Well, why don't you just tell them you're not feeling well?" she says. "Tell them you had a previous appointment. A family matter. Tell them your 80-year-old grandmother just pulled into town."

"Oh, come on," I say. I do sigh now. I hear my voice assume a thin, ugly edge, an ursine howl.

"Why don't I just tell them I'm a big, stupid pansy-ass?" I say. "Why don't I tell them I can't leave my house without permission? Why don't I tell them my fiancée keeps me locked up after dark?"

"That's not very nice," she says.

"You make it hard for me to be nice," I say. There is a long, ominous moment of silence as these words settle in.

"You're impossible," she says then. "Did you know that? Sometimes you're really impossible."

This is the first time she has said these words to me. This is the first time anyone has said them. I am hurt but angered also. This hardly seems fair. I'm the difficult one. I'm the one impossible? Something inside me snaps then. I lose my cool. I lose my very tenuous grip on the reins of this relationship.

"You know what?" I say. "I think you're impossible too, sometimes. You make it impossible for me to work. You make it impossible for me to have fun. You make it impossible for me to enjoy my day. You—"

You know—you always know—when you have gone one step too far. I hear her on the other end make a shrill, angry sound, a shriek, a noise that is like an ice pick to my soul. Then she hangs up. She has never hung up on me before. I sit staring at the phone as though it were a thing of horror, writhing with snakes and Medusa hair. Heart pounding, I pretend first that nothing has happened, that I can will things back to the way they were before. Two seconds in a life can mean so much. Two seconds can mean the rest of your life will be happy or the rest of your life will be filled with misery and regret.

Despondent, delirious, I call back, punching the numbers on the telephone face like a convicted felon hammering out a plea for mercy. I think that I may even say a prayer. The phone rings, and I know that her voice mail picks up at four rings. Her voice mail picks up. I punch out the numbers again. She answers on the third ring.

"What?" she says, in a heavy, blurred voice. She has been crying, no doubt. I think—"Why does she need to cry?" In retrospect, I recognize what a sorry jerk I am.

"Hey—" I say. "I'm sorry."

She says nothing.

"I said I'm sorry," I say.

"I heard you," she says—after a moment. "What an ass you are!" Her declaration seems to indict not only me in the present but my entire life history, my family, my upbringing, my religion. Then she reads me the riot act for five solid minutes, at least. She tells me what a clod I've been, that I'm uncommunicative, uncaring, too cool, full of myself, that I am a sinner and a bastard and certainly a very bad person. I sit slumped on my side of the phone listening in abject silence, a figure of remorse and repentance, like an old-time penitent in sackcloth and ashes. Or somebody with a Loser sign stamped on their forehead.

Sarah calls off the wedding, one brief, brutal week before we're due for our walk to the altar. We're standing in the kitchen of her apartment, finishing off the dishes. We've just had another argument, this one a doozy involving a different of opinion on the scope of her mother's role in our future together.

"Listen," she says, in a tone that I will associate forever with dire warnings and apocalyptic events. "This isn't going to work."

Prepped by weeks of foreshadowing, my mind grasps immediately the context of her words.

"It's going to be fine!" I say. "It's going to be wonderful. We love each other."

Sarah is unmovable, unassailable, intractable, and wickedly honest, as only a female can be.

"You've been wanting to get out of this for a long time," she says.

"No, I haven't," I lie. I know in my heart that I have been wanting to get out, that this must have been transparent to her, that I cannot now, suddenly, pretend otherwise. Daily life leaves evidence.

"It's obvious," she says. "You aren't interested when I talk to you. You're off somewhere else. You'd rather be doing something different. I have to drag you with me to go dancing or to see my friends. Sometimes I think it was only the sex."

"It's not only the sex," I say.

"Sex was a big part of it," she says. "I knew I shouldn't have let you sleep with me so soon. My mother always told me that."

"I'll change," I say. My voice assumes a pleading quality that even I find repugnant. "I'll be different. I'll go with you wherever you want to go."

"It's too late," she says. "I can't take this any more. I've changed now. I see things differently. It's like I'm starting over."

"I love you," I try pitifully. I reach out to pull her toward me, as if by physical contact I could change her mind. She struggles away.

"Well, I don't know if I still love you," she says.

"What about the wedding plans, our honeymoon and all?"

"Do you really think we should go through with that and then be miserable for the rest of our lives?"

"I won't be miserable."

"I will."

"You'll be miserable?"

"Yes, I will." Finally, I let go. I can think of no reasonable rebuttal to that.

I am well up into my thirties now, with a position as Assistant Publications Director for a Fortune 500 company in the children's textbook field and a girlfriend who doesn't want to get married. Claire doesn't think commitment is a good idea—she thinks it narrows you down. She wants to experience everything. She rises early to view the sunrise. Long walks through the forest on cold, blowy days make her feel safe and insulated from the world.

I am uncertain again. I think I want more from the person I am with, more pushback, more edge. I want somebody who will make me work harder for her affections. I see my life spinning away, my past receding into murky memory, my future dark and nebulous, a far corner of the cosmos, a metaphysical black hole. Whimsically, perhaps, I think now that I want to have children, a stable home, detailed plans for the years to come. But every time I plant a hint in that direction she diverts attention or pushes me away.

"How would you picture me as a dad?" I say, with a perplexed, inquiring smile on my face, my best, mixed message of a smile. It is a very complicated smile that I provide to offer tempting insights into my soul.

"Hey, wow, did you see that?" Claire replies, darting away, pointing toward a flowering bush or a little cat across the street or something on TV.

"I just thought it might fun to be a father," I say.

"Yeah, that might be fun some day," Claire says.

Reserving a cabin in the Sangre de Christo mountains north of Santa Fe, Claire and I travel to New Mexico right after Christmas Day. We depart early the morning of December 26, a cold, gray, dreary, grind-it-out sort of day, representing winter as the absence of warmth. Our 12-hour drive has few highlights, just the bleak memory of fighting headwinds for 700 miles and rushed, edgy meals at interstate fast-food stops. But our cabin is a beautiful place, it turns out, ridiculously beautiful, isolated, pristine, fresh, cold, clean. The inside is bare, like a fresh start, with a bed and built-in cabinets and a gleaming small kitchen, and smelling of its pinewood walls and the pine forests outside. A cold, clear stream runs swiftly just outside a window over the kitchen sink. Claire is like a kindergarten kid, alive, aware, wanting to gambol in the woods, taking my hand and running, falling into a bank of snow.

"Isn't this beautiful!" she proclaims. "Isn't this what life is all about?"

"It's beautiful," I say. But my soul is somewhere else. My soul is back home, far away, buried under a pile of computer printouts on the windowsill at my office. Tromping through the woods, eating dinner at a little roadside café, I think of things I should be doing, memos to be written, people to call, meetings to set up. I get antsy. I go dull. By the third day I am sullen, silent. I am ruining it for her.

"Why are you so quiet?" Claire says, looking at me pensively, eyes hard though glossy, as though making a calculation, that the hard numbers say that she must finally accept that I am not everything she thought I was.

"I'm not being quiet," I say.

"You are," she says. And for the first time, almost, her voice takes on an edge of exasperation, anger even. She has always been so even-tempered with me, so easy come easy go. I am surprised to hear her fervor. I feel like somebody trapped by a police surveillance net—a Truth Squad from life itself. "What's the matter? You don't like being here? You don't like me? You don't to be with me?"

"I want to be with you," I say. I reach for her, clumsily, to show by holding her that I care for her deeply, but I have little energy. I am like somebody moving in a dream. She pushes me away. She runs away twenty feet, puts her hand over her face. She begins to sob. I start toward her, then stop. I don't know why. For some reason, my eyes focus on pine fronds scattered through the sandy ground. Clad in white sneakers, her feet seem obtrusively clean and tidy, as if to mock me by their order.

"I can't believe I've wasted all this time with you," Claire says. "I thought you were the one. I thought you were the person I'd spend the rest of my life with. I love you. I thought you loved me, too." I stand arms by side, stunned and ineffectual.

"I thought you didn't want to make a commitment," I say, in a lament. "I thought you wanted to keep our options open, to be free to play and travel, to make new friends, experience new things."

"People say that all the time," Claire says. "I was protecting myself. I didn't want to get hurt. I wasn't sure how things would play out. But then I fell in love with you. I thought you could see that. I thought you'd catch on. Now I can see it was all a delusion."

Standing flat-footed, I try to regroup. I try to piece the picture of all of our time spent together back into a new context, reassemble it in a split-second into a new image, one that incorporates Claire's just-disclosed version of events. If she wants to make a commitment, I'll make a commitment. But it doesn't work. It's not possible. I can't switch psychological gears that quickly. All this time that I've been thinking things were headed nowhere has had its impact. I never took our relationship seriously. I never really thought of her as a life partner. How could I not know that she was in love with me? How could I not see?

"I'm writing a novel," I blurt out suddenly. It's almost as if I have disclosed that I am gay or that I was in prison for ten years.

"A novel?" she says. She tilts her head sideways with a narrow-eyed squint. "Is that what that thing you're always working on the computer is? I always thought it was some kind of work report."

"That's my novel," I say.

"Why didn't you ever tell me?" she says.

"I don't know," I say. "I guess I wanted to surprise you."

"What—surprise me when I'm eighty years old and in a nursing home? Nice surprise."

The novel is not enough to keep her at this point. I should have told her about the novel long ago.

When we part, back home in Austin, it is quick and sad, like the last leaves falling off a deadened tree. Claire packs up her belongings that have gravitated to my condo in a big blue sports bag and drives away. I sit in my den changing TV channels with a remote control. It is a big, new 51" flat-screen HD TV, silver and black, very modern, very chic. It is a luxury I can afford to purchase because I have few other expenses. If only I could afford to buy love, I think. If only I could fine love.

In my late forties now, I am reduced to flirtatious relationships with women who are either already married or much too young. I cruise the online dating sites, sometimes, searching for the perfect match, but nothing ever seems to click. I have a sweet, teasing relationship with one particular married woman at work—she is thirty, too young and married—accompanied by a fantasy that she will one day leave her husband and run away with me. She knows about my novel. She knows about my dreams. She knows everything about me, almost, and I know everything about her that she wants to tell me—but she and I both know deep down that nothing between us will ever transpire. Each year that passes new events occur that further reduce those chances. Her children will grow up and marry, enabling her and her husband to reestablish their relationship, alone, together. Grandchildren will be born.

At Christmastime she gives me a firm but chaste little hug and goes home to her family, surrounded by love. The bonds there are too strong. Our positions in life are too different. She will never run away with me. I don't think I would truly ever want her to. So I go home in the early gloom of December to my trendy little condo with the back deck overlooking a dry creek and city lights, and drink eggnog mixed with Courvoisier and stare. I print out a copy of the first chapter of my novel. The full novel, bloated now to 900 dense pages, is stored on the C drive of my laptop at home. It is my life's work—it is my life, in a sense, condensed down through some sort of modern magic into a series of binary numbers inside a plastic box. It will surely be published and make me loads of money when it is finished and ready to go. It is time to add another chapter, I suppose.

Ms. Payne, wherever you are, I want you to know that I am still writing, still polishing, still trying to get my manuscript just right. Some day, it will be.

The Shorthorn No.3

With my first quarter-century in the rear view mirror now, I would say I had settled into some pretty serious drifting. I had spent the biggest part of my adult life drifting. I understood drifting. My style was understated, but within certain parameters I could drift with the best of them. I might pretend otherwise, but I could see no other future but drifting.

A lot of people I knew wanted to stop my drifting. I'm not really sure why. I forced myself to hunker down against them. I became very good at hunkering down. As I told everybody, "Hey, I have a job. Maybe it's a career!" I worked in a late-night college-area greasy-spoon, the Shorthorn No. 3, waiting tables, bussing, cooking sometimes, serving as goodwill ambassador to our intoxicated but truth-seeking clientele of students and street people, all in sight of the University of Texas tower, icon of the illustrious institution where I had finished college thirty credit hours short of an English degree. (The establishment's name, while undoubtedly a takeoff on the university sports team mascot, was something of a mystery, there being no Shorthorn No. 1

or No. 2.) The institution that had prepared me well for my vocation of drifting. There—that's what it was—a vocation, a calling, a life choice, a ministry. I was ministering to the late-night minions, broken souls who needed a place to be and people to see.

Julio was Night Manager at the Shorthorn No. 3, and he was my friend, my mentor, my guide. Julio was not his real name—his real name was Al—and late-night restaurant work not his real profession. In real life, he was a songwriter and singer on the verge of breaking through big. One night I listened to a demo CD he had cut, and he was good, damn good, part progressive country, part Northeastern smart-ass protest poet.

Julio had drifted a lot longer than I had. With his 40th birthday coming around, he was balding rapidly, though he wore what hair he had long in back tied in a pony -tail, often with a scarf atop his head. His acne-scarred face was masked by a dark greasy beard, remarkably Castro-like. (I never told him this.) His upper lip, too, seemed unusually large and constantly sneering, though whether this was simply a physical trait or a symptom of some inner disdain, I could not be sure. What was great about Julio was that he didn't worry about unimportant things any more, or anything out of his control. He didn't worry about his parents. He didn't worry about what society thought. He had broken free of all of those chains. There were sporadic flare-ups with his ex-wife Rhonda when she showed up at the Shorthorn No. 3 to berate him about credit card bills, but he released the tension from these visits with Vodka shots and a few tokes of weed. Imbibing also, the rest of us helped him with his tension release. As for credit card bills, I had personally observed him shredding them unopened then tossing the shards away. It was a brave, powerful display. He was as close to a free man as I had ever known.

Jacqueline worked with us too, there at the diner. Somewhat older than myself, Jacqueline had a rich beautiful nest of straight platinum blonde hair—dyed, Julio informed me, though I chose to believe it was her natural color—and dangly earrings and a knockout smile that sometimes, occasionally, faded into a scary, tough-as-nails glare. She had a gorgeous face, delicate, model-quality almost, not sweet precisely, but very soulful, and a figure like a Rockette, long of leg and firm to the touch. She appeared to me as a beautiful gypsy girl who had wandered away from her tribe and landed here, a forlorn, dramatic character. Though filled with intense feelings, Jacqueline was inconsistent, maddeningly, endearingly inconsistent. Sometimes she moved quickly, making others catch up to her, other times she moved slow, making everybody wait. She expected you to follow her speed.

Julio and I both loved her, I had come to realize, but it was undetermined which of us she preferred, because although Julio was older and more experienced, I was definitely funnier. While Julio's attempts at humor were mainly duds, I don't mind saying that I could be hilarious at times. Funniness kept me going during bad periods of drifting. It was almost like a career of its own, unpaid, unrecognized. Jacqueline let me kiss her sometimes, when we were goofing off after work, on the lips. It was wonderful, but it was only kisses, nothing more. "I don't want to spoil you," Jacqueline said. "You're like a babe in arms, beautiful and innocent." I let her think that, because it seemed to make her want to kiss me, but I wanted to shout out: "Spoil me! Go ahead! I'll be fine! It won't ruin me!" I didn't know if she let Julio kiss her. I hoped not. I didn't want to think about it.

Jacqueline had married early, on her 18th birthday, June 21, three weeks after finishing high school. Her birthday was the first day of summer, the longest day of the year, and she took pride in that, as if it were some kind of omen. She ran off to Mexico that day to elope with a former quarterback from their high school football team, the Athens (Texas) High Hornets. Carl Lewis was his name, the same name as that of the Olympic sprinter. Carl was older than Jacqueline, twenty-five, and he claimed to have been offered a scholarship to play football at Texas A&M, but turned it down. So instead he went to work for Southwestern Bell, installing and repairing lines. Their marriage lasted five years, until Carl Lewis decided they should have a child. Jacqueline did not want to have a child with Carl Lewis. She did not want to continue living with him. She felt that she had evolved beyond Carl to a new, more refined plane of existence. "Carl wanted to control me," Jacqueline said. "He wanted to mold me into something I'm not." She didn't want to be controlled. She didn't want to be molded. She had seen enough of being controlled growing up in small-town East Texas with a conservative Christian father and a society that was as cloying as the humidity on a mid-summer's night. She came to Austin to break away from all that—Austin was a great place to come if you wanted to break away. After her divorce, Jacqueline had studied to become a cosmetologist, but withdrew from classes after the first semester. Now she wanted to become a massage therapist. I told her (boyishly, innocently) that she could practice her skill sets on me. I would never control her, of course. I would never try to mold her into something she wasn't.

We were all together one night after work, Julio and Jacqueline and me, at the Orange Bull tavern across the street from Shorthorn No. 3, drinking beer, when Julio said, casual-like, as if he had just thought of it, "Let's go to California."

"Sure," I said. "What for?"

"To live there," Julio said. "To start a new life."

"A new life?" I said. "When?"

"Right now," Julio said. "Not tonight, I don't mean, but soon. As soon as we can get organized. Next week maybe. The next few days."

"Next week?" I said. "The next few days?" I guess you could say I was stalling. I was trying to figure out how I would feel. I was trying to control my voice, too, because it seemed to be taking on a life of its own, high-pitched and squawky. Like all men, drifters or not, I wanted my voice to be strong and low and under control.

Julio looked exasperated. He looked at me as though I were some dense, dumb-butt ten-year-old who could not understand simple directions. My eyes got watery. Anytime somebody looked at me like that my eyes got watery. Julio was originally from Brooklyn, N.Y., but sometimes he acted a whole lot like my San Antonio, Texas, father, put out and obtuse about the reason I would or wouldn't do a certain thing. My father was of the mindset that pretty much everybody in the world should be of the same mindset.

"Why the hell not?" said Julio, leaning forward, leaning forward in such an aggressive posture that I was forced to lean back. His upper lip seemed to sneer at me. "What are you waiting for? What's going on here?" He spread out his hand to indicate this place, this city, this point in time. Well, nothing really, of course, but I guess that I felt somewhat in control here. I felt that I was in charge of the details of my own life.

We both looked toward Jacqueline, trying to gauge her reaction. She could be hard to read sometimes. She could pretend that she felt one way when she really felt another. She could make you feel like she was in love with you one minute and that you were a worthless pest the next.

Jacqueline nodded yes. Then she looked at me for a second. She wasn't sure. Damn, I wish I could have relayed some signal to her by ESP just then: "Go with me, me alone! Let's get a place together and start a family. We'll settle down. We'll live on a farm outside of town and grow our own crops and swim naked in the river. You can set up your massage studio there."

"I'll go if both of you are going," I said instead. I'm not sure why I said that. It was like somebody else, somebody with a trained theatrical voice, was saying it.

"I'll go too, then," Jacqueline said. I could see her saying that and then planning already to back out, leaving us in the lurch, leaving just Julio and me to go by ourselves. That I resolved not to do. If that happened, I could see myself disappearing at some godforsaken rest stop out in the boondocks while Julio waited for me and I never came back. Julio and me alone in California together would be a nightmare of unimaginable horror.

Sweeping floors at work the following day, the concept of going to California began to grow on me, like a dream of glory. I could be somebody in California, I thought. I began feeling excited. I was talking both extremely politely and incredibly fast. I had never done anything like this before. Though nobody realized this—I had never told anyone—I always worried about what my parents thought, and my siblings back in San Antonio, and even the Irish nuns who taught me in grade school, way back when. In some peculiar sense, I *had* followed the party line, what was expected of me, society's plan for old el Steve-o. Though I was drifting, I was drifting within the confines of somebody else's grand vision. I was ready, at last, to move beyond those outer-imposed limitations to a brave new world of triumphant self-actualization. This was the big break I had been waiting for. I was ready to be on my own. Plans and expectations formed in my head, like grand drama productions. For the first time in a long time, it was fun to dream. And with Jacqueline at my side, all things would be possible.

We agreed to meet at 6:00 one Sunday morning in the Shorthorn No. 3 parking lot, like vacationers getting an early start on a long first day. We would take Jacqueline's car, since she had the best one, a result of her divorce settlement—a big, powerful American car, an Oldsmobile or a Buick, with frigid, blasting A/C and a top-rate CD player and electric everything. I watched Jacqueline screech her way out of the parking lot every morning in that big white beast after work was over. The car seemed right for her somehow—she *needed* something big and powerful, something brawny. It wouldn't have seemed right her driving a hybrid or something.

The morning we were set to leave was cool and misty, the streetlights above our parking lot projecting cone-shaped auras of wavery yellow light, like halos of saints. I wore a light green windbreaker, New Balance basketball shoes, and tan calf-length cargo shorts, designed to make me appear both well-prepared and debonair. (My hair, unfortunately, was glazed over with an unglamorous coating of mist.) As I arrived, my sensitive, sensible eyes drank in the ramshackle white clapboard facade of the Shorthorn No. 3 for the final time, trying to assign this place a place among all the places in my life—homes, schools, playing fields, worksites. I couldn't quite get a fix at that point. I could only assign an incomplete. As I strode forward purposefully to observe Jacqueline and Julio loading a suitcase into the trunk of her car, I was filled with a sudden burst of energy and good cheer. I was all set to hit them with an impromptu joke I had prepared in my mind that morning, something about travelers driving west to the sea. These little jokes had become my trademark, my distinguishing characteristic, my signature move. People expected them. People remembered me by them. The laughter I received for them was like a warm embrace.

Only this time, the joke never came out. I raised my hand to announce my presence, but quickly put it down.

And then I broke down. I couldn't go to California, I realized. I just couldn't go. Even love couldn't overcome this. Everything and everybody I had ever known was in Texas, either here in Austin or seventy-five miles down the road in San Antonio, where I grew up. Though my parents drove me crazy at times I couldn't imagine being so far away from them. It felt like a betrayal. I still went home some weekends, hung out with old high school friends on Saturday night, ate a big festive dinner that my mother cooked on Sunday afternoon. On my way out of town, my mother loaded me up with groceries in plastic sacks. After haranguing me over my situation, my father sometimes slipped a $20 bill into my hand. With my two brothers and one sister lying in front of the TV I cut up while watching FOX News or CNN or some other show that provided fodder for our internal family jokes. Maybe I enjoyed having them gripe at me about drifting. They must have made me feel important in that way. They provided meaning to my life.

"What's wrong?" Julio said, lip sneering. "You got cold feet?"

"I can't do this," I said. "I can't leave."

"Why the hell not?" Julio said.

"I don't know," I said. "I feel at home here. I don't think I can live anywhere else."

"But you're not doing anything here," Julio said. "You're not going anywhere. You're working in a goddamn student diner, wasting your life away."

"I know," I said. My eyes were watering. I tried to keep him from changing my mind. I tried to let him change my mind. I tried to keep from dissolving into tears.

I stood there hoping somehow that Jacqueline would jump into my arms and that we would go back into the empty restaurant and make love on the cement floor. But instead she said to Julio, "Well, I guess it's you and me, Boss. Let's go to California." I didn't even get a final kiss, though I stuck my face in there desperately hoping for one. Jacqueline gave me a little hug and got in the car and they drove off together. Julio was driving. This hurt me more than anything else, almost. It looked like he had been driving her car all along. I had never driven her car. She waved as they screeched around the corner, one of those careless little fingertip waves. Julio gave me something like a military salute.

"No! Wait!" I yelled then. I began to run, legs pumping like Carl Lewis the sprinter. I ran to the end of the block, hand waving wildly. But it was too late. It was futile. They were out of sight. Gone. Winded, crushed, I turned to walk slowly back to the restaurant parking lot. I had never felt so desolate in my life. I wanted to pray for a miracle, but since I hadn't prayed much recently, it didn't seem quite right. I didn't think it would work, anyway. Kicking the ground like an angry horse, I pulled out my key to unlock the door to the Shorthorn No. 3 and went inside and began to set up tables. There was really nothing else left to do.

East of Paris, West of Berlin

The young woman who worked the morning shift at Jim's Coffee Shop in suburban San Antonio wore a crisp white uniform dress with matching cap, giving her a sophisticated, European ambiance—somewhere east of Paris, west of Berlin. Perhaps it was also her hair, long and dark and a deep, reddish brown, rolled on her head in several tight buns; perhaps it was her hands, small and delicate, pale and ringless. There was her voice, of course. To the sensitive ear, it betrayed a certain obscure Southern ancestry, but had developed far beyond its roots into something cultured, musical, and geographically neutral. Her voice was like a lyre.

As a 19-year-old college sophomore living at home with my parents, I would drop in at Jim's with it's sunlit floor-to-ceiling windows, glossy formica tables, and cheerful glassed-in displays of peach cobblers and cherry strudels and chocolate ice box pies; its aroma of grease and pork sausage; its master chefs, culinary giants trained to sear a chicken fried steak to perfection while keeping one eye on a "Penthouse" centerfold; and she would wait on me and smile. From a stiff, formal beginning, our relationship developed within the limited framework of Jim's art deco design into pure poetry.

Her name was Annette. I told her I wanted to be a writer—humorous in style, but with serious undertones. She told me as she poured coffee with a light but elegant touch that she painted, mostly impressionistic, some abstract. I told her I could tell by her hands, they were artist's hands, small but strong and precise. She blushed lightly, but delivered my biscuits and sausage without missing a beat. I asked her to draw me something and she doodled on an order pad a snow scene in Vermont, but with a triangle-faced, one-eyed woman with her ski stuck sideways in the snow. A reindeer with the face of a withered old man gazed down from a hillside. Obviously, this was powerful stuff.

"Compelling," I gushed, floating in emotion. "Hard but sleekly beautiful. Combines old and new into something modern but unique." She patted my hand and poured more coffee. I smiled with deep understanding. The life of an artiste can be extremely rewarding.

One morning in December I arrived at Jim's in the throes of a tragic artistic dilemma. It was, first of all, the day before final examinations commenced—always a sorrowful occasion for persons, such as myself, who considered themselves removed from such mainstream irritations as working for a living. What's more, a term paper, on which my entire semester's grade in Economics, was due; and, at the forefront of my difficulties, another semester had passed during which I had failed to become rich and famous, making moot the necessity of further study and mental anguish.

My mood was black as I settled into my favorite red-plastic molded dinette chair, delicate late-autumn tendrils of sunlight illuminating my right arm, and, by extension, my plight. My coffee was poured directly, with a terribly cosmopolitan flair. She smiled tentatively, a questioning look in her large, almond-colored, soulful eyes, a slight pondering tremor in her lips, before moving on gracefully, with the fluidity of an ice skater, to her other customers, whom she treated with a restrained but sensitive dignity. I brooded quietly as I sipped, a noble silence enveloping me like a purple cloak. She approached, delicate sensibilities attuned to my plight.

"Is there something wrong?" she queried with an air of professional restraint edged with just the right air of deep emotional understanding. "You seem upset."

"Nothing," I said primly, with an indifferent wave.

"Okay," she rejoined. "I just thought you looked a little—sad." A blush tinged her smooth olive complexion as she topped off my coffee and moved on to another table. Our dialogues normally lasted the amount of time it took her to pour coffee or remove my plate.

When she returned I cleared my throat softly, symbolically.

"Well," I said somberly, as she delivered my hotcakes with a fastidious panache. "There is something—maybe." My voice faltered, and we blushed together. "Could we talk later? If you'd like. I could pick you up..." My voice faded, my visage became terribly wan. Would she grind a biscuit in my cheek for such impertinence?

"Okay," she said in an incredibly feathery tone, someone's used breakfast dish grasped loosely in her fingertips. God, she had style when it came to culinary accouterments! Violin music seemed to float on the golden shafts of sunlight which now through the expansive window panes floating cubically in Picassoesque patterns. "That would be nice."

"What time do you get off work?" My voice danced up with the violins. "I could pick you up here."

"Two o'clock," she said, as flutes piped in and a cello trilled. A chorus of cherubs sang falsetto in the background.

At 2:00 o'clock sharp I pulled my battered green Ford Mustang, ravaged by years of adolescent misuse, rather lyrically into Jim's parking lot, a plump Muenster cheese and a bottle of chilled Claret brown-bagged at my side. Annette was waiting, per schedule, by Jim's glass doors, a trim, graceful figure, dark and pensive. Final exam preparations I had tossed to the gods—if I was ready, I was ready. If I wasn't—I could spend the remainder of my natural life bumming on the beach in California. That would be simple enough, after all.

The red fringed shawl over her white uniform smock made Annette seem even more European than before—I had it pinned down now to a small country village in the south of France, where they routinely gathered to dance and discuss Flaubert.

I greeted her with rampant hopefulness with a quote from Stendhal, which she seemed to ignore, oddly, or brush aside, or fail to understand. Her red lips remained fixed in a kind of deep, disapproving pout. Puzzled, I pondered this unanticipated breech of protocol. To my previous statements she had responded with uniform alacrity and a subdued, if distinctly sophisticated, good humor. Then she slid into the passenger seat with a tough, determined gesture that I failed to recognize from before, and tugged her shawl tightly around her shoulders—a sharp, space-defining motion. She stared straight ahead, her claret-brown eyes focused on some unknown, distant object. Something, at any rate, unrelated to me.

"So," I said, with my usual air of utmost civility, one hand resting rakishly on the apex of the steering wheel. I realized suddenly that I might appear too precocious, too worldly, too refined, and made a mental note to dumb down things a notch. "Where would you like to go?" But she sighed forcefully, like somebody resigned to a terrible, tasteless fate, and shrugged. I shrank inside—all my life I've disliked shrugs and noncommittal answers. Can't people know what they want?

"Christ, I don't know," she moaned. "Just get me away from this dump." Her tart and testy tone surprised me, and then she pulled a crumpled pack of Pall-Mall filters from her crocheted hand-bag. She lit one cradling a see-through yellow BIC lighter in both hands, cigarette dangling expertly between parted lips. After a moment, it clicked—I understood the sudden turnaround.

"Is there trouble at work?" I ventured. Of course, I reasoned, this was all a simple matter of a workplace contretemps. Members of the intelligentsia, like saints, are often misunderstood by Philistine associates.

"Shit," she said, shaking her head and exhaling through flared nostrils, two thin, powerful streams. "There's so many goddam problems in there I couldn't even begin to explain all of them to you. Everybody's stupid. Half of the people can't even speak English. And the manager makes a pass at me every time he gets me alone in the kitchen."

I nodded with extravagant sympathy, then attempted to defuse the situation with a sample of the rapier-sharp wit she expected, and appreciated, during our restaurant days. But her responding laugh was short and hollow, a pale reflection of her earlier, more robust self—a forced laugh. It was the first time anything she had done with me seemed strained or anything less than natural. Moreover, she seemed distant, distracted, drained. Frankly, she looked as though she would rather be scraping eggs off a breakfast plate than be with me.

I felt depressed. Finally I had her with me, alone, unencumbered by the prying eyes of Jim's patrons, and she already was slipping away, dropping into the vast nether-world of lost and unfulfilled relationships. I started the car and drove in tortured silence for an eternal series of city blocks as I searched frantically for a conversation starter. Then Annette started the conversation herself.

"Hey!" she blurted suddenly. "Wanta get some weed?" I looked at her as though she had asked me to undress in a grocery store.

"Weed?" I repeated, mulishly. "Weed?"

"Yeah," Annette said, impatiently, almost irritably.

She was probably thinking, "What an idiot!" "You know, dope. Pot. Marijuana."

"Hey, I know," I said, feeling somehow that I must prove my condition of advanced enlightenment. "I'm very familiar with that particular organic substance." Sure, I considered myself as counter-cultural as the next guy, but the fact is I had never actually smoked marijuana. A full-length explication may not be in order here, but essentially I feared that use of such illicit items might interfere in some delicate operation integrally related to my brain stem. Or perhaps I was just simply afraid. The truth is that underneath my cool, unharried exterior, I was a wimp. The truth is I probably had more in common with my father's accountant associates than with members of my own, peace generation.

Besides, I had in mind a peaceful picnic in a park with a gentle breeze wiffling through our clothes and our hair. Then we would lie down on a blanket and make out madly. Making out madly seemed to dominate my vision at the time.

"Well, then . . .?" she said.

"Yeah!" I said, with trumped up enthusiasm.

'Great," she said. "Drive."

I drove. I drove reluctantly, brooding and introspective, filled with disappointment and foreboding. I drove with a sharp-edged sense of loss. I drove as a young man whose dream of romance has been shattered.

"Take Broadway to Mulberry," she said. "Hang a left on Mulberry and a right on Magnolia. There's a laundry on Magnolia Street—it's right by that."

I nodded, silent, unhappy.

The houses in the Wilshire Woods neighborhood near downtown San Antonio were survivors of a Roaring Twenties building boom—tall and white with asbestos siding, stacked one against the other on deep but narrow lawns. Later, in the decade of the 1980's, the residences there were transformed by purposeful young professionals into trendy fixer-uppers, enthusiastically refitted with updated plumbing fixtures, track lighting, and sleek contemporary furnishings, but now, in the autumn of 1969, they looked merely careworn and old.

Parked cars lined both sides of the cramped streets, making navigation irritating and arduous. Giant leafy oaks spread a picturesque canopy, I feel certain, over the rough and rutted pavement, but I had no use for picturesque, just then. I was far too busy being crestfallen and petulant. I was basically wallowing in petulance.

"Here," she said, pointing.

I nodded and parked obediently between a dusty blue Buick with fins and a Harley-Davidson motorcycle with a windshield. I attempted a smile, which strained my face with its patent phoniness. She didn't seem to notice. And then she was outside the car before I could remove my hand from the ignition key. I followed her white uniform feeling foolish, unexplained, an interloper. I followed in despair.

Annette walked quickly along the sidewalk and up the steps and onto the high front porch, pinching her shawl around her shoulders. She turned the doorknob without knocking and we entered a cave filled with smoke and music and laughter—diffuse, dangerous, inappropriate laughter, floating on the edge of chaos. The lights were off and Venetian blinds closed to the sun, creating an uncertain world of hazy darkness.

This was precisely the sort of situation I struggled constantly to avoid. Strangers, strangers without inhibitions, strangers who could hone in on my weak points and vulnerabilities and imperfections. Strangers who could read my phobias like a line of type. Strangers who would recognize me instantly as inferior to them.

They were three or four young men, members of my peer group, each lean and lanky and overbearingly confident, and covered with hair. Their entire beings, in fact, seemed defined by hair, and the volume of hair contained on and about their bodies seemed to suggest a certain nihilistic swagger which I, in my pressed jeans and pullover Izod shirt, could never hope to match. By comparison, I felt ridiculously clean-cut, conservative, uncool—an unthinking, robotic product of the middle class, a holdover from a distant, discredited past. My ambition to write seemed as far removed from real life as Shakespeare from a 20th Century discotheque.

Annette embraced each friend individually while I hovered behind, mute, nameless, invisible. I longed for her embrace, but there was nothing for me, not even a rote introduction. When we sat on the floor, in a circle, Annette and I were separated by far more than several pairs of scuffed sandals and ragged blue jeans. We were separated by a million miles of cosmos.

I attempted to communicate by the angle of my shoulders, by the extension of my legs, by facial expression my profound and acute acumen, but it was hopeless. My tension built as the fat, lumpy marijuana cigarette made its way slowly around the circle, its tip glowing red. I felt queasy, irresolute, insecure—alienated. Lips pursed, I discovered myself disapproving primly. When Annette's turn came, she inhaled deeply, eyes closed, cheeks drawn in, seeming as remote as a dot of light in a distant galaxy. When my turn came, everybody glared as the cigarette, white-hot around the edges, dropped to the floor.

An hour or two later, we drove back to Annette's apartment in slow-motion silence. Everything was different, now—in our new roles, we were lost. I wished she would wait on me. I wished I could sit at my regular table and deliver jokes as she delivered my hotcakes. I wished she would tell me about her drawings and I could tell her about my latest piece of writing.

Instead, I saw her now as somebody different—a lower-middle class girl without much education or refinement, without ambition, plans or any real passion to understand the meaning of life. At age 19, I didn't know who or what I wanted, exactly, but I knew I wanted something more than that. Not that it mattered, anyway—the bond we briefly shared had snapped like a frayed rubber band. When I dropped her off, she left quickly, not looking back.

"See you later," she said rotely.

"See you later," I said back, to her back. I raced home then in a deep blue late-afternoon funk, drank down three cups of blistering black coffee, and laid my class books out before me on my desk.

I dropped in at Jim's a time or two after that, but it

just wasn't right, anymore. Annette had a different smile, a different way of approaching me, a different presence. She seemed to not quite remember—or want to remember—who I was or what had passed between us previously. I was just another customer, now. Somebody to serve. A potential tipper. But I was also a potential embarrassment, I guess, a reminder of something gone wrong, a source of discomfort and chagrin. I tried to wax nostalgic with her, using one of my old lines that she had always appreciated, but she didn't seem to quite get it. She smiled faintly and glided away. I had an order of biscuits and sausage, just to try something different, and I was gone.

Vietnam Vets

Steadfastly, valiantly, heroically, I believed, I manned a stripped-down, gun-metal gray battleship of a work desk in a windowless back room of the Registrar's Office at the University of Texas, a room filled with filing cabinets and piles of printouts and mature married women who clucked and cooed over me as if I were their grown child, their own little darling office worker. They sheltered me, they nurtured me, they mother-henned me into head-shaking bouts of embarrassed laughter. I confess that I rather enjoyed this special treatment, savoring the attention, relishing the embarrassment, while presenting myself as that rare representative of the younger generation who could be both talented and non-threatening. I wasn't just about free love or protests—though protest I did—I was about pride and potential, about helping our fellow man. Though my hair was long, my face was clean, my attire neat, my demeanor sweet and gentle. The year being 1973, the Vietnam War was still boiling, 8,400 miles away and at home on our TV screens. With the nation in turmoil, I was doing my best to bridge the generation gap.

I had taken the job after graduating from the university with a degree in English. It was a simple transition, from college student to office worker at the college. And the job was a simple one—processing GI Bill documents for Vietnam vets who had returned to college after serving their term in the military. But the task was complicated by the fact that these were military veterans while I was a measly civilian, an anti-war civilian, at that. It was kind of an odd, unsettling situation for me because I was part of the same generation as them, these tough, grizzled men. I felt odd and inferior alongside them, off-kilter, as if they knew some deep secret that I did not, some inside information, a special code for living life. Despite my political beliefs which I considered unassailably correct, I felt like a slacker in their presence, cowardly, spineless, weak. When my lottery number turned up as a very draftable "69," my mother lobbied my childhood pediatrician to write a letter to the draft board detailing my history of childhood asthma. It worked. I was reclassified first 1-Y ("fit for service only in emergency"), then 4-F, "unfit for military service." I was opposed to the war, philosophically speaking, of course, but as someone who grew up watching helicopter pick-ups and bombing runs on TV this view was no doubt colored by not wanting to be sent into combat and killed. I would be a terrible soldier, I was convinced, but it was impossible to know whether I would be more terrible than anybody else. There were undoubtedly a gazillion terrible soldiers out there.

At the beginning of the semester the vets all lined up at my desk for me to check over their registration forms and to enter their information into the computer system. They were a varied bunch. Some were tight-lipped, tight-assed types who couldn't hide their disdain for me, holding onto their superiority like a loaded M-16 rifle. Some wanted to be my pal, a little buddy to take under their wing. Others were brisk and business-like, brandishing briefcases like junior managers in training. Still others were super-determined, studious solid citizens with wives and children they were now obliged to support. More than anything else they wanted to just finish college and put this phase of their lives behind them. There was one former high school classmate I hadn't seen in years, back then a geeky, self-driven, too-smart-for-his-own-good type who got caught up in drugs and dropped out of college and ended up getting drafted and sent into the war zone. Scott Stephens was his name, and of all the vets I served he was the most accommodating, the most courteous, treating me as a kind of younger cousin who showed signs of promise but needed years of seasoning. But even Scott didn't want to hang around for very long. He would engage me for a few hurried moments of small talk and a slap on the shoulder before wanting to get out, move on, needing to get things done. His light blonde mustache and black-framed eyeglasses seemed like theatrical props, designed to add an air of solemnity to his boyish face. Like all the others, his life had urgency, meaning, consequence. One trait all the vets shared in common was a certain gravity of being, a sense that they had confronted life (and death) in ways that I had not. I was a mere child beside them, a gangly, pimply adolescent. Any drama in my own life was clearly minor, light comedy that would be resolved at the conclusion of a thirty-minute show. I served them graciously, almost courtly, wanting them to understand that I deferred to their superior knowledge and experience. I was there to serve.

The final Friday of each month at 1:00 p.m. Registrar's Office staff manned screened pay windows for the vets to pick up their GI Bill checks. This was a manual procedure back then, with a green-shaded printout list and a sign-in sheet with a line to mark "Paid"—and, for most, a happy time. Payday! A bright buzz of anticipation animated the drab, gray-walled premises while everyone moved quickly, purposely, diligently. There were intricate Power Shakes and loud, strident declarations of solidarity.

"Here you go, Man!"

"You got it, sir!"

"You're the man, Dude!"

"You're the dude, Man!"

"Take care!"

"I will!"

"Don't be a stranger!"

"I won't!"

"See you next time!"

"You bet!"

There was one regular paycheck recipient that nobody wanted at their pay window. He was an "older" dude—29 perhaps—with a wild aureole of curling red hair surrounding an arrowhead-shaped head and worry lines around the corners of his eyes and a handlebar mustache like Oakland A's pitcher Rollie Fingers. The ladies had warned me that he was a trouble-maker, a cranky dog that you walked around the block avoid. Samuel Leggett was his name, and intimidation was his game.

I scoffed at their warnings. I could handle him, I said. Before today, however, I had only glimpsed him from afar. Small-framed and wiry, he appeared suddenly, filling my pay window with a sudden sense of foreboding. He was dressed in a sleeveless, tie-dyed tee shirt and cut-off jeans, with huarache sandals that smelled of Mexican calves' leather and slapped against the scratched linoleum floor like paddles. His eyes burned with a kind of exotic, lizard-like energy, and his hands moved haphazardly, almost spasmodically, to and fro. I was immediately drawn into his force-field. We exchanged eye contact—intense, penetrating, allegedly a deep bonding experience. We shook hands dramatically, a vigorous Power Shake, his grip like a blood pressure cuff. I hollered out several high-decibel verbal exchanges to prove my manhood and my moxie. I moved forward to seize the initiative. It was my nature—I wanted to please. I wanted to avoid conflict and win him over.

"What's up, Dude?" I said, with worked-up enthusiasm, with that trademark good humor that made the ladies smile. Samuel said nothing, smiling cryptically. My opening salvo had fallen flat. Shaken but determined, I tried to recover with another hearty declaration. This was met by a second, gratuitous Power Shake.

Unfortunately, Samuel seemed even a bit more free-floating than usual today, possibly high on something or drunk. Back in the 70s, it wasn't altogether unusual for the vets to show up for paycheck pickup high or drunk. Friday afternoon—Beer Thirty!

"Ready for the weekend?" I tried, following up myself, making another pitch for acceptance. Per his reputation, Samuel tried intimidating me with flexed biceps and the angle of his stance. His military service had trained him in the martial arts, as I well knew. I felt a wave of exasperation wafting off of him to me. He leaned forward, almost into my booth.

"I am Samuel Leggett," he said. Almost like an old pirate stating, "I be Pegleg Joe."

"That's what I've heard," I said, soldiering on. (I could behave like a soldier in non-combat conditions.)~

"You are Kevin Milligan," Samuel said, reading the name badge dangling from my neck.

"Yes, I am," I said. I stood planted firmly on two feet, perspiring like an overweight lineman after a series of practice-ending wind sprints. Samuel bent forward menacingly again.

"I need my check," he said.

"Sure thing," I said, relieved that our little tango of introduction was almost over, digging into my shoebox of checks. "I just need to see some picture ID."

Samuel recoiled, as if I had karate-punched him in the gut. He struck a pose of affronted dignity. He pointed to his own chest.

"Samuel Leggett," he said. "I don't need no picture ID."

I paused, trapped in my cage. My hands shook. My heart stopped. Then it beat furiously, like a caught bird. I could feel the ladies staring at me.

"We're required to see a picture ID," I said, standing firm, though my legs buckled under me. "We can't give you a check without an ID." Samuel stood staring, eyes opening to a slant. A suave, sarcastic smile puckered his mustachioed lips.

"My signature is my ID, Man," he said. He held his hands apart slightly, as if this certified the validity of his case. I searched for logic in his answer, but could find none.

"I apologize, Mr. Leggett," I said, hiding behind formal language like a court order. "I cannot release your check." Standing behind the wire mesh pay window deep inside the bowels of the Registrar's Office, I felt like The Man himself—didactic, bureaucratic, rigidly authoritarian. Still, I felt that I couldn't back off now. I felt that I must follow the rules, do this right, show everyone that I was one really tough Administrative Assistant III. The space behind me seemed strangely deserted, desolate, like a beach at sundown after all the waders and the sand castle builders had drifted away.

"I want my check," Samuel said.

"You can get your check," I said, "if you show me a picture ID."

"I need my check," Samuel said.

"Please," I said softly but firmly, in a voice that I hoped only Samuel would be able to hear. I was pleading, really, begging for Samuel to comply or go away. He snorted, with a disgusted face, and, hands shaking, pulled a thin black alligator-skin wallet from a hip pocket and flipped it open to a laminated sheaf of plastic cards. I glanced at the top card briefly. I barely glanced at it, actually. I didn't know if the picture was really of Samuel Leggett or of Donald Duck. But it was something. It was good enough. I riffled through the box of cardboard checks spit out by a mainframe printer in alphabetical order and slid Samuel's over to him along with the sign-in sheet.

"Here you go," I said, my hands, my body, my entire being shaking. "Just sign on the line by your name."

Samuel leaned over theatrically, signing with a ballpoint pen attached to a clipboard by a string. He held his check from one end, like a landed fish, and turned abruptly, sandals slapping sharply as he stepped away.

"Dude," he shouted out. "I thought we were all brothers here. I guess not."

"Next!" I sang out. I had never said "next" before. My face flushed. My jaw clenched. The room tilted strangely, as though I were standing in the hull of a ship. I greeted the next person in line with a strange, spooky smile. He held out his ID gingerly, in both hands.

Shaken, shaky, I split from work promptly at 5:30 p.m., slipping out the battered back door of Main Building 1 without a wave or a word of farewell to the ladies in the office. Hopping on my utilitarian 3-speed bike, I peddled the short distance home through shady campus-area streets. Once there, I chained my bike to a metal rail and dashed upstairs, eager to unload my tale of courage and heroism to my live-in girlfriend Kat (for Katharine) O'Malley. I wanted Kat to hear my story fresh, to be proud of me for it, to throw open her arms and exclaim, "Oh, Kevin, you're so brave!" Kat's brother Nick was another kind of Vietnam War vet—a draft dodger on the lam. Kat's family in San Antonio hadn't seen him in three years. Though we had never met, he made me feel inferior, too.

But opening the door to our apartment I could see Kat on the portable phone, standing in the hallway between the living room and the bedroom. Her hoop earrings dangled from her delicate ears. A cup of hot tea lay steeping on the kitchen counter, steam rising. Braless in a white, scoop-cut peasant's blouse, barefoot, slender legs swathed in tattered jeans, she waved (and shrugged) at me: "My mother," she mouthed. My heart sank. My resolve wavered. I hovered for a few moments, hoping that Kat would recognize my need, but she merely smiled, turning her back as she moved into the bedroom. I was annoyed, of course, but more than that—jealous. Sometimes I envied Kat her closeness with her mother. I had hoped that my credentials as a member of the Woodstock Generation would have expunged such base emotions as jealousy from my emotional repertoire. Sadly, they had not. Downcast, depressed, I dropped my backpack and keys and sat down heavily on our brown naug-a-hyde couch, pushing aside a pile of washed, folded towels. Grunting dispiritedly, I got back up to switch on the television set, a table-top rabbit-ears model. The TV news was on, Walter Cronkite talking about a bombing run near Dà Nang that had gone off target and destroyed a village. Sapped, I tried hard to work up an appropriate degree of anger and angst.

Phone on ear, Kat wandered back over by me and put a hand on my shoulder and blew me a kiss. I sat back, temporarily content. The feeling didn't last. I felt restless, incomplete. My stomach rumbled. My mind raced. I slipped into a nervous, self-criticizing funk. I glanced about the apartment thinking, "I need to fix this. Damn, I've got to replace that. Shoot, that table is really crappy."

Kat eyed me quizzically as I stood, straightening the Rolling Stones poster taped above the threshold to the hallway. The poster represented everything that was wrong with my life. It was crooked, first of all, and stuck up like a 2nd grader's artwork on a classroom wall. More than that, the poster seemed to represent exactly how far I had come in life—not very far. We lived in squalor. Our apartment was a cluttered mess. Kat's school work—Kat was still in college—lay scattered around the awkwardly-placed, oval-shaped kitchen floor. We never ate there, we ate watching TV on the coffee table or on the floor. All our furniture was cheap and chipped, Goodwill or garage sale stuff. Our dishes didn't match. Everything was haphazard. We had no long-term plans. We had no plans beyond the coming weekend. All good things seemed far in the future, if anywhere at all.

One short decade previous, in the early 60s, Kat would be one of those brainy, serious-minded co-eds walking the campus determinedly in matching skirt and sweater, focusing in on one of the few career paths a woman could take—teaching, nursing, secretarial. Looking for a boy-friend. Saving herself for marriage. Now, like everyone else, she was caught up in this socio-political whirl-a-gig of change, this new world order. Graduate of St. Ursula Academy, a Catholic girls' school in suburban San Antonio, she was a young woman with a swath of purple in her shoulder-length brunette hair and a tattoo of a flower on her left hip, with a brother who was a draft dodger and on the lam from the law. There was a certain angle to her stance that was not possible in 1963, the way she walked, the way she held her hands and feet, the way her blue jeans hung beltless, loose around her slender waist. A political sciences major, her sights were set on becoming a civil rights attorney, representing the rights of the oppressed. We all wanted to represent the rights of the oppressed, back then.

Then there was sex. Sex! Kat had switched recently from birth control pills—they upset her stomach—to an IUD, and she talked about sex as if sex were as routine as buying groceries or ordering out for pizza. (It was anything but routine for me!) Sometimes, Kat would light candles and turn out the lights and put soft music on the stereo and we would sit naked on a pad in the living room of our apartment and rub on oils and make love. This was something beyond even my wildest adolescent dreams, unattainable, unthinkable, almost like a new development in the history of mankind. We were on the vanguard of history, in a movement, a part of the Sexual Revolution. Things would never be the same. We would never look back.

Finally, Kat finished the conversation with her mother and came over and sat down beside me, perching on the armrest of the couch. Her cup of tea she held between both hands, near her mouth. Reflexively, almost, I reached under her peasant's blouse for her naked breast. She wiggled away.

"Guess what?" she said.

"Your mom's moving in with us?" I said. Kat smiled sardonically. She r elocated her cup of tea over to an end table and rearranged herself on the armrest of the couch.

"You could only hope," she teased. She leaned forward provocatively, speaking softly. "No—they got a call from Nick." Involuntarily, I sat up straight. Nick was Kat's older brother, the draft dodger, the brother on the lam. My feelings I kept secret, but the mention of Nick made me uneasy, upsetting my delicate sense of equilibrium. My equilibrium seemed always on the verge of teetering over.

"Really?" I said, enthusiastically. "Where was he?"

"Some place out on the West Coast, they think," Kat said. "He wouldn't say exactly. He was afraid the phone lines might be tapped."

"Oh, shoot," I said. "Man." Kat reached over to take a sip of tea, watching me.

"He's so scared," Kat said. "He doesn't know what's going to happen to him. He doesn't want to go to prison He doesn't know when he's going to be able to come back."

I made a sorrowful, conciliatory face.

"This is the first time they've heard from him in a while, isn't it?" I said.

"It's been a year at least," Kat said. "Last time he called he was in New York ." I wracked my mind for something positive to say.

"I saw where there might be an amnesty at some point," I said.

"With Nixon in there?" Kat said. "I don't think so."

"Maybe Nixon'll get impeached."

"Yeah, right—like that's going to happen."

"Yeah, you're right," I said. "That won't happen."

For a few strained moments we sat staring blankly at

the TV screen, separated by mere inches but miles apart. My confrontation with Samuel Leggett this afternoon seemed insignificant now, too small, too subtle, narcissistic, buried under the more vital issue of Kat's brother Nick going AWOL. I couldn't say anything now.

It was foolish, but I leaned in impulsively for a kiss, pulling Kat down beside me onto the couch. It was a fine kiss, wet and sweet, shooting beams of desire and content-ment through me like warming tendrils of the sun. I loved kissing Kat. Our kisses were long and lingering, tender knowing, fond. No matter what type of thorny issues might be intruding on my life, I loved kissing Kat. I reached for her bare breast. She pushed me away. The Sexual Revolution had its limits.

"Big test tomorrow," Kat said. "Got to study."

"A test on Saturday?" I said.

"It's a make-up," Kat said. "I was sick during the first time it was administered. Remember when I was sick?"

"Oh, yeah," I said. "You had the flu. Later, maybe?"

"Maybe later," she said.

Mollified slightly, I settled into some serious TV watching, changing channels with an old-fashioned knob attached to the set itself. The first sitcoms of the evening were kicking in, and I selected "The Bob Newhart Show," hoping a few light laughs with Bob Hartley and friends would settle my nerves and ease my angst. I was just settling into a comfortable, sitcom-induced stupor when there was a knock on the door.

"Can you get that, Dar?" Kat said, not looking up

from her books on the table. She called me "Dar" as short for "Darling." "I really need to study."

"Sure thing, Katrina," I said.

I pulled myself up from the couch one leg at a time, catching a few more moments of Bob and neighbor Howard in a conversation about birds nesting outside their apartments. Determined, resolute, I prepared to dismiss summarily whatever uninvited visitor lurked. Located in the heart of the campus area, we received a heavy load of drop-in traffic here. I opened the door to a very large, very hairy, very earnest young man, dressed neatly if casually in a pullover white izod shirt and faded blue jeans—yet another type of individual I found intimidating, someone with a strong purpose. I wanted to discharge him quickly, go back to watching TV, light up a joint maybe, while waiting for Kat to finish studying so we could have sex again. Having sex loomed heavy in my mind. I glanced at the visitor inquiringly to see if he wanted anything, if he was selling anything, proselytizing, hoping for a handout. The new world order notwithstanding, there was a part of me, a part of all of us, I thought, that disdained those wanting a handout. We didn't want intruders in our lives. We didn't want disruption from those in need. We wanted to help others only on our own terms.

"Can I help you?" I said. I held the door gingerly, by the knob, prepared to shut it quickly if necessary.

"Are you Kevin Milligan?" the visitor said, with a nervous, awkward smile. He had very white, very even white teeth, and a certain texture to his hair that reminded me of somebody, somewhere—maybe one of my GI Bill vets, I thought. He seemed to be trying very hard to peer past me into the living room.

"That would be me," I said, uncertainly.

"I'm Nick," the visitor said. "Nick O'Malley, Katherine's brother."

I stood frozen for a few lost moments, hand on the doorknob. My heart raced. Then it stopped. I tried to perform a few quick mental calculations, but my mind would not compute.

"Nick!" I said finally, reaching weakly for Nick's hand. "Come in. Come on in!"

About the Author

Steven McBrearty grew up in San Antonio, Texas, in one of those big, rollicking Catholic families so common in the 1960s. On any given day, there might be games of pitch and catch in the hallway or tackle football in the back bedroom. He moved to Austin to attend the University of Texas and has lived in Austin ever since. He has published more than 35 short stories, humor pieces, and non-fiction articles and has received several honors for his writing. His story collection, *"Christmas Day on a City Bus,"* was published in 2011 by McKinney Press. He has two grown children and four lovely grandchildren.